THE TREE OF PERSEVERANCE

THE TREE OF PERSEVERANCE

CHRONICLES OF THE PROVERBS

BOOK TWO

INDIA MILLAR

Red Empress Publishing
www.RedEmpressPublishing.com

Cover Design by Cherith Vaughan
https://www.facebook.com/coversbycherith/

ALSO BY INDIA MILLAR

THE CHRONICLES OF THE PROVERBS

Frog in a Well

Climbing the Dragon Gate

The Tree of Perseverance

SECRETS FROM THE HIDDEN HOUSE

The Geisha with the Green Eyes

The Geisha Who Could Feel No Pain

The Dragon Geisha

THE GEISHA WHO RAN AWAY

The Song of the Wild Geese

The Red Thread of Fate

This World is Ours

WARRIOR WOMAN OF THE SAMURAI

Firefly

Mantis

Chameleon

Spider

Dragonfly

Scorpion

Cricket

Moth

HAIKU COLLECTIONS

Dreams from the Hidden House

Song of the Samurai

This book is humbly dedicated to Baizenten, the Japanese Goddess of writers and geisha. May both you and she enjoy the words written herein!

PROLOGUE

We had just arrived back home after traveling to Father's birthplace to celebrate Oban Festival. It was the first time I had accompanied my parents and brothers, and also the first time I had left our estate since I had contracted paralysis of the morning. I treasured every moment.

My family was Buddhist, although we were not regular worshippers at the temple. But in common with all Buddhists in Japan, we believed that the souls of our ancestors did not entirely leave us, but returned once each year to visit their relatives—Oban Festival. At that time, whole families returned to their birthplaces to honor their ancestors, just as we had done.

Oban Festival is held in the seventh month of the year, so the weather had been hot and humid. Mother had been tight-lipped the entire time we were away. The heat made her headaches worse than usual, and she hated traveling. But even she did not complain out loud; family and tradition are the basis of everything in Japan, so even though she loathed the annual pilgrimage, she held her tongue.

For me, it was a joyous time, when memories of those who had gone before were spoken of and families were united. Or, at least, that was what was supposed to have happened. In light of this weight of tradition, it was surely the most unfortunate of all days in the year for my brothers to betray our beloved Father.

CHAPTER
ONE

In the depths of night,
The wind sounds like the souls of
The dead come to call

"I have no sons."

Father pointed the forefinger of his right hand at my oldest brother. The gesture was unbelievably rude, as discourteous as his words.

I heard Mother gasp and then wail. The sound was cut off abruptly, and I guessed she had put her hand over her mouth. I did not turn my head to look. I was hypnotized by Father's hand. So great was his emotion that the pointing finger was quivering as if he had suddenly developed a palsy. I was bewildered and more than a little afraid.

Father was generally a silent, serious man. He was not given to dramatic gestures. This display of emotion was so unusual, so unexpected, that I wanted to creep away and hide under my kakebuton until things returned to normal. As they surely would! Father was often angered by his sons, but only ever momentarily. I could understand that—both of my brothers were, in my opinion, lazy. Although they were employed in the family business, they had no interest in any kind of work, instead reserving their enthusiasm for gambling, generally on sumo bouts. Father reprimanded them often, but they always won him over, and his annoyance was generally short-lived. I risked a sideways glance at my eldest brother, Ichiro.

As always, when Father was irritated with him, Ichiro's face was sulky. He stared at the tea bowl in his hand, his shoulders hunched. I felt a chill creep up my back as I understood that Ichiro was not greatly concerned by Father's anger. Was it possible that he could not know that this time was different? That this time, Father was not going to sigh and forget whatever had angered him quickly. Surely, even my brothers could feel the sizzling anger that enveloped Father like some dark and ominous cloud.

"Daughter." Mother's voice startled me. "Come, child. We will leave the men to sort this out between them. We have no place here."

I reached for my crutch, preparing to lever myself to my feet. Naturally, I had left my geta at the house entrance, so I was without my special built-up geta and the clever reins and stirrup contraption that enabled me to walk almost normally. Or at least, so I told myself. The paralysis of the morning had caused my withered left leg, but with the help and advice of my lover, Tengen, I'd had the geta and walking aid made, and when I was wearing them, I had no need of the support of my crutch. On bad days, when my leg ached and ached, I still needed a walking stick even when I wore the geta, but even then, it was far better than the heavy, clumsy crutch I was forced to seek now.

Father's voice reverberated with authority, stopping me before I could rise. "No. Emica, sit down. Mi, stay where you are." It was a brutal, sharp command. Mother whimpered; I bit my distress back. "This is a matter for the whole of the family. You will both stay."

I heard Satoru, my younger brother, clear his throat uneasily, and I guessed that the seriousness of the situation had finally gotten through to him. It was Satoru who spoke.

"Father, I—both of us—are deeply sorry that you are not happy with our actions. I assure you, we thought we were acting for the benefit of the family."

Father said nothing, just glared at his youngest son. After a while, Satoru dropped his gaze and stared at the tatami.

My initial fear began to give way to an intense curiosity. What *could* my silly brothers have done to make Father so very angry? Had their gambling debts become so great that they could not pay? I knew that recently Mother had begun to make plans for betrothals for both of them, and in truth, they were both of an age when they should have been married already. But both of them were suave, iki, men-about-town, and they had successfully convinced Mother —who doted on her fine, handsome sons—that they had plenty of time before they settled down with wives. Father had married relatively late, and in any event, he left such things to Mother to arrange. Was it possible that one—or both—of them had made some terrible match with a totally unsuitable girl?

As soon as the thought came to me, I knew it was nonsense. Father was a rich man. If my brothers had been so very silly, he would not hesitate to buy off the girls in question. No, it had to be something much worse. But what, I had no idea at all.

I began to wonder if Father's anger had started to die

down, but a glance at his expression told me it had not. His face was stone, but fury burned in his eyes.

"I have no sons." He repeated the dreadful words slowly and deliberately. "Mi is the only child I have now. She has never disappointed me. She would never betray the family. She is all I could have hoped to find in my sons."

I glowed with pleasure at such extravagant praise. But it lasted for only a moment. Ichiro spoke angrily, and I blinked in horror that he would dare to talk to our father in such a way.

"Father, you don't understand."

Father said nothing, and Ichiro went on quickly, his voice becoming condescending. It was not my place to interrupt, but I longed to tell him to be quiet before it was too late. If it wasn't already so.

"We have acted in the best interests of the family, I promise you. We were going to discuss the matter with you this evening. We thought it would be a pleasant surprise for you."

I watched Father's face carefully. I still had no inkling of what was going on, but I sensed that my brothers would do well to tread carefully.

Satoru nodded eagerly at his brother's words and spoke quickly. "We were going to wait until after dinner, Father, when Mother and Mi had left us. This has nothing to do with them. What do women know of business?"

Father's expression did not change, but a pulse lifted the corner of his lip. He rubbed his mouth as if he was angry that his body had betrayed him. Satoru either did not notice or chose to ignore it.

"Of course, we both know that Mi amused herself in the office before she was crippled, but that hardly counts as understanding the complex world of business, does it? It's a shame she's as she is. I daresay it will make finding a husband for her difficult, but I expect you'll manage to marry her off if you offer a high enough dowry. In any event, do you not think it would be better for Mi and Mother to leave us now so that we can discuss this important matter men-to-men?"

I sucked in a deep breath, feeling my pulse beat fiercely in my ears. Both my brothers were staring at me rudely, obviously waiting for me—and Mother—to stand and leave the room. Mother, traditional woman that she was, was clearly about to obey. She was gathering her kimono skirts together as she prepared to leave as her son had instructed her. She glanced at me and nodded fractionally, clearly expecting me to do the same.

For a heartbeat, I almost obeyed. Naturally, I should do so—the word of the men in the family was law. I was nothing but a girl child, and a useless, crippled one at that. Instinct made me glance at Father. He was watching me intently and unspoken words flashed between us.

"I will not leave. Neither will Mother." I was pleased to hear that my voice sounded firm. Satoru's jaw dropped. He stared at me, his expression as astounded as if he had seen the smallest of mice turn and confront a stalking cat. Mother wailed faintly. "Father said that Mother and I were to stay. Until he says we are to leave, that is what we will do."

Both my brothers began to talk at once, their indignation cut off abruptly as Father spoke.

"Mi is correct. I told her and her mother to stay. I want both of them to hear how you two have betrayed this family. Ichiro, you are the eldest. It is your place to explain to us all what you and your brother have done."

Ichiro flushed a dull red. He stared at the tatami as he spoke, his tone rebellious.

"Father, I really do not see what all the fuss is about. We have done nothing but act in the best interests of our family. Our actions will bring great prosperity to us, both now and for future generations."

He paused and sipped from his tea bowl. Or rather, he pretended to sip—from where I sat, I could see it was empty. My curiosity overflowed; Ichiro was speaking of future generations. Had I been right when I thought either he or Satoru had gotten themselves entangled with a totally unsuitable woman? Was it possible that they had been inveigled into a promise of marriage to one of the high-class oiran that both boasted of frequenting? Such women could be very rich indeed, but they also had hundreds—perhaps thousands—of lovers. Wealthy men who showered them with gifts and money. It was not unheard of for an especially beautiful and talented oiran to be taken as a premier concubine by a rich man. But marriage? Never.

I waited in tense anticipation, but I was disappointed. Ichiro seemed to have run out of words. Father waited for a moment and then spoke for him. His tone was so icy, I felt gooseflesh erupt on my arms.

"You do not wish to explain what you have done? Very well. I will tell my family how you have betrayed us. When we returned home from the festival today, the maid told me that Mikayo-san was waiting to see me. That he had been waiting for some time even though the girl had told him we were traveling home from the Oban Festival and that she was not sure when we would be back. I thought such behavior very odd indeed, but of course, politeness obliged me to see Mikayo-san as soon as I had washed and changed my dusty clothes."

"That is why we didn't tell you sooner, Father," Satoru broke in anxiously. "We thought it would be better to wait until you had cast off the dust of the journey and you had enjoyed your meal before we mentioned it. We had no idea that Mikayo-san would come to see you himself."

I glanced at Mother. She was frowning, her face puzzled. From somewhere, she found the courage to speak.

"How very strange of Mikayo-san to visit us without giving word. And today of all days. Did he not make a pilgrimage to his home village?"

"I asked him that," Father said crisply. "He explained that his family had lived in Edo for many generations, so he had attended the nearest Oban Festival and did not need to travel. He had assumed that we would have done the same and was surprised we were not here when he arrived. He was even more surprised—in fact, shocked is more the word—when I was forced to explain that I had not been expecting him. I had no idea what he had come to see me about. It was deeply embarrassing for both of us."

"I am sorry, Father. As I said, I—we—had not expected him to be here today." Ichiro was clearly about to say more, but Father cut him off abruptly.

"Really? Is that all you are sorry about? Emica, are these wretched creatures truly my sons?"

Mother's face was ashen. Her mouth opened and closed, but no sound came from her lips. I heard both my brothers take deep breaths that sounded like sighs. Although I still had no idea what they had done that was so very bad, I guessed that they finally understood how truly angry Father was with them. Even though his anger was not directed at me, I was apprehensive of what was to come.

I forced my mind to work, trying to make sense of what was happening. I knew of Mikayo. He was a wealthy, respected businessman. Unlike Father, his wealth was inherited—his family had been the most successful moneylenders in Edo for generations. Until Father had, by his own efforts and astute business dealings, stolen that position from him. Tanaka—Father's chief clerk—had told me that the two men were, as he put it, the best of enemies. If either could do a business deal that would be to the detriment of the other, then the deal would be done without a second thought. I gathered that Father disliked Mikayo for his inherited wealth and traditional ways of carrying out business, whilst Mikayo hated Father as an upstart who was trying to usurp his rightful place in Edo's business world.

So why had Mikayo been here, today of all days? And without an appointment? That was almost stranger still. Nobody simply visited someone's house without making arrangements first, not even close friends. And above all, what had my brothers been doing, associating with Father's rival?

My curiosity was soon satisfied as I listened to what Father had to say, and I began to wish with dawning horror that it had not been.

TWO

Rice will thrive as long
As its roots have cool water.
That life is so calm

"Despite my surprise, I was courteous to Mikayo-san. I offered him tea, asked after his family. His only son worked at his business, I knew. A good, steady sort of a boy. Not too intelligent, but I have no doubt that Mikayo-san is proud of him." Father broke off and raised his eyebrows as Ichiro made a noise somewhere between a gasp and a cough. When he remained silent, Father went on calmly, his voice betraying the tension in his body. "Mikayo-san said his son was well and thanked me for my inquiry. He stopped then and looked at me as if he expected me to say more. When I did not, he spoke cheerfully.

"'Well, my friend, I have no doubt you know why I am here.' He went on before I could reply, which, as it turned out, was just as well. "I am so sorry to simply arrive like this, and on the day of your return from Oban Festival, but I could not contain my happiness for another moment. I had to speak to you.'

"My bewildered expression must have finally told him I had no idea what he was talking about. His beaming smile faltered, and I gathered my wits and spoke quickly before he could begin to speak again.

"'Naturally, it is always a pleasure to meet such a close business associate as yourself, Mikayo-san, even if it is somewhat unexpected. Please, do tell me what has brought you here so urgently.'

"He spoke slowly, his expression suddenly wary.

"'Your sons have not said anything to you, Kono-san?'

"His voice was almost pleading. I shook my head.

"'My sons? They tell me many things," I said as pleasantly as I could manage. "But as far as I am aware, nothing that concerns you.'

"I knew my response was so blunt as to be rude, but I could say nothing else. I had no idea what he was talking about. But I should have known, shouldn't I have? Ichiro? Satoru?"

Both my brothers chorused, "Yes, Father," their eyes still fixed on the tatami. Their embarrassment was contagious; I felt their discomfort and squirmed with them.

"So, perhaps you would be good enough to tell your mother and sister what you have done? And me, finally. In your own words. Ichiro?"

Ichiro cleared his throat. "We thought we were acting for the best, Father," Ichiro repeated stubbornly. Mother made a movement toward her son, but Father's hand chopped through the air to stop her and she sat down again, her hands drawing her face down into a mask of anguish. Ichiro blurted, "It wasn't our fault. It was Mikayo-san's idea in the first place. We often met his son at sumo bouts and naturally, given that we were in the same line of business, we got talking. He—the son, that is—said his father wanted to expand his business, but the market just wasn't big enough to allow him. We knew he meant that was because you stood in his way, of course. We sympathized with him but did no more, even though we kept meeting the son at sumo bouts. After a while, he started telling us how beautiful and talented his sisters were. How it was very sad that they had not been betrothed years ago, but his father was such a proud man that nobody but the very best would do for his precious daughters. We shrugged his words off. Of course he would say his sisters were lovely. After all, if anybody asks if we have a sister, we always praise Mi-chan to the skies in spite of her withered leg."

I glared at him, but he appeared not to notice.

"Anyway, the son finally asked us if we would like to come to an event his father was holding for various business acquaintances. We thought we might pick up some useful information for you, Father, so we agreed to go. We were going to mention it to you, but it just slipped our minds."

Father smiled, or at least his lips moved, but the smile did not reach his eyes.

"Really? That was...unfortunate. Do go on, Ichiro."

"Well, it was an excellent event. There were many geisha who played and sang. The sake flowed freely. Mikayo-san was a very attentive host. He spoke to us as if he had known us for years, as if we were respected colleagues. He..." Ichiro paused and swallowed, as if he was unsure how to go on. The deadly silence must have prompted him, as he finally went on in a rush. "He mentioned his daughters. Said how lovely, how talented they were. Told us, as if in confidence, that they were not betrothed as he had never found anyone he would be happy to accept as his son-in-law. I—we—were flattered, Father. I don't really know how it happened, but suddenly I found myself agreeing that nothing could be more fortuitous than a match between his daughters and Satoru and me. And at the time, an alliance by marriage between our two houses seemed to be the most sensible thing in the world."

Mother cried out loud, and Ichiro stared at her miserably, suddenly no longer an iki man-about-town, but a small boy who knew he had done something very foolish. Father remained silent. I glanced at him, rather in the manner of one who feels the first drop of rain and looks at the skies, anticipating a thunderstorm.

Father's face was still grim, but the fire had left his eyes. I realized with a shock that left me cold that he was no longer a young man. That someday the unthinkable would happen and he would die. He was everything to me, the rock that supported me through each and every day, and the knowledge left me wanting to echo Mother's despairing cry.

My brothers had done this. They had demeaned Father, leaving him less than the man I knew him to be. Those stupid creatures had acted without a thought for anybody but themselves. I wanted to howl at them, to make them listen to me until they understood how deep the loss of face was that they had inflicted on Father. How terrible was the shame they had brought on the whole family.

Naturally, I did nothing of the kind. I was a mere girl

child, and a crippled one at that. For all Father's extravagant praise earlier, I knew my place. But that did not stop me from longing to shake both my brothers until their teeth rattled.

"So Mikayo-san told me." Father spoke calmly, and I saw my brothers relax. Did they really think they had gotten away with this? Could they be so stupid? "We had a long discussion. Mikayo-san is of the opinion that young men can be thoughtless, and he regrets that he intruded upon me before my sons had the chance to speak to me. Naturally, I agreed with him. I had no option."

"Perhaps it is all for the best?" Mother's voice was breathy and hesitant.

"I hear you, wife. And perhaps you are right." Her eyes flared with a hope that died as quickly as it came as Father went on icily. "What's done is done. If I had told Mikayo-san that there could be no betrothals, that I was unhappy with the match and had no intention of combining our two businesses, then I would not only be offering him a deadly insult, but I would appear to be an idiot. The whole of Edo would know of it in a day or two, and the loss of face would finish me. Nobody would wish to deal with a man who had been made foolish by his own sons."

"But, Father," Satoru broke in eagerly, "that will not happen. If you and Mikayo-san unite, then it would only be to your advantage. You do far more trade with the gaijin than Mikayo-san, but he has many clients from amongst the aristocracy. The union would bring great prosperity to both houses."

I shook my head in disbelief. How could my brothers not see that being forced into such a union was anathema to Father? Whatever he did, whatever he had accomplished, he had done himself, for himself. I remembered the accounts ledgers stored in the upper room of Father's business premises, remembered seeing the slim volumes that represented the modest business that Father had run so many years ago. He had taken that small beginning and changed it into one of the most respected and thriving concerns in the whole of Edo, all by his own efforts. That was his way, and always would be.

Father smiled, and I felt the tension ease in the room. Only I stayed rigid, holding my breath as I waited for the final act of the performance to take place.

"I cannot forbid the matches," Father said calmly. "If I did, I would be as a dead man in Edo. I have told your future father-in-law that I am delighted by the union of our families. But that is all I have told him. He is a subtle man, and I believe he understood that this was not the time to discuss business. All will be done as it should be, and you will leave this house with my blessings."

"Leave this house...?" Ichiro thrust his head forward like a snapping turtle about to pounce on its prey. Satoru was slower, his puzzled face turning from Ichiro to Father and back again. "Surely, your new daughters will come to live here, Father, with us. For us to live in Mikayo-san's house rather than his daughters moving in with us would be unheard of. People will think it very strange indeed."

It was my turn to smile. Father had called Mikayo-san a subtle man, but surely, he was far more subtle still.

"Tell me, Ichiro, why do you think Mikayo-san is so eager to make a match for you both with his daughters? Is it possible that you are vain enough to believe it is because he thinks you are such great catches?" Ichiro made an indecisive gesture with his hands, frowning. "You are wrong. The only reason he has pursued you both so cunningly is because he thinks that by gaining you as sons-in-law, he has also gained my business. He is a clever man, without a doubt. He must know that if he had approached me honestly, I would have refused him. This way, he no doubt thinks that I have no option but to surrender and appear pleased about it. That our businesses will combine to his great advantage.

"He is wrong.

"I have agreed that you and Satoru will marry his daughters. But that is where it ends. On the day of your marriages, you will leave this house. You will not live here, and you will no longer be employed by me. If Mikayo-san thinks it worthwhile, you may work for him. It means nothing to me, for from that day onward, I do not know either of you. From that day onward, I will have no sons."

Father spoke the last three words with great emphasis. Ichiro climbed to his feet. He was trembling; I could see that his hands were shaking violently. I could only admire his courage as he took the few steps that took him close enough to touch Father.

"That is unheard of. The world will think you have gone mad." He spoke loudly, as if he was talking to a deaf man or a fool. His behavior was so insolent I tensed, expecting Father to strike him.

He did not. Instead, he smiled, the slow grin of a wolf that knows his prey is within striking distance.

"The world will understand perfectly. It will be Mikayo-san who appears foolish. He will have gained two worthless sons-in-law, but not a single thing more. The people who matter will see that I no longer acknowledge my sons, and that our businesses remain distinct. There will be gossip, but it will be Mikayo-san who loses clients. Nobody will want to deal with a dishonorable man, still less a man who has failed so very badly."

Ichiro's hands clenched into fists. Father regarded him calmly for some moments and then bowed his head once. His meaning was clear, the audience was finished. He waited calmly until Ichiro turned and—gesturing to Satoru to follow him—walked out of the room silently.

CHAPTER
THREE

The moon's light is cold;
What does he care for the pain
We bring on ourselves?

The day of my brothers" wedding was perfect. Warm, but not disagreeably so, with just a gentle breeze to cool those who had perhaps taken just a little too much sake.

Everything was just as it should be. The only slight shadow was the obvious surprise of the many guests when my brothers followed their new wives back to Mikayo-san's house. Naturally, nobody dared to mention it, but I knew that tongues would wag, and very soon.

Father showed not the slightest displeasure at the event. If he was not concerned with what the world thought, then neither would I care. Mikayo-san was obviously less content. His smile was forced, and it looked as if he wanted to get the happy couples away before my brothers—who were amongst those who had drunk far too much—could speak. Nothing would be said directly, but when the rumors began to spread, Father would know how to handle the situation. In any event, I could not see how Mikayo-san could complain. The whole of Edo must know that he had chased my brothers as husbands for his daughters. He had gotten what he wanted, if not what he had expected. Truly, as the proverb has it—be careful what you wish for, you may get it.

In the weeks that followed the ceremonies, Mother stayed in her apartment. When I ventured in to see if she was well—happiness, I doubted was possible—it was clear that she had been weeping. She glared at me through reddened eyes and demanded to know if I was content now. My brothers had been driven away from her. Had I dared to come to try to take their place in her affections, as I seemed to have done with Father? I slipped away, saddened that she seemed to blame me for my brothers" stupidity, but still amazed that she could not see that her sons had brought their downfall on themselves.

But I couldn't help it. Now that my brothers were lost to the family, I was as happy as Mother was distressed. No more teasing from them. No more brutal games where I was always the target. No longer would I be made to feel even more ugly and deformed than I was by their cruel comments. And although I knew it could not really be so, I did wonder if the gods had decided it was time my brothers were paid back for their treatment of me over the years. Their new brides were far from the beauties their father had described, and it seemed to me that both girls were already deeply possessive of their new husbands—they never took their eyes off my brothers for the entire day of the wedding ceremony. There would be no more sneaking off to visit expensive women of pleasure for my brothers, their wives would see to that. I doubted if they would even stand for their husbands spending all their spare time and money at sumo wrestling bouts. I knew I should feel guilty about my spiteful pleasure in all this, but somehow, I could not.

And best of all, Father had spoken to me in a way that made it obvious that I was to go back to Edo with him, to be at his side in the family business. True, he had not said explicitly that I was to take my brothers" place, but surely, that would come. I was sorry for Mother's distress, but I was so full of joy, nothing could diminish it.

Even with my brothers lost to the family, I did not fool myself that Father would ever have acknowledged me publicly if I had still been obviously deformed. I accepted that without hurt. It would have been too much to expect that he would parade a crippled daughter in front of the important men who made up his world. I gave silent thanks whenever I thought of Tengen for his gift of what—to me—was life. I remembered now that his parting words to me were that he expected to hear of me spoken of admiringly in the future. I felt a surge of excitement as I wondered if perhaps this would be so.

The thrill lasted only a moment. I shook my head and laughed at myself. Was it not enough that I was to be given my heart's desire and finally be allowed back into my father's world? I could help him, I knew I could. I could read and write, and my skill with the abacus was as great as any of Father's clerks. More than that, I had a feel for business. I understood—in a way that my brothers never had—that money was one of the important things in this world, far more important than traditional status. In the new world that was opening to Japan, it mattered less who one was than what one could offer, and in that respect, money was truly one of the greatest gifts.

My brothers had taken it for granted that money was theirs for the asking. Although they both worked in Father's office, they were lazy, leaving when they had a mind to go, not appearing to understand that money had to be earned and did not simply appear when they wanted it. They were both gamblers and spent yet more on expensive women of pleasure. If they had not been his sons, I guessed that Father would never have tolerated them as employees. I tried—and failed—to suppress a deep glee as I wondered what Mikayo-san was making of his longed-for bargain. Be careful what you wish for, indeed!

A sharp wind slid through the open shoji, sufficiently vigorous to ruffle the pages of the book that lay on the chabudai table in front of me. It was not my book. One of Father's messengers—Gen—had been instructed to teach me to read and write. To help me, he had loaned me a book of haiku written by the great poet Bashu. I had thought nothing of it at the time, but Tengen had explained to me that the book was old and very precious, and I had realized belatedly that it must have been very important to Gen. The paralysis of the morning—the dreaded disease that had left me crippled—had left me confined to our house for many, many months, and I had forgotten I still had the book for a long time.

Now, I stroked the binding lovingly. Tengen had taught me to appreciate the beauty of its words and illustrations. But to me, of far greater importance than its contents was the fact that Gen had freely loaned me his most precious possession.

We had parted on bad terms, Gen and I. Hindsight is a wonderful thing. At the time, I had had no idea that it would be more than a year before I would be well enough to think about seeing him again.

In the days just before my illness struck, I had realized that I had been unfair to him. In fact, my behavior toward him had been almost insulting. I had been full of plans to make amends, but the gods had seen fit to arrange things differently.

But at least I had the chance now to make things right. On my return to Edo, I would return his book and apologize to him for my unreasonable anger at our last meeting. For some reason, the thought of seeing Gen again made me uncomfortable. I could concentrate on nothing but what I would say to him. How he would react.

I told myself firmly that it was of no consequence. Clever as he was, Gen was a mere messenger boy. Father's chief clerk, Tanaka-san, had told me that Gen was one of the best calligraphers in Edo but had chosen to enter Father's service because he understood the way the world was changing, and he perceived that only men like my father had the drive and determination to succeed in that new world. Grudgingly, I admitted to myself that I owed him an apology for my behavior, and also thanks for giving me my first lessons.

No doubt he would be delighted to get his book back. It was a great credit to him that he had not asked Tanaka-san to enquire of Father if it could be returned to him. Apart from his book, I had no reason to suppose he had wasted a moment thinking about me. I would do well to follow his lead.

But the more I tried to push Gen from my thoughts, the more persistently did he intrude. Oddly, I found that I could not recall what he looked like. He was taller than me, much taller, I could remember that. And slender. Now that I came to think about it, he was too thin. His mother was very poor, I recollected. Was he thin because he could not afford to eat properly? That had never occurred to me, and now my conscience smarted.

I remembered he had always been very neatly dressed—naturally, anybody who worked for Father would be expected to be presentable, even a lowly messenger. But although clean, his clothes had been old.

His face I could not recall at all, no matter how I tried. I was distressed; how could this be so? The more I tried to recall Gen's features, the less I could see. I became so frustrated that my stomach began to knot. It was only when I found that I had clenched my fingers so tightly into my palms that the nails were hurting me that I forced myself to stop.

Perhaps if I thought of something—somebody—else, it might calm me? Immediately, I recalled Tengen sitting opposite me and instructing me that my mind was the greatest asset I had, if only I could learn to use it properly.

He had told me time and time again, "Do not try and force your thoughts to go down a path they are reluctant to tread. If they will not obey you instantly, there is a reason for it. Let whatever is worrying you go. Sit quietly; allow tranquility to be your guide."

It had made no sense to me for the longest time. I was—still am—a stubborn creature. It always annoyed me greatly if I misremembered something, and my first instinct was to worry at it until the answer came to me. How could forgetting about it help?

But Tengen was persistent, and eventually—grudgingly—I tried to follow his advice. At first, it was almost impossible. After a moment or two, my thoughts always veered from the path of meditation and tried to return to the question that was perplexing me. But I was determined that this new philosophy would not get the better of me, and finally I began to find it quite simple to sink into a state of ease, where everything—Tengen's presence, the songs of birds in the garden, the warmth of the sun in my face, even whatever had been bothering me so intensely a moment ago—swam around me without intruding on my thoughts in any way.

I found that once the state of oneness with nature became possible for me, I would emerge from my meditations refreshed and no longer at all concerned with whatever had eluded me. Better yet, often the answer to the conundrum that had worried me was there for the asking.

Alas, once Tengen had gone from my life, I got out of the habit of meditating and now I found it difficult to relax. I stared into space, concentrating on seeing Tengen's image opposite me, where he had sat so many times. I was not at all helped by the knowledge that I was using the image of my lover to recollect another man, but in spite of the discomfort that thought gave me, gradually I felt peace wash gently over my body and mind.

I was startled out of my meditation abruptly by the sound of my amah's voice. Even though Anzu had been my nursemaid from the day I had been born, she still treated me with great formality, and now she was calling respectfully from outside my room, asking if she could come in.

"Of course, Anzu," I called out. As she entered, she let a shaft of sunlight through the shoji that made her no more than a dark silhouette. And in the shadows I saw, not her dearly familiar face, but that of Gen, smiling with hidden amusement as my temper flared. My pleasure must have shown in my face as Anzu beamed back and asked if I needed anything.

"Not a thing, Anzu," I answered sincerely. "I have everything I need. Thank you."

Enlightenment is
Always around the next bend,
Hidden from us both

My left knee ached terribly. It only allowed me a little comfort if I stretched my leg out in front of me and flexed it almost constantly. But I was determined that I would not fidget. Still less would I complain.

Father had gestured for me to sit on the tatami as soon as we entered his private office, and I had obeyed without question. If I had known then that I would be expected to sit in the same position for hours, I would have tried to get myself in a better position from the start.

I watched Father constantly. I had nothing else to do. His office was enclosed on three sides by silken shoji. The fourth side was the bare stone of the building's outside wall. Although the room was very spacious—twelve tatami in size; I knew that as I counted each mat to occupy my mind—it held no furniture other than a chabudai table, which bore orderly piles of ledgers and stacks of papers, together with an ink brush and ink pot.

Father had seated himself behind the table and paused for an instant, as if collecting his thoughts, and then drawn one of the ledgers toward him. For the time it took the sunlight to advance halfway across the room, he did not speak.

This was not what I had expected. Not what I had hoped and longed for. Before my illness, when Father had brought me to Edo with him, I had sat in the outer office, enjoying the bustle of the constant comings and goings of clerks and messenger boys. Father's chief clerk, Tanaka, had kindly taken the time to show me how to use an abacus. He had been delighted when I had quickly mastered the art of complex calculations using the beads and frame. But once I knew how to use the abacus to its fullest extent, I was eager for more. I coaxed Tanaka into allowing me to learn to read and write, which was how I had met Gen.

I had loved those busy days. Reading and writing had proved unexpectedly difficult, but I am stubborn and was determined to learn. I reasoned that if a mere messenger boy like Gen could master the art, then surely I could not fail. And oh! How grand were my dreams in those lost days. I saw my future as being here, in Father's thriving business, becoming so invaluable that I was seated at Tanaka's right hand.

And now I was here, next to Father. But, alas, my dreams were now bitter memories. I had done nothing at all for almost half a day. I had learned nothing, spoken to nobody. Was this to be my future? I was so miserable I had to keep my eyes wide open to force the tears back.

The soft tap at the shoji distracted Father from his

ledgers, and I took the chance to straighten my back and ease my knees a little. Father called out for the clerk to enter.

"Kono-san." A rush of sound—voices, the clack of abacus beads, feet scuffling over tatami—came in with the clerk. He spoke quite loudly to be heard. "Goto-san is here for his appointment. Shall I show him in?"

"In a moment." Father turned his head to me and smiled. He had ignored me for so long, I was relieved that he had not forgotten I was there. "Mi., would you leave us, please? I am sure Tanaka-san will be pleased to see you. Come back when my visitor has gone."

"Of course, Father."

I was relieved to move at last, but also more than a little hurt that I was not to be allowed to stay for Father's meeting. The thought fled as I tried—and failed—to get to my feet. My withered leg was angry with me, and it refused to support my weight. I levered myself to arms" length and then paused, helpless. The clerk obviously saw my predicament. He took a step toward me but was checked instantly by Father, who spoke to him as if I did not exist.

"Botan-san, before you show my visitor in to me, I will need details of his account. Please bring them to me at once and apologize to Goto-san for keeping him waiting."

The clerk bowed deeply and walked back into the main room. His face was stone, but I could see from the rigidity of his back that he felt he had been reprimanded. I wanted to call out to Father, to ask him—no, beg him—to help me to my feet, but he had already turned his back and was shuffling the papers on his table into a neat pile.

My cheeks burned with shame. Without meaning to, I had brought dishonor on my father. The clerk had clearly seen that I was unable to rise unaided. I was grateful that

Father had intervened. How much greater would my loss of face have been if I had been forced to accept the man's help.

I set my teeth so hard I felt them grind. No matter, it was nothing to the pain I was about to bear. I had no idea how long it would take for the clerk to return with the papers, and probably Goto-san as well. I had to get to my feet, and quickly. I had no idea where my strength came from, but somehow, I managed to lever myself to my feet by thrusting my palms into the tatami and pushing as hard as my muscles could manage. I teetered on the edge of balance for a moment and then recovered in time to bow deeply to Father as he turned toward me. Did I see a glimmer of respect in his eyes, or was I grasping for the stars? I walked out with as much grace as I could muster. My fixed smile hid my pain, which was very great.

"Tanaka-san." I bowed deeply to the chief clerk, grateful that the movement eased the pain in my back.

"Mi-chan!" The elderly man got to his feet with a suppleness that I envied. "How lovely to see you again after so long. Has your honored father released you to me? I am just about to take tea. Would you like some?"

"Yes, please." Tanaka turned and raised his finger to a messenger boy, who came at a trot. I used the opportunity to sink to the tatami, but this time in as comfortable a position as I could manage.

"Tea for both of us," Tanaka instructed him briskly. The boy bowed and left without a word.

We were both silent then. I knew I was smiling foolishly with pleasure and, glancing at my companion, I was delighted to find that he was beaming at me. We both spoke at once, but Tanaka gestured politely for me to continue.

"It is so very good to see you again, Tanaka-san. I have been ill for a long time."

"Yes. Kono-san told us that you had contracted paralysis of the morning. We were all greatly concerned for you and delighted when he told us that you had begun to recover. It is a very serious illness. You were fortunate to recover." A twinkle came into his eyes as he added, "Although, I was never in any doubt that you would let a mere illness get the better of you."

I laughed with him. Was my stubbornness really so obvious? At that moment, I didn't care. I glanced around, drinking in the bustle of the outside office with enormous pleasure. This was what I had missed—the signs and sound of a prosperous business going about its normal routine. To be sure, sitting alongside Father was a very great honor, but this was better.

Our tea arrived and I poured two bowls carefully.

"So little has changed."

Tanaka-san twisted his lips. I stared at him suspiciously, guessing he was hiding a smile.

"Apart from the fact that your brothers are no longer here?" His tone invited a response.

"There is that," I said cautiously. "I hope they are happy in their marriages and, of course, working for Mikayo-san."

I thought Tanaka was struggling to suppress amusement.

"Who can say? Although it seems they have brought Kono-san great good fortune by their marriages. I have noticed that a number of Mikayo-san's more important clients come to us now."

I smiled with him. I had always been confident that Father would know how to handle the situation. Was it possible that my brothers had been foolish enough to complain about their treatment, even told anybody who would listen that Mikayo had expected to join his business with Father's as a result of their marriages and had been deeply disappointed? I would hardly have been surprised if they had, even though to do so would have caused Mikayo intolerable loss of face. I was about to share my thought with Tanaka when a deep hush fell on the room.

All of the clerks bowed, as did Tanaka. I supposed I had better do the same but raised my eyes to watch as Botan ushered a man through the silence and opened Father's shoji after a brief tap on the frame. As soon as he closed the screen, the normal hum of conversation rose again.

I was astonished. Father's client was a samurai.

What did a samurai have to do with the world of business? The man was in his middle years, I thought. Not fat, but prosperously built. His hair was shaven over the temples and scraped back in the traditional samurai topknot, and his robes were of the first style. I sipped my tea thoughtfully, trying to decide what—apart from the fact that he was here—was wrong about him.

It came to me suddenly. His walk was odd. He walked stiffly, with his hands held slightly away from his sides, his elbows bent, and his fists clenched. I recognized that walk; just so had I moved when I had first tried to walk without my crutch. Uncertainly, as if something important to me was missing.

His swords. That was it. Neither the long katana nor the shorter wakizashi swords hung from each side of his waist, and Goto obviously felt their lack.

I turned to Tanaka in astonishment. "Goto-san is samurai?"

"Indeed, he is. Although a recent client, Kono-san holds him in very high esteem."

I was puzzled and blurted out my questions without thinking. "But, Tanaka-san, why is a samurai concerning himself with business like a commoner? And why isn't he wearing his swords?"

I knew at once that my words had been impertinent, but Tanaka seemed not to notice. He sipped his tea and I guessed he was ordering his reply.

"Many things have changed recently, Mi-chan. A few years ago, the government issued the Danpatsuei Edict. Have you heard of it?"

I shook my head. Politics had never been discussed at home, and I had no curiosity about something that did not concern me. But I reasoned if Tanaka was aware of such things, then they must be important to Father's business, so now I listened with interest.

"Well, that edict allowed samurai to cut their topknot if they wished to. The noblemen didn't have to do that, but it was encouraged as it was more in the Western manner."

"But Geto-san hasn't cut his topknot," I protested.

"Obviously not, but you see, that was only the start of the changes. Two years after that edict, the Imperial Japanese Army was created, and all men below a certain age were forced to serve in the national army for a certain time."

I frowned, not understanding what this had to do with samurai. Seeing my confusion, Tanaka went on quickly.

"Before that, only the samurai and daimyo were allowed to recruit soldiers, and then only for their own service. At the same time, the hereditary stipends granted to the samurai by their own lords, the daimyo, were abolished." He paused, waiting to see if I understood.

"So the samurai were no longer wealthy?"

Tanaka's smile nearly split his face. "Exactly so. Of

course, many of the samurai families had built up wealth over the centuries, and the richest amongst them have farms and whole villages in their gift. But even so, the loss of the stipend had an effect, and also it was a most serious loss of face. It may seem a trivial thing, but recently, samurai were forbidden to wear their swords in public, and for many of them, that was the greatest blow of all. Daimyo may still walk this earth fully armed, but samurai—" He shrugged. "—may not."

My mind was working furiously. Goto might still consider himself a noble, but to have lost centuries of position in such a short time must have been an unimaginable loss of face. I guessed if Father considered him an honored client, then he must still be rich, but not so rich that he had not been forced to borrow money. How are the mighty fallen!

I sighed with satisfaction. Of course, Father had not wanted me present when he discussed business with Goto. A samurai would never countenance having a girl present under such circumstances. It was as unthinkable as a samurai being seen without his swords, I thought gleefully. Truly, the old order was changing. I found the thought enormously exciting.

Realizing belatedly that Tanaka was waiting for my response, I nodded. "I understand." I leaned forward to pour the last of the tea out of the pot and felt an uncomfortable obstruction in my obi. Gen's book of haiku. I had tucked it carefully in my obi and then forgotten about it in the disappointments of the day. I waited politely until Tanaka had lowered his bowl before I asked, "Tanaka-san, it seems that not only my brothers are absent, but also Gen."

Tanaka raised his eyebrows, his expression suddenly

wary. Even though I sensed that something was wrong, I plowed on anyway.

"Gen was kind enough to loan me a book of haiku to help me with my reading. Of course, as I have been so ill, I was unable to return it, but I have it here now. Is Gen upstairs with the ledgers? I would like to give the book back to him before Father calls for me."

My tone was far too bright. Tanaka was looking at me thoughtfully, and I was seized with the ridiculous idea that he was embarrassed by my questions.

"Gen no longer works for your father. He left some months ago."

FIVE

See the eagle soar
Far above the earth. What does
He make of mere men?

A messenger approached Tanaka at that moment, and the chief clerk put his tea bowl down at once and turned his attention to the boy. I was certain he was relieved by the interruption. I was also disappointed and puzzled by what he had told me.

Gen himself had spoken of how honored he was to work for Father. I had gathered that he saw his future here, and I could not understand how he had left in what were obviously odd circumstances. I waited impatiently for the messenger to leave so I could probe Tanaka further, but a glance at his set lips and stiff back told me I could hope for little more. Very well, I would try another tack.

"I am so sorry to hear Gen is no longer here. I know that the book he loaned to me is very valuable, and I have already kept it for far too long. I seem to recollect Gen saying he lived with his mother, who was in very poor circumstances. Perhaps you know her address and I could arrange to send the book to her?"

I hoped my expression was suitably unconcerned. I realized I was holding my breath in expectation of an answer and forced myself to let it go slowly. I had no idea how I would be able to find my way to Gen's home. Even as the thought came to me, I acknowledged to myself that it was ridiculous, that I was as a drowning man clutching at reeds. But suddenly, it mattered greatly that I explain to Gen that I had been unable to return his book because I had been ill and had not simply kept it selfishly.

"Gen no longer lives with his mother." Tanaka's tone said the subject was closed. I searched frantically for some way to find out what had happened to Gen, but Tanaka was already turning aside, reaching for the first in the pile of papers at his side. He spoke kindly but firmly. "I understand that you have kept up your studies, Mi-chan. Perhaps you could help me by telling me what this says? My eyes, alas, are getting old and it would not do to make mistakes."

He was lying. We both knew that. But courtesy commanded me to take the paper from him and read out loud what it said. When I finished, Tanaka immediately pushed the ink pot and brush to me and asked if I would write a reply for him.

Distracted as I was by Gen's mysterious disappearance, time passed quickly as I became drawn back into the fascinating minutiae of the world of business. I only noticed that Father's client was leaving when a sudden silence fell and the samurai strode through the office as if he owned it. Fascinated, I noticed that Father had not escorted him personally, and I wondered greatly at that. With or without his swords, the man was samurai and of such a superior caste to my family that it was almost unbelievable that my father was doing business with him. Not so long ago, the samurai would have sent an intermediary to do his bidding rather than soil his aristocratic hands with discussions about money.

Tanaka nodded at me, smiling, and told me to go tap on Father's shoji. "It is time for the mid-day meal, Mi-chan. Your father often forgets to eat, he is so preoccupied by business matters. It would be no bad thing for you to remind him that he needs to eat for the good of his health."

Because I had been sitting more comfortably and, I supposed, was not afraid of showing my deformity in front of Tanaka, I got to my feet quite easily. Not gracefully, but not too hesitantly either. As Tanaka had instructed, I tapped on the shoji and slid it back at Father's command.

"Mi-chan." I thought Father sounded vaguely puzzled, as if for a moment he had forgotten I was there. My spirits plunged but revived at once as he smiled and beckoned me in. "What time is it? My client's business took rather longer than I expected."

"Time for the mid-day meal, Father." I spoke boldly, buoyed up by the knowledge that I was speaking for Father's good. "Tanaka-san and the clerks are eating, so I am not needed at the moment."

Father frowned and I wondered if I had overstepped the boundaries of politeness. Then his face cleared. "Is it so late? I daresay you will be hungry, then. Would you like to go to the teahouse we went to on your birthday?"

"Yes, please, Father."

He was right. I was very hungry. My stomach groaned loudly at the thought of food and—rather than politely ignoring it—Father laughed. He was a man who smiled rarely and laughed even less. I guessed his meeting had gone very well, indeed.

The teahouse was full, but just as on the day of my birthday, Father was shown to a table immediately. He seemed to be in such a good mood that when he asked if I would like some mochi, I found the courage to say I would prefer sea vegetables and rice.

"So, have you been of use to Tanaka-san?"

"I think so. I read some papers to him and wrote down the replies he dictated. Tanaka-san has been telling me of the many changes that have been taking place recently." Wondering if Father would disapprove, I added cautiously, "I was surprised to see a samurai in a place of business, and without his swords, so I asked Tanaka-san about it."

"Many things have changed in the last few years." Father nodded thoughtfully. "Goto-san is not the only samurai who does business with us now. He was the first to come to me, and I am deeply privileged that it appears that he has spread the word amongst his fellow samurai that I am both an honorable and discreet man. Who knows? Perhaps some of the daimyos will follow their example!"

He chuckled softly at his own words, and I laughed with him, although I did not understand what was funny about it. More for something to say than because I was really interested, I asked, "Do many of the gaijin still come to do business with you, Father?"

He looked at me oddly, as if I had asked an unexpected question.

"I doubt there is a business in Edo that could thrive without the gaijin's custom these days. Did Tanaka-san tell you why the samurai have been encouraged to cut their topknots?"

"Yes," I answered quickly. "He said the government wanted to encourage them to appear more western." Encouraged by his approving expression, I blurted, "But I do not understand why that is so. Why would samurai want to look like gaijin?"

Father paused as if collecting his thoughts and then spoke slowly and carefully, watching me as if to make sure I understood what he was telling me. "You know that for many centuries, our country had nothing to do with the outside world? Very few gaijin were allowed into the country to trade, but they were kept together and not allowed to mix with our people more than was necessary."

I nodded. Gen had told me this.

"That all changed when the gaijin black fleet sailed into Edo harbor—before you were born, Mi-chan—and their leader, Commander Perry, demanded of the shogun that Japan be opened to the outside world, that trade be freely undertaken between us and the gaijin. I was a young man then, but I remember to this day standing in Edo harbor and wondering at their ships and the arms that the men bore. I knew at that moment that change was inevitable, whether we liked it or not." He paused, staring at the table. Obviously worried that there was something wrong with the food, a server bustled over and bowed deeply. Father ordered more tea and waited until the man had gone before he went on.

"Did your tutor tell you of such things?" he asked.

Tengen had not, but Gen had. For some reason, I was reluctant to bring Gen into the conversation, so I lied.

"Yes, Father. He explained to me why there are so many gaijin in Edo now. I remember meeting one of them in your office, before my illness, Dickson-san. I still have the gold coin he gave to me."

"Dickson-san is—for a gaijin—a courteous man. He is still my client; I see him often. He was kind enough to enquire about your health frequently while you were ill.

Would you like to see him next time he comes to the office?"

I agreed eagerly, sensing that it would please Father. I remembered him saying that all gaijin liked children. Alas, I was no longer a child. Would that mean that Dickson-san no longer liked me? I would worry about that later. For the moment, Father had still not answered my question. I asked cautiously, "I understand that there are many gaijin in Japan now. But I don't see why the government wants samurai to look like them."

Father seemed amused by my question, so I went on boldly, "If they are here in our country, wouldn't it be more polite for them to try to look like us?"

A sudden, long forgotten memory came back to me of Gen saying bitterly that the gaijin were superior to us in many ways. That their ships could cross oceans and their weapons could kill men with the ease of a scythe cutting rice stalks. Did I already know the answer to my own question? I was sure when Father went on.

"We have always thought of ourselves as a great nation. But the bitter truth is that compared to the wide world around us, we are nothing. The gaijin possessed means of making goods and shipping those goods around the world that were unknown to us. We could not hope to match the ease and cheapness with which they produced things. It seemed, at the time, that they were superior to us in every way. Their weapons were more advanced. They could communicate with each other across continents. Even their medicine could heal better than ours. At first, we thought it was all magic. But when we got to know the gaijin better—and that was soon, for the shogun in his wisdom knew that he had to allow them into our country or else they would simply come anyway and take everything that was precious to us—we saw that there was no magic behind it all, just techniques we could not have imagined.

"And the more the gaijin came, Mi-chan, the more important they became to us. We need to trade with them. More than that, we need to know their secrets so that, in time, we do not just compete with them, but we become superior. And that is why the government wants us to appear more like the gaijin in appearance and in our ways. They need to trust us, to no longer see us as backward foreigners. Do you understand?"

"Yes, Father," I responded at once. I didn't really understand, but the habit of obedience was deeply ingrained in me, and I would never dream of questioning anything Father said to me. He stared at me without speaking for so long, the silence became uncomfortable. When he finally spoke, his words left me confused.

"My sons are lost to me, Mi-chan. Your mother is too old to have more children, and I have neither time nor inclination to take a second wife." He paused, and then went on, "Do you understand what I am saying?"

"Yes, Father." It seemed to me that we were going round in circles, but it was not my place to break the endless chain. I was relieved when Father seemed to go off at a tangent.

"You have often heard me say that prosperity grows on the tree of perseverance." He raised his eyebrows, apparently expecting an answer. I could not bring myself to say "yes, Father" yet again, so I simply nodded. "And this is a true saying, to be sure. But there is also a proverb that says it is better to be like the bamboo and bow to the prevailing wind than a great tree that will not yield and is blown down. Do you see the truth of that, Mi-chan?"

He leaned forward slightly, holding me rigid with the intensity of his gaze. I was bewildered, but I knew that Father was deadly serious, and I thought that my answer mattered to him. I took a deep breath and said firmly, "I understand what you are saying, Father."

He stared at me for a moment longer and then—when I nodded seriously—he smiled and sipped his tea silently. I waited in vain for anything further.

SIX

Day will follow night
As surely as the birds will
Sing with each new dawn

I could make nothing of the strange episode with Father, so eventually I shrugged it aside, telling myself that I was making far too much of it. I was not used to the company of adults. No doubt it was something I would come to understand when I was a little older—and wiser.

Besides, I had so many other things to keep my mind occupied.

I rode on my own pony, following Father into Edo every day. At first, I wondered if Mother would be annoyed that I was not left with her, but it soon became obvious that she barely noticed my absence. In the whole house, only Anzu missed me. As soon as I came home, she would be waiting for me, ready to rinse me, help me into the bath, and then dry me carefully afterward. When I asked her what she did with her day, her face fell.

"Nothing," she said simply. "All the other servants have their work to do, so they have no need of any help from me. Now and then, your mother shouts for me when she needs something, but other than that, once I have tidied your clothes and cleaned your room, I have nothing to do. And that takes no time at all because you are so very neat," she added reproachfully.

I felt sorry for Anzu, but I had no idea how I could help her, other than to tell her of my own day. She listened eagerly, but always seemed vaguely disappointed.

"And you have met no one you like?" she asked hopefully.

I stared at her, not understanding what she meant. "There are lots of people who work in Father's office." I shrugged. "And many clients come and go. But I can't say I know any of them well enough to say if I like them or not."

"Oh. That is a shame." Anzu seemed very sad at my answer, and in a flash of insight, I understood what she meant.

"I go to Edo with Father to learn the business, not to meet a young man who might want to marry me, Anzu."

"Oh, I know that Mi-san. But I thought perhaps…"

Her voice tailed off and I hid a smile. Naturally, Anzu hoped I would marry, and quickly have babies. Babies that she could care for just as she had cared for me and my brothers. Did it hurt her, I wondered, that my brothers were lost to her? That she would never have the chance to be the amah to their children? I asked, "And what about you, Anzu? Is there no nice young man amongst the servants that you might want to marry?"

I had spoken jokingly, so I was amazed when Anzu blushed and kept her gaze firmly fixed on the tatami.

"I have never had time to think about it, mistress," she muttered.

I was instantly intrigued. I looked at Anzu carefully, seeing not my loyal amah, but a woman. She had been nursemaid to my brothers, but I guessed that she had probably been no more than a child herself when she had been sold into my family's service. She was probably no more than thirty or so, and was a small, slender, pretty woman. Astonishingly, I felt a pang of jealousy. Anzu had always been there for me, night and day. How was it possible that she now had a life of her own?

"Who is he, Anzu?" I demanded. "One of the other servants? Tell me!"

"Nobody, mistress. At least…" She took a deep breath, her hands fidgeting together like birds fighting. "Since you have not been here, I have been about the kitchen more and I have had time to speak to some of the tradesmen who come to the estate."

My thoughts darted. Surely not the fishmonger, who came every other day? I had seen him occasionally, on the days when I had nothing better to do than wander to the kitchen to see if there was anything to eat. He was a young man, well set-up, but stinking of fish. Or perhaps the tradesman who brought us fresh vegetables? No, I seemed to recollect that he was an older man, and very deaf besides.

"Who, Anzu? Who has taken your fancy?"

"It's nothing like that, mistress. I promise. I would never leave you, you know that. It's just that, with nothing much to do, I've let it be known that I can run errands if the other servants are too busy or can help them out in any other way. I like to be occupied. And…" She paused, clearly unsure how to proceed.

"And?" I nudged.

"Well, a good while ago, the house steward asked me to run down to the stables. It was the blacksmith's day to visit to see if any of the horses needed attention or to do any repairs that were needed in the way of kitchen or garden tools. Cook had found that his favorite copper pan had a loose handle, and he wanted the blacksmith to mend it. So, I took it down to him."

Anzu looked at me anxiously, and I realized I must have made a noise. She obviously took my astonishment for disapproval, so I spoke quickly to reassure her, even as my thoughts whirled.

"That was kind of you," I said lamely.

The blacksmith! The last man I would ever have thought of as attractive to Anzu. Or any woman, at that. I knew him to be a deeply kind man—he had made the reins and stirrup that worked with my built-up geta to help me walk so much better. And when I was a child, he had always been friendly and helpful. But he must have been at least ten years older than Anzu, and—just as the fishmonger stank of his fish—the blacksmith always carried the warm smell of horses with him. Nor was he in the least handsome. He was quite small and strongly built, his hair was receding, and he had some teeth missing. But a kind man, I reminded myself hurriedly, and he had surely been a good friend to me.

But. I had always assumed he was a married man. At his age, it would have been very odd if he was not.

"The blacksmith is a very nice man," I said cautiously. "But isn't he married already, Anzu?"

She spoke eagerly, and I felt a wash of pity as I understood that my amah was delighted to have the chance to talk about him.

"His wife died last year. Unfortunately, she could never have children, although Mori-san would have loved to have had a large family. He feels it very greatly that he will have no son to pass his skills along to."

I was deeply ashamed. I had known the blacksmith since my first faltering attempts to ride. He had helped me greatly, asking no questions, when I had no one else to turn to. Yet, I had not even known his name. Perhaps because of that, I spoke warmly to Anzu.

"I see. Clearly, you like Mori-san a great deal. Does he also like you?"

"Oh, yes." Anzu was so eager, it was almost embarrassing. "After that first time, we have spoken each time he has come to the estate, and recently he has begun to talk about how lonely he is and how it would be very good to take another wife before he is an old man."

That, I supposed, was how such things worked amongst the lower classes. And who was I to say it was not better—far better—than the arranged marriages and long betrothals forced on to the children of the rich? I thought of the man I was to have married, before the paralysis of the morning had left me deformed, and righteous anger boiled in my stomach. I would have hated every minute of every day I was his wife, but if his mother had not declared that her precious son could not wed a cripple, I would have obeyed my parents" wishes and married him.

I spoke hotly, without thinking. "If Mori-san likes you, and you like him, then let nothing stand in your way. Nothing."

Anzu's mouth fell open. She blinked rapidly, and I thought she was struggling to hold back tears.

"But what if you marry and have children of your own, Mi-san? Who would be their amah if I was not here?"

Her loyalty made me want to cry myself. I spoke briskly to hide my emotion.

"I will not marry, Anzu. I am sure of that." I did not speak simply to reassure her. As soon as my future mother-in-law had released me from my promises, I had decided that I would never want to marry a man who was willing to take a hopelessly deformed cripple as his wife. What woman with any pride would be willing to wed such a man? Anzu looked stricken, so I added quickly, "And if by some chance I did, then surely you will still be nearby? Still able to look after my children just as you did me?"

That was a lie. Our blacksmith was a prosperous tradesman and so of much higher cast than a mere servant. He would never countenance his wife continuing to work. Naturally, he would expect her to be at home, cooking his food and keeping the house clean and sweet. And—in time—caring for her own children.

"Oh, of course!" Anzu was so overcome by happiness she forgot to speak formally. It was that which convinced me that her affair with the blacksmith was serious.

Although she was many years older than me, I found myself speaking strictly to my amah. This news was so unexpected, so unlike the Anzu I thought I knew, that I was deeply concerned for her.

"I will not stand in your way, Anzu. But please, be careful. You barely know Mori-san. Give yourself time to get properly acquainted with him before you commit to anything. Has he actually asked you to marry him?"

"No, Mi-san, not exactly. But we get on so very well, I'm sure it will just be a matter of time."

"When he does propose, make sure I am the very first to know," I said firmly.

For once, it was quiet in Father's business premises, and I remembered the amazing conversation with Anzu vividly. I almost envied her. She had little in her life—so much less than I did—yet, I felt that in her own way she had achieved a happiness that eluded me. All nonsense. I had what I had wanted for so very long. A place at Father's side. The chance to help him in his business.

After much thought, I had come to understand that that was what Father had meant when he had told me so very seriously he had no sons. I was to take the place of my dishonored brothers. The knowledge made me very proud. I was certain I could help Father far more than either of my lazy, wastrel brothers ever had.

I glanced up idly and my pulse quickened with pleasure and surprise as I saw one of the senior clerks usher a tall, fair-haired man toward Father's private office.

I recognized him at once. Dickson. The friendly gaijin who was such a good client of Father's and who had given me a costly gold coin as a memento of our first meeting. I had not seen him since my illness, but I had never forgotten his kindness toward me on that occasion and I had hoped to see him again. He had another, much younger man, another gaijin, with him, but I had eyes only for Dickson.

I prayed that Father would call me into his office, and a moment later, my prayers were answered as the clerk who had escorted Dickson in hurried over to me and bowed deeply, whispering that my Father wished me to join him at once.

For once, I did not bother to try and stand gracefully but scrambled to my feet as quickly as I could. Taneka smiled at my enthusiasm and gestured for me to hurry. I wished that I could.

The men were all seated by the time I tapped on the shoji and entered Father's office. From the corner of my eye, I saw the younger man begin to rise—almost as clumsily as I had done a moment earlier—but Dickson put his hand gently on the other man's arm, forcing him to sit down again.

"Mi-chan," Father greeted me affably. I was immediately anxious that I would do something wrong and cause him to lose face in front of this important visitor. "You remember Dickson-san, no doubt?"

I bowed formally. Dickson bowed in his turn, the precise amount that courtesy demanded of a man greeting his host's young daughter. Unusually for a gaijin, his manners were perfect.

"Mi-san, how very good to see you again, and looking so very well. If it pleases you that she is to join us, perhaps Mi could be permitted to sit down, Kono-san?"

"Of course." Father lowered his head, and I sat down as gracefully and carefully as I could at an appropriate distance from the men. "I have ordered tea. My daughter will be pleased to serve it for us."

Immediately, the younger gaijin leaned across to Dickson, tugging at the sleeve of his robe urgently. He said something in a language I could not understand, and Dickson responded curtly, shaking his head in obvious exasperation. I stared from one to the other in confusion, wondering if I was the cause of his sudden irritation.

A breath of wind shakes
The blossom of the peach tree,
But the bee clings on

I had no time to consider the exchange further. A soft tap on the shoji heralded the arrival of our tea, and I was on my feet as gracefully as I could manage as soon as the tray was placed on the chabudai. If I had not understood before that moment how important Dickson and his companion were, I knew now. I had never seen the table bare of papers before, although I supposed it might have been so for the samurai's visit.

Generally, I am the least vain of women. With my disfigurement, it could hardly be otherwise. But I am proud of my skill with the tea ceremony, and today I took extra care = whisking the green matcha tea powder, filling the bowls just full enough to allow them to be served and sipped in comfort.

Father and Dickson took their bowls with murmurs of thanks while the strange gaijin simply smiled. I watched him with interest as I sat carefully on the tatami, arranging the skirts of my kimono to hide the awkward angle of my left leg.

He was dressed in Western-style clothes, and I thought how very uncomfortable he looked. Dickson was kneeling effortlessly in his loose robe, but the younger man clearly could not get himself comfortable. He sat rather than knelt, and shifted from side to side constantly, his long, thin legs appearing to be even more ungainly than they probably were as each was wrapped in cloth from his thighs to his ankles.

Thinking myself unobserved, I glanced at his face and was shocked to find he was staring at me so intently, I flushed with embarrassment.

His rudeness simply reinforced what I had already decided—I did not like him. His face was glistening with perspiration, and even though I was some distance from him, I could smell his sweat. Had he not bathed today? Surely Dickson would have ensured that he was clean. His hair was so very fair that I thought it looked like a dandelion seed head, waiting to be blown away by a puff of wind. All of that was unfortunate, but it was his eyes that had my toes curling with instinctive repulsion.

They were very light blue. I thought they looked like pebbles seen through water, and for a moment, I wondered if he was blind. The idea was silly, of course. He was glancing around with apparent interest. As if he had read my thoughts, he turned his head and smiled widely at me. Although I lowered my own gaze respectfully, I had seen that his eyes were not only a disturbingly strange color, but were also rather large and very protuberant. I shuddered involuntarily, hoping nobody had noticed my distaste.

"Mi-chan." Dickson's voice broke in on my distress and

I turned my attention to him gratefully. "I am so very glad to see you again. Although your father assured me that you were restored to full health, I am delighted to see that is so with my own eyes. But forgive me, in the pleasure of seeing you again I have forgotten my manners entirely. Please allow me to introduce my nephew to you. Unfortunately, he has not yet learned to speak more than a word or two of Japanese, but of course, I intend to remedy that as soon as possible. I have already told him about you, so you have the advantage over him. His name is Ian-san. Like so many young men these days, he likes to be informal."

I gathered from that remark that Ian must have preferred to use his given name rather than his surname, which was odd, but could, I supposed, be excused as he was gaijin and, hence, naturally had no manners. I rolled his name around my tongue silently, grateful that it was short. Ee-yan. Yes, I could remember that. Before I could respond, I was appalled to see that Ian was climbing clumsily to his feet and bowing jerkily to me.

"Mi-san, I am very pleased to meet you."

I was amazed that he was speaking in Japanese. He obviously found it difficult, as he spoke slowly, concentrating on every syllable, and I had to listen very carefully to make out what he was trying to say. The overall effect was rather false, as if he was an actor repeating his lines. That bothered me not at all—I supposed I should find it touching that he was making such an effort to speak in my language, but any pleasure I might have felt was swept away by his insolence.

How dare he rise and speak to me directly like that, without a word of instruction from either of the two older men? I was a young woman who was unknown to him. It was unheard of. And worse still, my only option was to also stand and bow politely to this oaf who had no idea of how to behave courteously.

I heard Father clear his throat nervously, but it was Dickson who intervened and smoothed over the awkward situation. He spoke in fluent Japanese, so colloquial that he might almost have been a native of Edo.

"Mi-chan, please forgive my nephew. Our ideas of courtesy in the West differ very greatly from what is polite here in Japan. He will learn, I assure you, and the sooner the better. And you must make allowance for the fact that his parents are missionaries—not here, but in Africa—and he learned his manners there."

The name meant nothing at all to me, which made me think the country must be very far away. I managed to keep the polite smile on my lips as I thought about Dickson's words. Although I had never encountered a missionary here in Edo, I knew that generally they were disliked. Tanaka told me only yesterday that he had actually been stopped in the street by gaijin missionaries that very morning.

"A man and a woman—his wife, I suppose. I only stopped when they stepped toward me because I thought they were lost and wanted directions. As soon as I saw the big, black book tucked under his arm and the ornament around his neck, I realized my mistake. But it was too late by then. I could hardly just walk away."

I was fascinated and asked, "Did they actually speak Japanese, Tanaka-san? What did they say to you?"

"The man spoke quite good Japanese," he admitted grudgingly. "He wanted to know what my religion was." I gasped in disbelief at the rudeness of the question from a stranger, and Tanaka nodded, clearly pleased at my reaction. "I had to give some answer, so I told him I was Shinto, as had been my forebears for many generations. You would have thought that common decency would have made him apologize and step away, but no. He actually put his hand on my arm to stop me from leaving."

This was too much! If it had been almost anybody but Tanaka who was telling me this, I would never have believed it. As it was, I breathed, "What did you do?"

"I glared at his hand until he seemed to understand that he had overstepped the mark very badly and finally he took it away. But still he had not finished with me. He said, "Forgive my presumption in stopping you, honored sir. But I can see that you are no longer a young man. Have you given any thought to what will happen to your soul when you pass away?'"

"No!" This was beyond belief, but Tanaka was nodding.

"He held the black book out to me before I could find breath to tell him what I thought of his behavior and tapped a page.

"'If you will only allow me to read to you from the Holy Bible and reflect upon the words of our savior Jesus Christ, then you will no longer have any fear of death and the hereafter, sir.'

"Now, as you know, Mi-san, I am a patient man."

Tanaka was nothing of the sort. I had seen many clerks and messengers reduced almost to tears under the lash of his tongue, but now was not the moment to disagree.

"And, of course, everybody in Japan is tolerant of other religions. But even so, I felt that this was just too much. This strange gaijin had questioned my religion, even touched me, and now he was telling me that his god could save my soul for me. Now, I know that your family is Buddhist, but I expect that you know that those of us who follow the path of Shinto, we believe that after death, the soul becomes a spirit deity and eventually passes on to become part of our collective ancestral spirit. Had this gaijin been a little less rude, I might have taken the time to explain that to him, but as it was, I was so furious that I simply told him that my soul—before and after my death—was my own business. I walked away from him before he could say another word, but I am still astonished at his presumption. As if it isn't bad enough having gaijin here in Edo without them trying to convert people to their silly religion."

I agreed with Tanaka completely. Why the gaijin wanted to convert everybody to their religion, rather than allow us all to live happily side by side, I—in common with all my countrymen—could not understand. But I knew that it made the gaijin missionaries deeply disliked and distrusted, and I looked at Ian carefully to make sure he had not hidden a big, black book inside his clothes somewhere.

I guessed that Dickson understood my concerns when he barked what was clearly an order at Ian and the younger man sat down quickly, his pale skin flushed an ugly brick red. I felt quite sorry for him.

"Please, Dickson-san, convey my thanks to your nephew for his greeting. I am naturally delighted to meet him," I offered.

Dickson smiled and said something softly to Ian. To my horror, his blush deepened, and I was certain that his bodily odor grew even stronger.

"As, of course, am I," Father broke in smoothly. "Tell me Dickson-san, is Ian-san going to be here in Edo for some time?"

It seemed to me that there was more in his tone than the words—innocent and polite as they were—suggested.

"Yes, indeed. Ian is fascinated by all things Japanese, as are many of my fellow countrymen. It is my sincere hope that he will learn the ways of your country and also learn to love it as much as I do."

Father nodded with apparent satisfaction and the conversation quickly drifted to politics, all of which meant nothing to me. It appeared that Ian-san was as lost as I was. Every time I glanced up, I found that he was staring at me intently.

I was relieved when Father lifted his tea bowl and I could get up to make more tea in response to his signal. I was deeply puzzled. Although nothing at all to do with business had been discussed, it seemed to me that both Dickson and Father were very pleased.

As was only correct, I filled Ian's tea bowl last, and it took a great effort not to wrinkle my nose as I stood at his side. I was right. He smelled of spoiled pork. Tanaka insisted that all gaijin smelled like that. He confided in me that he was sure that they did not bathe every day. The thought horrified me, and I wondered what Ian would smell like later in the year. It was barely late spring yet. What on earth would he smell like in the hot, humid, Edo summer?

I jumped as he spoke to Dickson, apparently urgently. Dickson pursed his lips and then spoke hesitantly.

"Kono-san, this is rather difficult." He broke off and smiled at me kindly.

I was instantly concerned. Had my expression betrayed my distaste of Ian? If it had, Father would have picked up on it instantly. I wanted to wail out loud. Dickson—and hence any relative of his—was important to Father. If I had been discourteous, surely it would be the end of my visits to Edo, and it would all be the fault of this thoroughly disagreeable young gaijin. How very unfair all this was! I relaxed slightly as Dickson went on.

"Although my nephew is a young man, he is a very experienced doctor. He specializes in diseases that affect young people. Naturally, I knew he would be interested in the fact that Mi-san had survived the paralysis of the morning, so I told him all about her."

I risked a glance at Father and saw he looked as puzzled as I felt.

"It is very kind of you to take such an interest in my worthless daughter, Dickson-san." He smiled to show how honored he was, and I felt a stone roll away from my chest. "I am sure that Mi-chan would be delighted to tell your nephew all about her illness, if that would be of interest to him. But I am afraid it will be very difficult as she does not speak any English at all, and I think you said your nephew has very little Japanese."

Father spoke decisively, obviously pleased that the situation had been settled with such ease. Ian and I could not communicate, so that was surely an end to the matter.

But he was wrong. Ian was still staring at me with intense interest. He did not turn away from me as he said something rapidly to Dickson, who nodded.

"My nephew is a young man, Kono-san, but also very clever and skilled in the art of healing the sick, and he is deeply committed to helping his patients. He has listened to all I could tell him about Mi-san with great interest and he is certain that he can help her to walk better and relieve any pain that she may still suffer. He would like to examine her leg."

As soon as he finished speaking, Dickson folded his hands together in his lap and stared down at them intently. I realized that my mouth was sagging open with shock and closed it so abruptly that my teeth clicked together. I looked toward Father helplessly, wondering how he could answer such a grossly dreadful request politely.

"Dickson-san." He cleared his throat and hesitated before he went on. "You understand, the best doctor in the whole of Edo has attended to Mi-san. This man is so very well-respected that he cares for the shogun's health. We are fortunate that he also attends to my family. He knows Mi-chan very well, and I am certain that nothing has been left undone that should or could have been done."

He trailed off, and I understood the sub-text of his words perfectly. The shogun's own physician had cared for me. To allow an unknown young man—and a gaijin at that —to not only examine me but perhaps also give an opinion that differed from our doctor's was unthinkable.

"Of course." Dickson was nodding briskly.

I was relieved; clearly, the discussion was over. But I was wrong.

"I mean no disrespect to your own doctor, Kono-san. But my nephew is very widely respected in our own country for his skill. Cases that have been thought impossible of a cure have been referred to him, and he has been able to help many young people recover from dreadful diseases such as paralysis of the morning. Our medicine is very different from what you are used to, and it may be that in this case it is superior. I realize it is unusual for a man of your status to consider allowing a gaijin doctor to treat your daughter, but I feel it could do no harm and could even do Mi-chan a great deal of good. Nobody else need know."

If I had not been so amazed by Dickson's response, I would have found his last words extremely odd. As it was, I kept my eyes firmly focused on the tatami as I waited for Father's blunt refusal.

It did not come.

"Dickson-san, you understand this is very difficult for me."

His voice was soft, almost pleading. I was confused. There was no mention of me at all. Clearly there was something going on here I was not meant to understand, yet instinctively I did. This discussion was not about me at all. It was about a subtle balance of power between Father and Dickson. I was no more than a bone that was disputed by two dogs.

"But of course," Dickson said promptly. "For myself, I can see no harm in allowing Ian to examine Mi's leg. Do not let his youth mislead you, there is none better in his area of expertise. I realize the issue is one of protocol or, perhaps it would be better to say, trust?"

Father's expression was stone, but I could feel the anger beneath his calm. This was important, even if I could not understand why. I had hated being examined by our own doctor, a venerable man who had treated me since I was a baby. The thought of this gaijin probing my body made me shudder. For a moment, Father shifted his glance to me, and I read a mute appeal in his gaze. I spoke instinctively.

"Father, I know that our own doctor is the most respected practitioner in Edo, and a very important and skilled man. But surely it would do no harm for Ian-san just to examine me? As Dickson-san has said, nobody outside this room would ever know."

At that moment, I cared nothing at all for myself. All that concerned me was saving face for Father. Agreeing that Ian could examine me put the responsibility for this strange situation squarely on my own slight shoulders, and if it helped Father, then I was content.

"Out of the mouths of babes and children," Dickson breathed softly. "I congratulate you on your daughter, Kono-san. She is truly the child of a great man."

I gathered from his words and Father's silence that the matter was settled. It was only then that I realized that in order to examine me, Ian would be very close to me, indeed.

How long, I wondered, could I hold my breath?

Your touch on my cheek
Is as soft as the summer
Breeze that cools my skin

Days and days passed with no further mention of Ian, and I convinced myself that all my concerns about him treating my withered leg had been for nothing. Alas for my confidence, my hopes melted like snow at the touch of spring when the day came that Father sent for me immediately after the morning meal and told me that today I would not be going into Edo with him. His voice was calm, but there was a defeated air about the way his shoulders were slumped and he avoided my gaze. I knew instinctively what was to come and began to shake.

"You will have the honor of a visit from Dickson-san and his nephew today."

In spite of my distress, it did not escape my notice that Father did not call Ian by name. Was it that he did not like the young gaijin, or was it more a dislike of the situation he had been forced into?

"I'm sure you remember that Ian-san was interested in your condition. Dickson-san tells me that his nephew is certain he could help you walk better, so I have decided to allow him to examine you. It is for your own good."

Father's final words sealed the situation. I would never have argued with his decision anyway, but as it appeared he was sure that he was acting for my benefit, I understood that I should not just accept the situation, but also that I must appear pleased and grateful.

"Thank you, Father," I said colorlessly. A thought gave me hope. I blurted, "But Ian-san does not speak Japanese. How can I explain to him what treatment I have received? How my leg feels? I would not like to waste his time." My confidence was dashed at once.

Father said woodenly, "Dickson-san has very kindly agreed to be present while Ian-san examines your leg, to translate for you. Anzu will also be present to help to answer any questions that Ian-san may have about the time when you were taken by the fever."

The thought of Ian looking at my leg, perhaps even touching it, was bad enough, but at least he was a doctor and presumably would take a professional interest in my deformity. But the thought that Dickson—a relative stranger and not even a doctor—was about to see my body filled me with horror.

My mouth formed the word "no" soundlessly, but Father appeared not to notice as he turned away and left me without another word. I longed to call him back and plead with him, at the very least to ask that he stay with me, but I did not. Even in my misery, I reasoned that he must have important business in Edo that day. If he had not, then surely he would have stayed with me. Of course he would have.

Anzu ushered my visitors into my apartment, her expression anxious. Of course, Anzu had never met gaijin before, had probably never even seen one. Because of that, I was careful to speak to her pleasantly, doing my best to keep my voice reassuringly calm.

"Thank you, Anzu. These gentlemen are colleagues of my father. Ian-san—" I inclined my head politely toward the younger man. "—is a doctor who is very skilled in treating my illness. He has been kind enough to offer his services to help me to walk better and have less pain. Please stay, I may need you to explain what treatments I have already had."

Anzu bobbed her head nervously, but I thought some of her initial terror had evaporated at my explanation. I was about to get to my feet to greet my visitors formally when Dickson spoke gently but firmly.

"Please do not trouble yourself to rise, Mi-chan."

Anzu's mouth gaped with shock at hearing fluent Japanese emerge from a gaijin's lips.

"It will be necessary for Ian to examine you, and to do that, you must be sitting down. He has a number of questions to ask you, if you will permit me to translate?"

"Of course, Dickson-san."

I stayed exactly where I was, trembling so hard that it would have been impossible for me to get to my feet even if I had tried. I had a sudden, clear vision of myself getting as far as my arms could support me and then falling back to the tatami as my strength failed. The thought was almost as ignominious as the act would have been.

Dickson spoke briskly to his nephew and then turned to me, his expression business-like rather than concerned. I decided at once I would follow his lead and treat this examination as something that did not concern me greatly.

"Ian would like to know how long ago you became ill and what was the duration of the disease."

That was easy enough. I checked with Anzu—after all, I had no real idea how long my illness had lasted before my fever broke and I regained awareness—and then answered Dickson carefully.

Before he passed on my response to his nephew, he paused, his lips pursed. When he spoke, his words were very far from what I expected.

"Mi-chan, I understand that this first examination will be very difficult for you. But perhaps it would be a little easier if we could all be more informal? After all, this is hardly a business meeting. My given name is Tom. As you know, my nephew is called Ian. Shall we do away with formality when we are private together? Would it not be good if we were simply Tom and Ian? And if I called you Mi?"

He was smiling as if his words were no great thing. But I was appalled. I had never even called my brothers simply by their given names. Such a thing was unheard of. But what could I do? I had no option. Father honored this man, so I must offer him equal respect.

"Of course... Tom." There, the dreadful word was spoken. "If that is what you would like. But not in front of Father," I said firmly.

"Naturally." Tom seemed very pleased. I was relieved I had apparently done the correct thing. "We will be formal when your honored father is present. This will be our little secret."

He smiled, his eyes twinkling. Yet I was certain there was something more behind his smile, something I could

not understand. Something I was not supposed to understand. I glanced at Anzu, wondering if she had noticed
anything. Her expression was fearful, but when I smiled at
her, she relaxed visibly. I shrugged my concerns aside. It
was obvious that Tom meant to put me at my ease and had
no idea how outrageous his request was.

I had no time at all to brood over the strangeness of the
situation. Ian shot question after question at his uncle,
who translated equally rapidly. How had I been treated
initially? What medicines had been prescribed for me? Did
any of my treatments help? And, finally, the dreaded
moment, could he look at my leg?

I twitched aside the skirts of my kimono unwillingly,
turning my head aside. I had long ago become immune to
my leg's ugliness, but now the knowledge that it was being
inspected by two strange, gaijin men made me deeply
conscious of its deformity once again.

Ian spoke sharply, his voice urgent. Tom translated
quickly.

"That contraption on your shoe, Mi. Did the doctor
order that to be made for you?"

"No." My voice was a whisper. I was reluctant to talk
about Tengen, my friend and lover and the person who had
explained to me how the built-up geta for my withered leg
would help me walk better. Reluctantly, I decided I had no
choice. "My special geta was designed for me by a very
clever man. He was a monk who taught me to read and
write. Without it, I cannot walk without the support of a
heavy crutch. But the stirrup and reins were my idea," I
added proudly.

The two gaijin chatted back and forth. I watched them
both, trying to read an outcome from their expressions and

failing. Although I knew it could not be so, I thought they were both trying to hide amusement.

Tom spoke finally, his tone soothing. "As you know, Ian is a very skilled doctor. He has dealt with many cases of paralysis of the morning. Unfortunately, he is certain that all of the medicines that were prescribed for you—and also the hot cloths and ointments—were all virtually useless."

Anzu gasped out loud at such terrible bluntness. I should have reprimanded her, but I was so angry myself that I could not. Ian, a young man who was barely out of childhood himself, thought he knew better than a venerable doctor who was so skilled he cared for the shogun? I took a deep breath, ordering my thoughts, before I spoke calmly.

"I thank your nephew for his opinion. But what is done is done and I am certain that my doctor did the very best he could for me. Can he do anything to help my leg now?"

I was triumphant. Of course, the answer would be "no," and the loss of face for him would be unbearable. His shame would be so great he would never be able to return. Such was my pleasure that I felt a flash of pity for him. My smugness was short-lived.

Tom corrected me with his smile still in place, but iron in his voice.

"Ian is certain that he can help you greatly. He thinks your built-up geta and stirrup are good ideas in principle, but unfortunately, they can only help you to *appear* to walk better. They can do nothing at all to make your leg stronger, or to help bring the knee joint into better alignment, which is the vital thing. From that point of view, they are causing further damage. He thinks you should stop wearing them at once."

Horror made me dumb. Discard my wonderful geta?

Throw away the only thing that allowed me to have the appearance of normality? Was this stinking gaijin being deliberately hurtful to me? Or was he so puffed up with his own pride that he could not believe anybody could better him in his profession? It must be the latter, I decided.

Anzu broke in before I could speak. Her face was working, and I could see she was holding back tears with an effort.

"Dickson-san, it is not my place to interfere, and I am most sorry if I seem impolite. But I have cared for Mi-san since the day she was born, and I know how brave she is. She has suffered so very much from the day she came out of her long sleep after her terrible illness. Can you really help her to…to be like everybody else again?"

Anzu broke off, obviously terrified that she had dared to speak out of turn in such a way. I was about to soothe her, but Tom spoke first.

"It is good to know that Mi is in such safe hands as yours, Anzu. I cannot help Mi. But my nephew is a very skilled doctor, who has helped many young people who have suffered paralysis of the morning. I trust him. If he says he can help Mi to walk better, without pain, then he will do it."

"Then he must help her."

Anzu spoke simply, and it seemed from that moment that it was a done thing.

NINE

Field of rice, bowing
To the morning wind. Tall and
Straight in the evening

If it had not been for Anzu's joyful expression, I might have found the courage to refuse to allow Ian to help me. But Anzu had been a mother to me for the whole of my life, and I could not bring myself to crush her hopes.

So, I told Tom I would be most grateful if Ian could find the time to help me and sat passively as the two men conversed. I was surprised when Tom spoke to Anzu, not to me.

"Anzu, please bring a large bowl of very hot water, some soap, and a clean towel."

Anzu's face radiated pleasure, this was surely more like what she had expected. Our own doctor had ordered that my leg should be poulticed with hot cloths every day. I guessed she expected something similar was about to happen now. She scurried off at once.

"Now, Mi, Ian needs to examine your leg very carefully

before he can decide what is to be done." He paused delicately. "Would you like me to leave the room during the examination?"

"No!" The word was torn from me. I was going to hate being touched by Ian, but in spite of my earlier concerns, I would be happier to have Tom present. If Father trusted him, then so should I. "Please stay. I will need you to translate what he wants me to do."

"Then, of course, I will stay. This is a little difficult, Mi-chan, but I must ask you. I wonder if it appears to you that Ian does not seem to be quite clean?"

I was appalled. I had tried so very hard to not to make it obvious that his rank stench turned my stomach. I avoided Tom's glance as I muttered that I had noticed nothing of the sort.

"You are very polite, Mi. Even to Western noses, he sometimes smells rather of perspiration. He is very aware of it, and I can assure you that he is very grateful that here in Japan everybody is far too polite to even notice it."

"But he is a doctor!" I exclaimed. "Can he not cure himself?"

"I'm afraid not." Tom shrugged his shoulders. "It appears there is no cure for what ails him. I assure you, he really is very clean. No matter, as the saying has it in my country "what cannot be cured must be endured." Fortunately, this is not the case with you. Let me explain what Ian is going to do for you. He has already taken a good look at your leg. Now, he wants to see how much range of movement you have. He will ask you to bend your leg in various ways and try to straighten it. He will feel certain parts of your body carefully to see which muscles need special care. Then he will ask you to walk without your special shoe so he can assess the differences between your legs and whether your hips and back need additional care."

"Our own doctor has already done all that," I said stiffly.

"I'm sure he has. But Ian needs to check for himself."

Anzu arrived back at that moment with the hot water. We both stared in astonishment as Ian took off his jacket and rolled up his sleeves before soaping his hands and fore-arms and drying them carefully. Had he washed my leg, it would have been understandable, but to wash himself? This was beyond strange.

I had no need for Tom to translate as Ian pointed at my leg and then made a crooked arm. I guessed he wanted me to move my leg from the knee as much as I could, and I did my best to oblige. Alas, the knee refused to budge. Before long, I was soaked in perspiration as I desperately tried to move muscles that defied me and refused to so much as twitch. Finally, Ian held his hands up in a gesture that I took to mean I should stop.

He knelt beside me, and I stared straight ahead as he pushed my skirts firmly out of his way. His hands were surprisingly cool and his touch efficient. I tensed as he began to feel my leg, beginning at the top of my thigh and working down to my ankle. Finally, he put his hand on my buttocks. I was rigid with horror before I realized he was indicating he wanted me to turn over onto my stomach. I was grateful I could bury my burning face in the tatami as he began probing again, this time down the length of my leg at the back.

Finally satisfied, he sat back on his heels and spoke to Tom, who then asked me to stand and walk about the room.

Anzu darted forward at once and held her hands out to

me, just as she had done when I was first learning to walk again. She leaned back and I levered myself to my feet, using her as a counterbalance.

At that moment, I hated myself even more than I hated Ian. I felt violated. I wanted to shout *no more,* even though it would have disappointed Anzu and caused Father to be angry with me. It was only the memory of Father saying, so very deliberately, *I have no sons,* that kept me silent.

I was all Father had left. He had invested his hopes for the future of the family and the business in me. Dickson—Tom—was important to him. I could not bring myself to betray his immense trust simply because of my dislike of Ian.

Once the decision was made, I was grateful that I could take refuge in trying to balance. Without my special geta or crutch for support, I was forced to totter with my arms held stiffly out at shoulder height for balance, swaying with each step. I was like a puppet barely controlled by unskilled hands and I hated my obvious deformity. After only a few steps, I found I was exhausted and was secretly delighted when Anzu clucked her distress and insisted on helping me to sit down again.

I found a bitter satisfaction in knowing that after such a display of deformed weakness, even Ian would have to admit that he could do nothing for me. I stared at Tom stonily, waiting for the words that would release me from this torture.

"Excellent. Ian says it is just as he would have expected after so long without proper treatment."

My mouth dried; I could not speak.

"He asks me to congratulate you on making such an excellent recovery with regard to your bodily strength. He would like to begin your new treatment as soon as he can get the correct brace made, which will be crafted exactly to your measurements. It will take some time to find a craftsman who can do the work, so please do not think we have forgotten you."

Brace? I had no idea what he was talking about. My head was reeling. Both men stood, obviously preparing to take their leave, and courtesy made me attempt to rise. Ian moved forward quickly, putting his hands on my shoulders and forcing me—quite gently—to remain seated.

It was the final indignity. All spirit drained from me. I wanted to weep, but even that consolation was denied to me as both men smiled at me with obvious pleasure, clearly expecting me to share their delight.

TEN

See how quickly our
Footprints in the sand are lost
To the rolling tide

It would surely have appeared to the casual observer that my life had returned to its new and delightful normality as my daily rides into Edo with Father resumed as if nothing had happened. But I was not fooled. Every time a clerk went to the door to escort a client into Father's private office, my heart bore the weight of a stone as I wondered if it was Tom coming to tell Father that Ian was ready to fit my brace. Whatever strange, gaijin contraption that turned out to be.

But when the blow came, I was not in Edo at all.

Father sent a servant to tell me that my presence would not be required in the office that day, as Dickson and Ian would visit me later, here at home. I heard Father's horse clatter briskly onto the road, and I nursed the silent hurt that his action had caused. How much easier would it have been to bear if only he had taken a moment to tell me himself!

I waited silently, refusing to allow even Anzu to be with me, as the morning hours crawled past. With each moment, I retreated almost into a stupor. When I finally heard the clatter of the house bell, I felt nothing but relief that the moment had finally come.

"Mi-chan, here we are at last!" Tom's voice was hearty. I bowed my head in response, too exhausted to even attempt to rise.

"Dickson-san, Ian-san, thank you for sparing the time to come all this way to see me. I am honored," I said formally.

"Now, Mi," Tom scolded me, "didn't we agree that there was to be no formality between us? No matter. Here is Ian, and he has great news for you."

I glanced at Ian, noticing the hefty package cradled in his arms. He kneeled by my side at once to unwrap his parcel, peeling layers of paper and silk bindings aside with such care that I understood that whatever was inside was obviously of great importance.

Finally, he unpeeled the last layer of wrappings and shook them aside.

I stared and stared and felt the blood run from my face as I choked back a gasp of horror. I had thought that using my old, heavy, ugly, *obvious* crutch the worst thing that could ever happen to me. Now, I knew I had been wrong.

In comparison to the thing that Ian cradled lovingly in his arms, my crutch was almost beautiful. At first glance, I thought it was some sort of life-sized toy leg, constructed clumsily of iron and leather. Ian hefted it in his arms and with the change of angle I realized that it was actually a hollow cage.

He intended that I should wear that hideous thing? My lips moved, but no sound came from between them. Horror had left me both numb and dumb.

Obviously, Ian saw nothing of my distress. He squatted beside me quickly and whisked my kimono to one side deftly, at the same time holding the cage against my leg as if he was measuring me. Satisfied, he spoke urgently to Tom.

"Ian asks that you make yourself comfortable, Mi. Fitting your brace make take some time. Will you stretch your leg out as well as you can?"

I obeyed numbly. I sensed that Ian was excited. His meaty smell was worse than ever. The stench forced me to breathe through my mouth. He ran his cold hands down my leg, and instantly I was certain that the gesture was not necessary, that he simply wanted to touch me.

His grip was firm as he lifted my leg and pulled the hideous cage over my knee. I was deeply uncomfortable at once, and it took all my willpower not to push it away. Ian rotated the cage around my leg and began to adjust a number of screws that fitted beneath the leather padding at the top of the cage.

It felt as ugly as it looked. I could restrain my disbelief no longer.

"This will help me walk better? I doubt I can even stand in it, it's so heavy."

Ian must have heard the incredulity in my voice as he began to speak quickly. Perhaps it was his tone of voice, or more likely that I understood that he was trying to justify inflicting this thing upon me, but I knew almost what he was saying before Tom translated for me.

"Ian says he understands that you will find it heavy to begin with, and it is not pretty, but given time it will help to straighten your leg. He also wishes to instruct you in certain exercises that will strengthen your back and leg muscles. He is certain that if you are willing to work with him, eventually you will be able to walk without support."

I stared at him incredulously.

"This...thing will help me walk again? How? It is heavy. It is ugly. It hurts. I was far better with my special geta and stirrup."

In truth, I had endured worse hurt since my illness, but I wanted to impress on Ian how very much I hated his cage. To my horror, I sounded like a spoiled brat mewling about taking my medicine.

"Ian says it will help, if you are willing to work with him."

There was a definite change in Tom's voice. It was no longer kind, but rather he sounded hurt. I stiffened, deeply worried that I had offended this man who was so important to Father.

"I will try," I whispered.

Tom nodded. He was smiling again, and I was relieved.

"I thought your father handled your brothers" unfortunate situation remarkably well."

I glanced at him in surprise, amazed that Father had discussed the affair with him, and also wondering why he had chosen this moment to raise the subject. His expression was open and encouraging, so I responded quickly, relieved to have something to distract me from Ian's searching fingers.

"It was very difficult for Father. If only my brothers had thought to discuss the matter with him before it was too late, I'm sure all would have been well."

"Indeed. I had heard rumors that Mikayo-san's business and your Father's were to merge as a result of the family unions, but I guess that is not so."

It was not a question exactly, but there was a note in Tom's voice that said he expected an answer. Flattered that he thought I knew so much about Father's business, I nodded and answered him quickly.

"My brothers clearly thought that would happen, and I believe Mikayo-san also expected it, but Father was adamant. He knew nothing of what had been agreed upon until Mikayo-san came to see us unexpectedly, and he was deeply disturbed by what my silly brothers had done behind his back. In fact, he was so angry with them that he disowned them. He told me he no longer had any sons."

My voice rang with pride as I said the last words. Tom was a subtle man for a gaijin; I hoped he would understand how important that made me to Father. I was sure he did when he responded.

"Then he must be very proud to have a daughter who is so useful to his business. Times are changing very rapidly, Mi. Very soon, I believe that women in Japan will begin to take their place alongside their menfolk, just as was the case in times long gone."

I nodded eagerly, delighted by his comments. I had vaguely heard of women who had fought alongside their men in the past, women who had been acclaimed warriors in their own right. But those women had been aristocrats, not normal girls from lower-caste families such as I was. Yet his words re-ignited the fire in me.

My lover Tengen had said that he was sure that at some time in the future, he would hear my name spoken with pride. Father must see some quality in me, to accept me in place of my brothers. For myself, I longed to be able to help Father with his business in any way I could. Tom seemed to simply accept that this should be so, and I was deeply grateful to him for it. If this important man believed in me, then the very least I could do to repay him was to accept that his nephew was doing his best to help me.

"Ian says that he is satisfied. May I help you to stand?" Tom offered his arm courteously, and I took it without hesitation.

Alas, all my doubts had been correct. The brace felt like a stone around my leg, anchoring me to the spot. The best thing I could find to say about my cage was that it was so heavy I was sure I could balance easily with its support. But as for walking! That was surely impossible.

I was absurdly disappointed. Although I had never really expected that Ian's efforts could help me, now that the moment had come, I felt like crying.

Ian said something quietly. Tom did not translate, but from the sympathetic tone of his voice, I understood the gist of his words instinctively. *The brace is strange to her. It will take time.*

"Come, Mi. Ian and I will both help to support you. Try and take a few steps. We will not allow you to fall."

Tom spoke kindly, yet my anger flared at once. I had already taught myself to walk again—first with the aid of a heavy crutch, and then again with my geta and stirrup. I neither wanted nor needed their help, nor would I let this strange gaijin contraption defeat me.

Wordlessly, I shrugged off Tom's arm. He opened his mouth to say something, and I was surprised when Ian broke in, his voice authoritative. Tom grimaced but stood aside.

With my arms held out stiffly on each side for balance, I moved my right leg forward in a short step. I clenched all the muscles in my withered leg as best I could and ordered the leg to move. I hissed in frustration as the weight of the brace defeated it and nothing happened. I tried again, but failed to even lift my foot off the floor.

Ian rose and moved to stand a little way in front of me. He held his hands out, not quite touching me. I understood at once what he expected, and I nodded.

I tried again, and again. I clenched my teeth tightly with frustration, close to screaming as the leg refused to move.

Tom murmured, "Perhaps your crutch would help, Mi?"

I did not look at him but concentrated on Ian. His strange, light eyes were staring coolly straight at my face, and I understood that he would not help me in any way. That pleased me for some reason, and I tried again.

This time, my foot left the floor. I could not take a step, but at least it moved. I was panting with the effort, and furious that I had not been able to do more.

"Again." Tom had translated the word so often that I understood it effortlessly. But formerly, it had been a polite request. This time, it was an order.

"Yes." I hissed the single word and put all my strength into moving my caged leg. This time, I managed to lift my foot and shuffle perhaps half a step. Because my good leg was further forward, the movement upset my balance and I wobbled.

Tom was at my side instantly, grabbing for my arm. I resented his help deeply, but courtesy made me accept his tight grip. For a moment, I wondered what the strange noise I could hear was, and then I realized that it was Ian laughing, an unpracticed, creaking bark of sound.

Whether at me or his uncle, I had no idea.

ELEVEN

When the heron stoops
In the flooded field, he is
As silent as death

I showed Father my leg, clad in the hideous brace, at the evening meal. Mother—for once—was present. Although she made no comment, I saw that her expression was sour as she glanced at it.

I had pinned all of my hopes on Father hating the device as much as I did. How could he not? It was ugly. It emphasized my deformity in a way that my clever built-up geta never had. And clearly, it would do no good to help straighten my leg. If it were possible, then our own doctor would surely have suggested it at once. I conveniently forgot that it was Tengen and not the doctor who had told suggested my lovely built-up geta.

"Ian-san had this made for me." I spoke timidly into the silence. "He says it will help straighten my leg, but I don't believe him. It is so heavy I can barely lift my foot when I am wearing it, and it is hideous. Everybody who glances at me will know I am a cripple."

My voice rang with defiance, and Mother stared at me with wide eyes.

Father took so long to reply that I was sure his thoughts had drifted elsewhere. Finally, he said, "Dickson-san has told me that his nephew is greatly respected in his own country. Although he is a very young man, I understand that he is consulted by colleagues who are much older than he is because his knowledge is so great."

My spirits sank to nothingness. I knew what was to come and that I had no argument against it.

"If Ian-san says that—" He waved his hand at my leg, clearly lost for the right word. "That contraption will help you, then it will. And I am very distressed, Mi-san, to find that you are so lacking in gratitude for all the time and care that such a distinguished doctor as Ian-san has spent on you. I am sure he has far better things to do with his time than attend an ungrateful girl."

Father might as well have slapped me as chastise me with such cruel words. I had angered him, and I knew the only thing left for me to do was to fall to the tatami and know-tow full length, saying nothing until he chose to speak to me again, praying that he would accept my apology. But I did not move. I was so aghast at the unfairness of his words I stayed on my feet until he turned stiffly to stare at me.

"I am in error, Father."

I spoke with my head bowed. I knew I had no doubt made things worse by daring to complain, but I was so disappointed and frustrated I had to say *something*. Had I said what was running through my mind, I had no doubt at all that I would have found myself in a monastery the next day.

To my astonishment, Mother spoke timidly into the crackling silence.

"Husband, I am sure Ian-san is a very skilled doctor...in his own country, anyway. But is it likely he will have ever tried to heal a Japanese person? We are not gaijin. It may be that his cleverness does not work for us. I am sure that our own doctor did his best for Mi-chan, and if this *thing*—" She spat the word with distaste, pointing rudely at my brace. "—could help her, then he would have had one made for her at once." Clearly shocked by her own daring, Mother then fell silent.

Father did not reply, and I wanted to weep. As if it wasn't bad enough that I had brought Father's wrath down on my head, it now appeared that he was angry with Mother, as well. Yet I dared not speak. I felt, miserably, that whatever I said would only make the situation worse.

"Mi-chan." Father's tone of voice gave me hope. I dared to raise my gaze to his face. "Your device appears to be very heavy. Is it painful for you?"

I was tempted to say instantly that it gave me great pain, but I could not lie to Father.

"It is very uncomfortable, and it makes it very difficult for me to walk. But it is not very painful."

"And you can take it off at night?"

I nodded miserably.

"Then you must not be a monk for three days, as the saying has it. You will persevere with it. It will not be forever."

Father spoke gently, but I wanted to wail out loud as I understood that his mind was made up.

"I respect Dickson-san's judgment. If he believes that

Ian-san can help you, then it will be so. I know that it is an ugly thing, but other people cannot see it; your kimono hides it very well. And surely a little discomfort is nothing at all if, eventually, it means you can walk again unaided?"

Father turned his head away and picked up his tea bowl, tipping it meaningfully toward Mother to show her that it was empty. She rose at once and poured him more. Before my illness, it was I who served Father his tea, but now I was too slow, especially when wearing my brace. Walking was so difficult for me that the tea would have been cold before he could sip it.

By that simple action, I knew my fate was sealed. Father had made up his mind. I was to wear the hated brace until Ian was satisfied that I was either healed, or he admitted that it did not work and I could discard it.

At that moment, I hated Ian more than I could ever have thought possible. I wished I could explain to Father that it was not just the brace—hideous though it was—that I found repulsive. It was Ian himself. Every time he touched me with those cold hands, I wanted to flinch away. When I was forced to meet his gaze, those protuberant, pale eyes filled me with distaste. And as for his smell! The memory of it made me shudder.

And now, Father had condemned me to suffer all that, as far into the future as I could see. I thought miserably that I would rather wear my special geta forever than tolerate Ian for one more day. But now, I had no choice. I knew that I had escaped lightly. If it wasn't for Father's love for me, then he might have put me aside for my shameful rudeness, just as he had cut off my brothers. I was, I knew, the most fortunate of girls.

But that knowledge did not stop me from hating every

moment I was forced to spend in Ian's company. And there were so very many of those.

He came to the house frequently. Sometimes, Tom came with him; sometimes, he was alone. Not that it mattered to me. Tom lingered only long enough to say hello and enquire after my health, then he vanished into Father's apartment and I did not see him again until Ian had finished with me.

Each visit was the same. He adjusted the brace minutely and watched me as I did the exercises he had shown me. I did not dislike them; apart from the fact that they concentrated on my back, they were not unlike the exercises I had done with Tengen.

I thought of my lover often, wondering where he was and if he had finally rediscovered happiness. Was there a woman in his life? I supposed there would be, and I was pleased that I felt no jealousy. What, I wondered, would he make of my brace? Of Ian, come to that? Knowing Tengen, I rather thought he would be tolerant of the gaijin doctor; his only question would be if he were helping me. If so, then all was well. I wished I could think the same way.

The brace was doing me no good at all. I was certain of that. Grudgingly, I acknowledged that the exercises had strengthened my muscles, as I found it easier to walk, even with the massive weight of iron and leather dragging me down.

Anzu insisted that the brace was helping. "Only look, Mi-san," she pleaded. "Your knee is much more like it used to be, and your leg is far shapelier."

She was, of course, seeing what she wanted to see. She was looking at my leg with the eyes of love, and as the saying has it, eyes dazzled with love see a pimple as a dimple. But I knew she was deceived and eventually forbid her to comment on my leg as her enthusiasm annoyed me.

For myself, I simply did not look at the brace at all. Anzu took it off for me before I bathed and when I went to bed, but I turned my head away from her, refusing to look until the ugly thing was put away.

I was determined that the contraption could not help me, and I longed for the day when Ian was forced to agree with me. Surely, that day must come soon!

"Mi. Please stand for me."

Ian explained his words by raising his hands, palms up. He had no need; as far as I was concerned, the only good thing that had come out of his repeated visits was the fact that I had learned to understand his language. I dared not try to speak it for fear of appearing stupid if I made mistakes, but with so much repetition, I now found it easy to understand his instructions. It was just as well, as Ian still could speak hardly any Japanese.

Father would be very pleased when I told him of my new skill, I was sure. I guessed that he would hate having to rely on an interpreter when he spoke to the gaijin. I sensed that he was not really happy that Tom spoke such excellent Japanese when he had not a word of English. I could help him. The knowledge filled me with delight.

My thoughts had wandered—I found it easier to accept Ian's close presence if I thought of something else—and I glanced at him in surprise when he cleared his throat and repeated his instructions, pointing at my brace, which lay on the tatami. Would his manners ever improve, I thought sourly?

"We will leave it off for the moment. Would you like me or Anzu to help you to your feet?"

He looked surprised when I shook my head and scrambled to my feet unaided. It was only when I was standing that I realized I had betrayed my knowledge of English by acting on his instructions, but all embarrassment was driven out by Anzu's cry of pleasure.

"You see, Mi-san! I was right. Look, you can stand. You are not leaning sideways at all. Not even holding your arms out for balance." She clapped her hands with pleasure.

I wished I could share in her joy, but I knew she was wrong. I was only standing well because I had been taken by surprise at Ian's command. If I tried to walk without support, I would lurch along like a lame horse, my deformity obvious to the world.

It appeared that Ian thought differently. He stood— quite gracefully considering his ridiculous clothes—and walked to the other side of the room. He turned and held out his hands to me.

"Walk toward me, Mi. Don't think about it, just do it."

I was so angry, I did not even bother to pretend I didn't understand what he was saying. I was absurdly pleased. At last, the moment had come when I could show him that all of his treatments had been for nothing. I was crippled. I always would be.

With no hope at all, I put one foot in front of the other —my deformed limb first. I expected to stumble. I would hardly have been surprised if I had fallen, I had become so accustomed to the support of my hideous brace.

But it did not happen.

Without the heavy brace to tie me to the earth, my leg

felt so very light that I found myself walking almost effort-lessly. I limped, certainly, but hardly more than I had done when I wore my built-up geta.

I was so shocked, I cried out loud.

Anzu rushed to my side at once, grasping my arm and peering anxiously into my face. I put her aside gently and turned, walking back to the center of the tatami. I slid to the floor and—for the first time since Ian had put the brace on my leg—pulled aside my kimono and looked at my withered limb.

I had no words. Anzu had been right all along. The knee was still out of alignment, but it no longer appeared as if it was back to front. Ugly, but not so hideous that it made me want to cry. Almost as wonderful, my leg was no longer flabby and clearly useless. Rather, it was shapely and appeared strong.

Anzu was staring at me. She had tears of joy in her eyes. I could not bear to look at her and glanced at Ian instead. He was smiling, although whether because he shared Anzu's pleasure or because he was delighted with his own cleverness, I had no idea.

"Anzu, you may leave us now," Ian said.

I translated his words without thinking.

Wind moans ceaselessly
At this time of year. I long
For the peace of spring

Ian waited until Anzu had closed the shoji behind her before he spoke. "You shame me, Mi."

I stared at him in astonishment and shook my head. "I do not understand," I murmured in Japanese.

Whether Ian understood what I had said or guessed from my puzzled expression, I could not tell.

"You understand a great deal of what I say when I speak English." His tone was so certain, I knew there was no point in denying it. "Can you also speak English? How did you learn?"

I took a deep breath before I replied, in English. "I listen very clearly when Tom speaks at you. When he translates what you say for my father, I try to think the words he used."

The words sounded all wrong. I was sure I had made no

sense at all and felt very foolish. I was amazed when Ian nodded.

"That was very good. It is correct to say "carefully," not "clearly;" and "remember," not "think;" and "speaks to you," not "at you." But no matter. I'm not really surprised that you have learned to speak English so well. I understand that you are a self-taught musician?"

I did not understand what he meant and shook my head apologetically.

"I believe that you taught yourself to play a musical instrument?"

Ah, but that was better. I nodded.

"And also that you are very good with figures?"

Another nod. I was secretly delighted. Father must have praised my skills to Tom, and in turn, he had passed the information on to Ian.

"I should have realized that you would be quick to learn a new language. Skill with music and figures often go with an ability to do that. I would be very pleased to help you understand—and speak—even better English. From now on, when we are alone, will you speak to me in English, please?"

He was smiling pleasantly, so why was I flustered? "I shall try."

"Good. Now, Mi, did you wonder why I sent Anzu away?"

I had been so delighted with the changes in my leg, I had given it no thought at all. But Ian seemed to expect me to be puzzled, so I nodded. "Yes, Ian. Did she..." I paused while I searched for the correct words. "Did she make you angry? Anzu was my amah. She is very fond of me."

"That is obvious," he said dryly. "But no, Anzu did not make me angry. She does not annoy me in the least."

Ah, so that was the word I wanted. Annoy, not angry. I tucked the knowledge away in my mind carefully.

"In fact, I find it very touching to see how much she cares about you." He was rubbing his hands together while he spoke, and I looked at them rather than at his pale eyes.

"I sent her away because there are things I wish to discuss with you, and it would be difficult to speak of them in front of Anzu."

I had no idea what he was talking about. Anzu did not understand a word he said—not even on the rare occasion when he attempted to speak in Japanese—so what did it matter if she was present or not?

I put the question of Anzu aside. I should, I knew, be deeply sincere in my thanks for all he had done for me, but the words hesitated in my mouth. Finally, I forced myself to say, "I thank you for helping me. I am very grateful." There, it was said. As I spoke, a thought came to me with blinding suddenness, and I went on very carefully, hoping Ian would think I was hesitating because I was searching for the right words. In truth, I could barely conceal the triumph that was surging through me. "You are most kind to help me so much, to grant me so much of your time. But now that my leg is healed, I do not need the brace, and I need take no more of your time. Thank you," I added again.

To my astonishment, Ian's expression was suddenly very serious. He shook his head and put his hands into each side of his waistcoat in a gesture that struck me as being extremely comical.

"Oh no, Mi. It is still early days. Your leg is very much better, certainly, but it will get much better still. And I am delighted to say that I will be here for you, always." His voice was tender, but I stared at him in dismay. "Uncle Tom has made Japan his home. He loves it here, and I can see why. I have decided that God guided me here. There is so very much I can do for the people in Edo. The medical knowledge of even the very best of your doctors is centuries out of date. I believe that I have been sent here to help heal the sick. I intend—with Uncle Tom's help—to set up a small hospital here in Edo. Eventually, I hope to take the best of your young doctors and pass my knowledge on to them."

He stopped, his expression rapturous. I remembered Tom's comments about his parents both being missionaries and I wondered uneasily if he, like them, was passionate about his religion. I could think of nothing else that would account for his strange comments about God guiding him to Japan. I remained silent, deeply embarrassed by his obvious but, to me, misplaced sincerity. I could hardly believe that any Japanese doctor would allow himself to be taught by a gaijin, still less a gaijin who did not speak Japanese.

"That is good, Ian." My voice was far too high-pitched. I sounded as if I was placating a child. "But I do not understand why you could not speak of this when Anzu was here."

"That is by the by." I had no idea what he meant; the phrase was new to me, but I nodded politely anyway. "This is not the time to talk to you about my plans for my work here."

He began to pace back and forth. My room was not large, so it took no time at all for his long legs to reach the shoji, turn, and come back. I wondered absently if he was nervous; his smell was getting worse.

"I would be most interested to hear of your plans," I said politely.

I watched him warily. Perhaps his nervousness was

contagious. Certainly, his pacing was beginning to irritate me, and I wondered if he would find it extremely rude if I suggested that I should call Anzu back and ask her to bring us some tea.

Tiring of watching him, I flexed my leg, marveling as it responded. I ran my hands down my thigh, delighting in the smooth muscles I felt beneath my skin. What on earth was Ian talking about, insisting that I needed either him or his brace for a single day longer? But good manners dictated that I had to listen to this man who had done so much for me, and I smiled brightly. Surely, I could tolerate him just a little longer!

"You would like tea? Shall I call for Anzu to bring some?"

"No." His voice was suddenly husky. "No, I do not want Anzu here for the moment. I need for us to be alone. You understand what I am talking about, Mi-chan?"

I had no idea what he meant. Yet, suddenly, I was deeply uneasy. Today, Ian had come alone. Father had gone to Edo as usual and would not be back until just before the evening meal. Even Anzu had been sent away. This was the first time I had been entirely alone with Ian, and it made me nervous.

I shifted my position on the tatami and stretched my left leg a little more than was comfortable. My knee gave a sharp, warning pain and I cried out loud.

Ian was beside me in an instant, kneeling on the tatami, his face concerned. "You have pain?"

I was deeply relieved. It appeared to me that the healer in him had swept aside all else. My pain was not at all great, but instinctively, I decided to exaggerate it. If nothing else, it would give me a reason to pretend that I needed Anzu.

"Yes, great pain. When I moved, my leg…" I was unsure of the word I needed, so I made a wringing motion with my hands. "I will call for Anzu and ask her to make up my futon for me. A little rest will make me good again."

"No, there's no need to trouble Anzu. Lay back, please. I think the muscles in your leg must have tightened when you moved. I will massage it for you."

When you come to me
At night, will you whistle like
The wind at my door?

This was not what I wanted, not at all what I had expected. I laid back warily and tried to make myself comfortable. Although I still had a sense of undefinable disquiet, I told myself I was being silly. Ian had seen my legs times beyond counting. He had touched my legs and my back repeatedly, pinching and feeling the flesh without causing me any great alarm. He was a doctor. This was his job. He was obviously about to touch me again. Why was I suddenly concerned?

The answer was simple—because neither Anzu nor Tom was present. Always, whenever Ian had examined me or manipulated my leg, even if Tom was missing, Anzu had been hovering close by. I almost laughed aloud at the thought. Anzu was tiny. Although she would fight like a tiger for me, what could she hope to do if Ian tried to cause me harm? In any event, I was being silly. Ian was a doctor, a healer. He had devoted a great deal of his valuable time to helping me. Why would he suddenly want to hurt me now?

I tried to get myself comfortable, lacing my fingers on my stomach and watching Ian over them.

He had risen to his feet and was looking at my leg carefully, just as he always did before touching me. He caught my glance.

"First, do no harm." He smiled. "That was the very first thing I was taught in medical school. Before you touch a patient, you must look very carefully."

That made sense to me, and I began to relax. Ian kneeled beside me, and, instinctively, I began to breathe through my mouth.

"What do you see, Ian?" I enquired politely.

He took a sudden breath and sat back on his heels. I thought about my words nervously. Had I said something impolite?

"I see a patient who is improved beyond anything I could have hoped for."

I had no answer to that, other than to wonder, if it were truly so, then why had he insisted earlier he must keep on treating me? It would, of course, have been incredibly discourteous to ask him, given his great kindness toward me, so instead I murmured, "My leg feels much happier now. Perhaps it was not very bad?"

"Possibly so. But in any event, I intend to give you a strong massage. It will relax your muscles and contribute to your feeling of well-being."

Ian had never suggested massaging my leg before. But I remembered the delightfully soothing massages that Tengen used to give me, and I was pleased. Without giving it any thought, I flicked back my kimono, wriggling until it was bunched well out of the way, leaving my legs entirely naked. Once he had started the massage, Ian would not want to be distracted by the heavy silk.

He was breathing heavily. I glanced at him enquiringly, waiting for him to lay his hands on me.

"Could you turn over, please? On to your stomach?"

I flipped over as gracefully as I could manage. Ian put his hands on my thighs, just above both knees, and I flinched. I could never get used to his cold hands.

"Am I hurting you?" he asked anxiously.

"No, no. Your hands are a little cold, is all." It was not polite of me to say that, but it struck me as silly to be formal in a situation where I was half-naked and Ian was about to run his hands over me.

"I am sorry." I heard him blowing on his palms before he put them back in place. "Is that better?"

It was no better at all, but I murmured that it was. I had expected the same sort of massage as Tengen had given me. Slow and deep, so delicious that I had almost been lulled into sleep by the time he had finished.

Ian's massage was very different.

His touch was so light that it almost tickled. I squirmed and could barely keep still as his hands moved up my thighs. But I was struck by how much sensation I had gained back in my withered leg, and I sighed with pleasure.

"Thank you," I said, and this time I meant it.

Ian paused fractionally but did not speak. When he resumed, the massage was much deeper. His fingers were making small circles on my upper thighs, around and around and around. The sensation was deeply enjoyable, and I groaned with pleasure.

"Is that good?" His voice was so close to my ear that I flinched with surprise.

"Very good."

"And that?"

Suddenly, I was no longer relaxed at all. His fingertips were flirting with my black moss, touching it and then darting away. My mouth was very dry, and I had trouble speaking.

"Thank you, Ian-san." I hoped desperately that the formality would make him understand that he had gone too far. "I am much better now. I will call for Anzu to help me order my clothing."

"No." His voice was trembling. As was I. "I want to be alone with you. I have dreamed about this moment almost from the first time I saw you, Mi. You were so tiny, so very beautiful, but at the same time so determined that your dreadful disease would not control you in any way. I knew then that God had sent me to you, to make all of you as beautiful as you were before you were struck down so cruelly by the paralysis of the morning. I prayed, Mi-chan. Prayed that I would be the one to help you, and God answered my prayers."

He took his hands away from my flesh for a moment, and then they were back on my shoulders, turning me over. I was terrified but forced myself to look at his face, hoping that I could read his intentions in his expression. All the while, a single thought was running through my mind. *Why, oh why, hadn't I listened to my instincts and refused to allow him to send Anzu away?*

"I am very grateful for all you have done to help me, Ian-san. But I think you need to go now."

His face was rapturous. I had seen an expression like that only once before, on the face of one of our servants. I was very young at the time, and being left alone in the house, also very bored. I heard an unusual amount of noise coming from the kitchen and wandered down to see what was going on. All the house servants were gathered around a man. They were all laughing loudly and soon I could see why. The man in the center of the ring had his eyes closed and his head thrown back. He was singing loudly, his voice terribly off key but obviously—to him at least—totally delightful. He had a sake flask in one hand and paused to take a swig from it. Anzu saw me at once and hurried across to usher me out.

I shrugged her off and asked what was going on. The man was a half-wit, she explained to me, but harmless. He did all the heavy work about the house and was normally very quiet and biddable. That day, he had been told to clean out the storeroom and had found the stock of sake. He had cleaned the storeroom before, but for some reason, that day had decided to sample some of the drink and was now very drunk. I would not tell my father about it? Anzu asked. The man would have a very bad headache when the sake wore off, and that was punishment enough.

I assured her I would say nothing, and truly, I had forgotten all about the trivial incident until today, when I recalled that the servant's rapturous expression had been exactly the same as Ian's was now.

Had he also taken leave of his senses? I feared he had, the more so when he spoke again.

He leaned toward me, his hands clasped in front of his chest. His bulging eyes were wide and shining, his lips parted. A thin drool of saliva ran down his chin. He looked not just joyful, but as if he was experiencing some wonderful spell that had swept over him and against which he had no defense. I recoiled, and his hands fell on my shoulders, gripping so hard that I winced.

"Mi-chan. My dear Mi-chan, you have no idea how very beautiful you are." He paused, as if he was searching for the right words. Suddenly, he began to whisper hoarsely. I was terrified, the more so as I found I could barely understand anything he said. "Oh, prince's daughter! The joints of thy thighs are like jewels, the work of the hands of a cunning workman. Thy navel is like a round goblet, which wanteth not liquor; thy belly is like an heap of wheat set about with lilies. Thy two breasts are like two young roes that are twins. How fair and pleasant art thou, oh, love, for delights! Thy stature is like to a palm tree and thy breasts to clusters of grapes. I said, I will go up to the palm tree, I will take hold of the boughs thereof; now also thy breasts shall be as clusters of the vine."

Was it poetry, I wondered? Or, at least, what passed for poetry in Ian's country? It seemed to have the rhythm of verse rather than ordinary speech. Was it possible that it was something from the gaijin holy book? I could not believe that. I was sure that these words were the gloating desires of a lover, or—in Ian's case—a would-be lover.

The thought made me feel nauseous.

I stared at him in horror as he paused, gasping for breath. His hands were like a bear's claws on my shoulders, holding me fast. I opened my mouth to scream for Anzu, but nothing came out but a croak. It wouldn't have mattered if I had found my voice. It was already too late.

Ian thrust himself toward me, his mouth fastening hungrily on my lips and his hands releasing my shoulders to clench on my breasts. He held me so tightly that if my mouth had been free, I would have screamed with the pain and indignity. His left hand held my breast fast while his right began to rove down my belly until his nails scratched at my black moss. He groaned loudly, and I had no need to look at his ridiculous trousers to know that his tree of flesh would be thrusting toward me.

Until this moment, Tengen had been the only man who had deliberately touched my black moss. Ian's fingers had brushed against it now and then, but only accidentally, and his touch had been cool and clinically detached. When Tengen had touched me there, it had been with love, and I had welcomed it. Ian was grabbing at me as if he were a madman, and I hated his touch with a depth of loathing I had never before thought possible. I could taste his breath in my mouth and I wanted to spit the stink back at him.

I was terrified and confused and worried, all at the same time. Was Ian as drunk as our servant had been? His breath did not even hint at alcohol, so I dismissed the thought. Was he mad, then? Surely, that was the case. Perhaps some malicious spirit had come to him in the night, feasting on his breath and infecting his mind. Such things were far from unknown.

But at least the thought gave me some hope. If he were truly possessed by a spirit, then his madness would pass when the spirit left him, and in the strangest of ways, it made his assault understandable. Yet still, I must get away from him. His grip was terribly strong, but that was surely to be expected. It was a well-known fact that those possessed by spirits also have superhuman strength.

I wrenched my lips away from his mouth and took a gasping breath. "Ian, you are not well. You are a healer, but you are hurting me. Let me go, please." My voice was trembling. That made me very angry. So close, his bulging, shiny eyes held my gaze and I found it difficult to look away.

"I could not hurt you, Mi. Never. I have longed for this moment. Now that it has come, I will never let you go again."

I closed my eyes, dizzy with the smell rising from his hot body. Nothing Tengen had taught me had prepared me for this. I was held too close to Ian to jab my elbow into his ribs. It was impossible for me to stiffen my arm and thrust my rigid hand at his temple. His arms pinned mine. I could not even free myself enough to grab for his kintama. Even had I been able to move, my bare feet could do little damage to him.

I would scream, I decided, at the top of my voice. Anzu would come running. He would surely be so embarrassed that he would let me go at once. Even better, he would never dare to show his face here again.

There was barely time for me to take comfort from the thought before I knew I was deceiving myself. I could not scream and draw attention to what was happening to me. I was nothing but a girl. Ian was an honored guest in my father's house. Whatever madness had infected him had to be my fault. He was a doctor, a learned man. If Father heard about what had happened, he would instantly think that I must have led Ian on, encouraged him to try and violate me. And if Mother insisted that a midwife examine me, as she surely would, she would find at once that I was not a virgin.

My disgrace would be complete. I had dared to make love to one man already. Now, I had enticed another man away from the path of his good intentions. I would bring shame on my family and on this man, who was an honored guest in our home. Almost worse, Tom would surely turn his kindness from me, and Father would lose one of his most important clients. The loss of face—and income!—would be unbearable, worse even than my foolish brothers" marriages.

FOURTEEN

Speak to me of the
Summer fruits we will share, not
The cold of winter

I was filled with complete despair. Father held Tom in great regard. Naturally, he also honored Ian as Tom's nephew, and I was sure he sincerely believed that Ian was working for my good. A thought chilled me. If Tom no longer wanted to trade with Father because of my actions, then who would he turn to in Father's place? Mikayo, naturally. His was the only money lender in the whole of Edo who was anywhere near as important and successful as Father. And if that happened, then Father's loss of face would be complete. Mikayo would not only have stolen his sons, but also his most important client.

And it would all be my fault, mine alone. Father had shown me such honor as had never been known to a mere girl child. I would break his heart. I wanted to cry out loud at the injustice of it all, but Ian was whispering again, and I shut my lips tightly on my anguish.

The strange hoarseness in his voice made me shudder. It was if he was running jagged nails down a slate. Abruptly, he released his grip on me and slid down my body to kiss my feet. My toes curled in disgust, but he seemed not to notice.

"How beautiful are thy feet in shoes!"

All at once, I was angry. What strange game was he playing? I was in the house, so naturally, I was not wearing shoes. Was he making some obscure reference to my built-up geta? Was he making fun of me? The irony of it—this man teasing me about my deformity when he had always pretended that he wanted nothing more than to help me walk again—whipped my anger to raging fury.

He had his arms wrapped around my legs. Although he was thin, he was possessed of a wiry strength, and I knew —I tugged carefully to make sure—I would not be able to free myself from his grip. Very well. I would find another way out of this intolerable situation. And it would be one that would not reflect badly on me.

I thought furiously, running through all the ways Tengen had taught me should I ever need to defend myself. Alas, none of them had involved a madman who was declaring his admiration of me and kissing my feet while he clung on to me tightly. But there was a way, a way that Tengen had dismissed.

It would work. It had to work, for I had no other alternative.

Had Ian still had his arms wrapped around my body, I would have gasped and gone limp, hoping that this man who spent his life healing would assume he had hurt me and would immediately loosen his grip. As that was not possible, I would try to make the maneuver work, but in a different way.

I spoke very softly, my tone high-pitched and breathy. I allowed my voice to hesitate and falter to a halt, as though I was deeply afraid. "Ian, please. Please, stop. You are upsetting me."

I realized with amazement that the less I thought about what I wanted to say in English, the easier the words flowed. I shrugged the thought aside to better concentrate on making Ian come to his senses. I even managed a sob as I ceased speaking. To make my act even more convincing, I put my face in my hands as if I was afraid to even look at him.

"Mi-chan?" Ian sat back at once. Although I could not see his face, I could tell from his tone that he was shocked. I pretended to choke on another sob, and I heard him snatch at a deep breath. His voice wavered. "Mi, have I hurt you?" I stifled a cry and took one hand away from my face to wave it in front of my bare breasts, as if I had no words to answer him with. "My God, what have I done?"

Ian's voice twisted with anguish. I peered through my fingers. His normally rather high-colored face was as pale as tofu. His mouth was open, his eyes shiny with what I thought were unshed tears.

"I am so sorry, Ian-san," I murmured. "Any fault must be mine. I am nothing but a worthless girl child. Please forgive me for my error." The words were no more than any Japanese man would have expected, but Ian was obviously horrified by my response.

"Mi-chan." He put his hands to each side of his face, dragging down his skin. "No blame for anything that I have done can attach to you. I...I cannot understand what came over me. You must know that my regard for you is very great, and that I could never hurt you. But this is not the time to discuss such matters." He rose, towering over me. I tensed, worrying what more strangeness might be yet to come. "I will leave. Please, accept my apologies for my behavior today. It was, I know, unforgivable." His mouth opened and closed soundlessly until finally, he blurted, "I must go."

I stayed very still until I heard him putting on his strange, ugly shoes in the entrance, and the shoji opening and closing. Only then did I relax. Suddenly, I was almost giddy with relief. I fastened my kimono and obi and straightened my hair quickly, for I knew that Anzu would appear as soon as she knew Ian had gone.

Gone, and surely forever.

I sighed with pleasure at the knowledge and smiled warmly at Anzu as she entered.

"Ian-san has gone?" She frowned in surprise as she glanced at my brace, lying discarded on the tatami.

"Yes, he has gone. He has done all he can for me and I no longer need to wear that." I flicked my finger at the brace. "Take the horrible thing away where I don't have to look at it, Anzu."

She picked the brace up carefully and then turned to look at me reproachfully.

"Forgive me for speaking out of place, Mi-san."

I smiled; when had that ever worried my amah?

"I know you don't care for Ian-san, but he has tried to do his best for you, and your leg is much, much better than it was."

The knowledge that I would never see Ian again buoyed my spirits. I responded equitably. "I'm sure you're right, Anzu."

I almost laughed out loud at her suspicious glance.

FIFTEEN

All that is of the
Earth is surely as one, as
We are also one

"A man has asked for permission to marry you."

I had been surprised by Mother's summons to her apartment. Only rarely did she call me to her, and when I was younger, it had always meant a scolding of some sort. I had, I supposed, been a clumsy child, and often left behind me a trail of broken ornaments that seemed to have gotten in my way with no help from me. But As far as I was aware, it had been many years since I had broken anything she treasured, so I was unconcerned by her call.

My thoughts had been far away. I was not wearing my brace. With Ian gone, why should I? The petty defiance delighted me at first, but my pleasure dwindled when I tried my built-up geta and I was upset to find it no longer fitted me properly. The geta still sat comfortably on the contours of my foot, but the height was all wrong, and as a result, my leg ached terribly and my limp was far worse than it was before I had been made to suffer the brace. I threw the geta from me in a fury.

"Mi-san." Anzu spoke timidly, but her tone was firm. "I think perhaps your geta was very good for you when your leg was badly twisted out of shape, but now, it is not very useful at all." I glared at her, and she twisted her hands together but went on anyway. "Perhaps you need a new geta made for you? One that is not so high?"

Her words were so sensible, they cooled my anger. She was probably right. She often was, in her own, quiet way.

"I can't wear that one any longer," I admitted. "And I don't want to wear *that thing* anymore." I pointed a disdainful finger at the tube of iron and leather that made up my brace.

Anzu looked at me reproachfully. "It is ugly, to be sure, Mi-san. But it has done its job. Ian-san must surely be very clever to know things that our own doctors do not."

She sounded so admiring, I glared at her. "Not so clever. My special geta and my stirrup worked very well to help me to walk. Tengen and I worked that out between us, and neither of us are doctors," I pointed out.

"No, but you are both very clever," Anzu soothed. "I don't think that your special geta has stopped working for you. It's just that now your leg is so much better, it doesn't fit properly. Perhaps I could speak to Mori-san, and he, in his turn, could have a word with the carpenter, and they could make you a new geta that fit your foot and had a lower sole?"

She was blushing ripely by the time she had finished, and the last of my anger evaporated. So, her romance with the blacksmith—Mori—was still alive, then? I felt terribly guilty that I had not asked her about her affaire for many, many weeks, but I had been so preoccupied with Ian and the wearing of my dreadful brace that it had slipped my mind completely.

"You and Mori-san are still...friends, then?"

I would not have thought it possible, but Anzu's blush deepened. She avoided my gaze when she answered.

"Mori-san has done me the honor of asking me to be his wife," she whispered.

I clapped my hands together with pleasure, even as I felt a pang of—not jealousy, exactly—a feeling that I was losing something precious. Anzu had been my nursemaid as soon as I passed into her care from my wet nurse. My first memories were of her. She had always been there for me, on good days and bad. She had smiled when I was happy and had sympathized when I was upset. And now, she was about to leave me to follow her own path.

"Anzu, that is wonderful! You said yes, of course. When is the happy day going to be?"

"I have said neither yes nor no, yet." Anzu raised her face and I saw deep pleasure tempered by worry in her expression.

"But you like Mori-san," I pointed out. She nodded quickly. "And I know him to be a good man, in a fair way of business. He can easily support a wife, and no doubt a family," I added slyly.

Anzu nodded, her brows knotted. I waited as patiently as I could while she gathered her thoughts.

"All that is so, Mi-san. He is a good man. He has his own house and a decent business. I have never heard any man speak ill of him. And I like him a great deal. But..." She hesitated and then blurted, "But how can I marry before you do? How would you manage without me? We have been together for so many years. I could not leave you all alone in the world."

I was deeply touched by her words. Because of the depth of my love for her, I spoke briskly. "Anzu, what nonsense is this? How am I alone in the world? I have my father and mother. You know I have vowed that I will never marry. I will not have you waiting forever for something that is not going to happen! Go, marry your Mori and have many children and be happy. You will still live on the estate. I am sure your new husband will have no objection to you coming to visit me whenever you want. We will not be parted, I assure you."

Anzu, dear, simple creature that she was, brightened at my words, but then shook her head. "Mori-san has said he is happy to wait for me. I will leave it a little longer. Who knows, Mi-san, now that your leg is no longer so badly crippled, you may change your mind. You are very beautiful and very clever. There must be many men who would be delighted to have you as a wife."

And no matter what I said, she would not be persuaded otherwise. I gave in eventually, torn between amusement and exasperation with my dear amah. I would, I decided, speak to Mori-san about making a new geta for me. And at the same time, I would casually let him know that I was very happy about his proposed marriage to Anzu. I thought he would be only too willing to try and make her change her mind.

So, I'd responded to Mother's summons with a light heart.

It was Anzu I thought of when I first heard Mother's

words. Wryly, I supposed that at least for her it would be good news. Her worries would be set aside and she could marry her blacksmith. Then all trace of pleasure left me as I realized Mother was completely serious. I stared at her incredulously.

"Someone wants to marry me? How can this be? Who is it? I see no one. I am either here in the house or with Father at his office. Is it one of his clients?"

I hoped not, with all my heart. I had never seen anybody ushered into Father's private office who was not an old man. If I was with Father when clients arrived, he politely asked me to leave. I was not offended. Traditional Japanese men would have found it strange for a woman to be present at a business meeting. Most—if not all—would simply refuse to discuss anything of importance in front of a woman, particularly one who was little more than a girl. Generally, the men were very polite, smiling at me and showing no impatience as I bowed and walked out as gracefully as I could.

Now, I was thinking furiously. Naturally, those clients who were important and rich enough to be attended by Father personally had to have attained a venerable age. Had any of them ever been accompanied by a younger man, perhaps a son, or even a grandson? Occasionally a companion had walked respectfully behind the client, but it had been obvious from their dress and manner that they were servants, probably secretaries who had come to take notes of the meeting, or who would be instructed to run errands as necessary. Certainly not the sort of man who would ever consider approaching Father for permission to marry me.

My mouth crowded with questions. Who was it? Was it

possible I did know the man? Was I to be a wife, or what was euphemistically known as a "second wife," in other words, a concubine?

But I did not speak. There was no need. I had vowed I would never marry any man who was prepared to take a deformed cripple for his wife, and I had not changed my mind. If the day ever came when both my legs were straight and strong and I could walk as well as any other woman with no support, then on that day, I *might* change my mind about taking a husband. And if I did, it would have to be a man I both liked and respected.

But that day was far in the future, if it ever happened. I stared Mother full in the face and waited for her to speak. All this would be her doing, I knew. It was tradition for the mother to arrange such matters. I would let her have her say before I refused my prospective bridegroom.

Mother refused to meet my gaze. She was reclining on her Western-style sofa, plump and pretty on a pile of cushions. Somehow, she even managed to look comfortable on the strange furniture. She played with a tassel on one of the cushions, pursing her lips and knitting her brows.

My sense of unease deepened until I could wait no longer. "Who is it who wants to marry me, Mother? Is it somebody I know?"

Oddly, I thought that it was Mother who was being shy and awkward rather than me. Suddenly, fear gripped me fiercely. This should be the happiest of occasions for Mother. Finally, somebody wanted to marry her crippled daughter. It was even more momentous in that—since Father had disowned her sons—I was her only chance to have grandchildren. She should be the happiest of women, yet instead, she was clearly reluctant to break the good news to me and appeared to be deeply unhappy about it.

I began to speak and then had to stop to clear my throat as the words lodged behind my tongue. "Mother? Who is it?" I demanded.

She did not raise her eyes to me when she replied. Her voice was toneless. "Ian-san."

SIXTEEN

Some nights I cannot
Sleep for the beguiling call
Of my lover moon

I laughed. Loudly.

It was both unkind and disrespectful to my mother, but as relief flowed over me, it was an instinctive reaction and I could not help it.

Ian! I could have counted every man I had ever seen in the whole of my life and still never have thought of him. No matter. Had my prospective bridegroom truly been one of Father's important clients, then I would have been worried. No matter how old the man was, Mother would see it as an excellent match. The man would be well-known to Father and would undoubtedly be rich and of good reputation. But Ian was neither.

I guessed that this sudden proposal arose out of Ian's bewildering behavior on the day he had thrown himself—literally—at my feet. Was it possible that he felt he had committed himself to me in some way? What a fool the man was if that were so. If I thought about the incident at all, it was with distant amusement. And I was vaguely flattered that I had caused Ian to lose both his dignity and his wits in such a spectacular fashion. But for him to think that as a result of his actions he had to ask me to become his wife! That was beyond my understanding.

Still, at least I now understood Mother's ambivalence. Ian had done so much to heal my withered leg, she must have been grateful to him, but that would not prevent her from being distressed by his ridiculous proposal. As a gaijin, he could not be expected to understand how difficult a situation he had created.

For a passing moment, I considered telling Mother about Ian's outburst. How she would laugh! Then I glanced at her face and quickly decided that to do so would be inappropriate. Ian had put her—and Father—in an almost impossibly difficult situation, and it must be troubling them both as to how they could respond politely. Had Ian discussed this with Tom, I wondered. I doubted it. If he had, his uncle would surely have pointed out the error of his ways to him.

As I waited for Mother to speak, I ran through all the reasons why such a match was laughably unthinkable in my head. Of course, there was the glaring, inescapable fact that Ian was a gaijin. I had never heard of a Japanese girl marrying a gaijin. Naturally, it was not uncommon for a gaijin to visit houses of pleasure, even to take a Japanese concubine for the time they were in our country. But marriage? Never.

And there was no getting around the fact that even had Ian been Japanese, he would not have been a suitable match for me. Tom had casually mentioned several times that Ian had no money of his own. His parents were penniless missionaries. Tom had paid for his nephew's medical training; Ian lived in his uncle's house, ate his food. To Japanese eyes, Ian had nothing. He was on par with the burakumin, the very lowest caste who undertook work that nobody else would dream of doing. Cesspits were emptied by burakumin; undoubtedly, a worthwhile task, but beneath most people's notice.

I realized my thoughts were distracting me from the matter in hand and jerked them back abruptly.

"Mother, no," I said finally.

"It is very difficult."

I understood. However my parents phrased their refusal, it would be, indeed, difficult. It would cause a huge loss of face for Ian. I hoped, sincerely, that Tom would not be offended on his behalf.

"Yes, I understand that." I made my face grave.

"Do you? Do you really understand the trouble you have caused, Mi?" Mother was staring at me openly, her face working as she tried—and failed—to control her obvious anger.

"I have caused trouble?" I echoed numbly. "I have done nothing. I told you and Father all along that I didn't want Ian-san to treat me." Suddenly deeply anxious, I blurted, "What has he said? Why does he want to marry me?"

"He says he is deeply in love with you. That he fell in love with you the first time he saw you."

Exactly what Ian had said to me. But what nonsense was this? Men married for many reasons—to take advantage of a good dowry; to ensure that their family line would continue; because the match was compatible and would do both families good. It was often the case that lower caste men married to have a wife who would cook and keep the house clean. And the woman, of course, married because she had no option—an unmarried woman was no more than a burden to her family.

All those reasons were perfectly understandable, but for a man to declare he wanted to marry for love of his bride! What nonsense was this? I spoke firmly.

"Well, I don't love him. In fact, I hate him even being near me. He stinks of spoiled flesh, Mother! And those cold, blue eyes make me shiver. I don't know why he thinks he's in love with me. I've never been more than polite to him."

Mother was tapping her closed fan on the arm of the sofa. Her lips were set in a straight line, and she was glaring at me. "What makes you think it matters whether you love him, or tolerate him, or hate him for that matter? Do your think I married your father for love? Could you really be that naïve?" Before I could reply, Mother went on fiercely. "I had met him only twice before my mother told me we were to be married. I agreed, naturally. He was of the same caste as us, and it was clear even then that he was an ambitious man who would go far in the world. I could have done far worse. Not that it mattered at all. I would never have dreamed of going against anything my mother had arranged for me."

I knew she was right. Still, I could not believe that she really intended that I should marry a gaijin who was no more than a pauper. It could not be. Surely, she was simply angry with me for daring to argue with her.

"I am sorry, Mother," I said humbly. "I spoke out of turn. I was just so shocked by hearing of Ian-san's proposal..."

She sniffed. "You young people seem to think you know better than your elders these days. I suppose it's the influence of all these gaijin one sees everywhere in Edo, strutting about as if they own the place."

I risked a quick look at Mother's expression to see if she appreciated the irony of her own words but saw nothing but righteous indignation. I swallowed a sigh. Clearly, this nonsense was going to take some time to resolve.

"Yes, Mother. I am very sorry Ian-san thinks he is in love with me, but I promise I have done nothing at all to encourage him. I have never even been alone with him; Anzu has always been in the room with us."

Except for once, but I was not about to tell Mother about that.

"That doesn't matter, child." Her tone was suddenly weary. "I'm sorry you dislike him so much, but that is the lot for us women. We have no choice in the matter of husbands. It is, I know, unheard of for a man to marry for love, but think yourself fortunate that it is so."

I heard what she said, but it took a long moment for me to understand her words.

SEVENTEEN

When the spring blossom
Loses its scent, and I am
Blind, I will know you

"No," I whispered. "I cannot marry Ian. I will not. You can't make me. I will speak to Father; he will tell you that I'm not going to marry him."

Mother's face was stone as she replied. "Your father thinks very highly of you, Mi. I am sure he will be distressed when I tell him how undutiful you are being in refusing to take Ian-san for your husband."

I stared at her in disbelief. "Father knows about this?"

Mother nodded smugly. "But of course. I would hardly be speaking to you now if he did not."

"I don't understand, Mother. You hate the gaijin. I have heard you say many times that they have no place here. Apart from anything else, Ian-san doesn't have any money except for what his uncle is kind enough to give him. He doesn't even speak Japanese! How can you want me to marry him? Such a thing is unheard of. People will laugh at us. They will think Father has taken leave of his senses. Why, Mother? Why?"

She stared at me silently. Finally, she spoke so icily, I flinched back. "If it hadn't been for you, I would still have my wonderful sons."

What had my brothers to do with my marrying Ian? I was taken aback and spoke without thinking. "My brothers betrayed Father. He had to put them aside."

"If there was any betrayal, it was you who did it! Don't think I haven't watched you all these years, oiling around your father. Why else did you want to learn how to use the abacus and learn to read and write if it wasn't to impress him?"

She was right, I could not deny it. Yet there had been so much more involved. I had wanted nothing more than to be able to help Father, to make up for the fact that I was deformed and useless otherwise. Surely Mother could see that?

"I wanted to be of help to him," I said simply.

"You wanted to take the place your brothers should rightfully have held! If you had been a normal daughter, they would never have had to do what they did. They thought they were acting in the best interests of the family, that your father would be pleased with them. If you hadn't been here, taking the place they should have held in his affections, taking the place of them both with your constant questions about the business and showing how clever you were, he would have seen that my poor sons only acted out of consideration for him. He would have understood that it was your brothers who were the clever ones. He would have had no choice." Her voice rose shrilly. "Without your brothers, he would have had no one else. But no, you were here. Waiting like a cunning snake to strike. You turned him against them. You put the stupid idea in his head that you could take their place."

Through the fog of my own hurt, I saw her put her hand to her chest. At once, I was worried that she might have injured herself with the strength of her emotions.

"Mother, I'm sorry. You are wrong. I never spoke to Father about my brothers. I had no idea what they were planning. But in any event, I don't understand what this has to do with Ian."

I was deeply hurt by her words, but that was for consideration later. All that mattered now was finding some argument to convince Mother that the thing was impossible.

"Selfish to the last," Mother said flatly. "All you care about is yourself, daughter."

I wanted to tell her that if anybody was selfish, then it was surely her, not me. I mastered my temper and spoke gently.

"Please, Mother. I am deeply sorry you feel that I drove my brothers away. But I don't understand what that has got to do with Ian. And why I am to marry him."

I saw the glimmer of a smile drive the distress from her expression. "Didn't you say your brothers deserved to be cut off from the family?"

I sighed; back to them again.

"Well, daughter, as the saying has it, bad causes, bad results. Your own cunning has come back to bite you, and I can't say I'm sorry."

"Perhaps it would be better if I discussed this with Father." I spoke firmly, and I was surprised when Mother laughed softly.

"You still don't understand, do you? Your father knows all about Ian-san's proposal. The gaijin have no idea how such delicate matters should be handled. The stupid man spoke to your father first rather than me."

Even if it was true that Father knew about the proposal, I was certain that he would simply have asked Mother to deal with it. She was trying to punish me, that was all.

"I will speak to Father this evening," I said firmly.

"Of course you will." Mother sounded pleased, and I felt my assurance falter. "You will run to him and bleat that you don't want to marry a penniless gaijin. And what do you think he will say in return, my daughter? I promise you, he will tell you what he has already told me. That you should give thanks that Ian-san desires you. That you will marry him whether you like it or not." She sat back on her cushions, her gaze fixed avidly on my face.

"I don't believe you," I whispered. "Why would he say that? Even if Ian were Japanese, such a match would be unthinkable. He has no caste. He is penniless. The loss of face for Father would be beyond anything."

"You think you know your dear Father so well, don't you? But you know nothing about him that matters. If anybody understands him, it's me. Your father and I have been married for many years. He has been a good husband to me, I admit that. Unlike virtually all other men, he has never chased after women of pleasure, never even wanted to take a concubine."

"Surely that should please you?" I interrupted angrily.

"If I thought that it was my allure that kept him away from other women, then I would be delighted. But that is not so and never has been. Your father is a cold man. He gave me children, but not out of passion. He wanted sons to carry on his business after he was gone." She glared at me and said spitefully, "But thanks to you, he has lost them. He cares nothing at all about you, or me for that matter. All he cares about is that we are of use to him. I ensure his house is clean, his food is tasty and served on time. I entertain his clients when he brings them to the house. If I did not do these things successfully, then he would have had no hesitation in putting me aside many years ago. He uses both of us, Mi. It amuses his gaijin clients to see a pretty, young girl in the office. Your brothers told me how he boasted to them about how clever you are, how educated. The gaijin think that is wonderful and praise your father for his progressive ideas. And that is why you must marry Ian-san."

"I don't understand. Just because the gaijin like to see me in Father's office, why does that mean I have to marry one of them? You said yourself, I am of no importance at all." I glanced at Mother and saw she was gloating. Suddenly, I understood what all this was about.

She was jealous of me and would be happy to see me gone.

CHAPTER

EIGHTEEN

Winter rice grows tall
And strong, yet still it falls to
The sharpened sickle

The thoughts tumbled through my mind like leaves blown by a sudden wind. I took a deep breath and forced myself to think. If I was good at nothing else, then at least I could do that.

Was it possible that my own mother could hate me so much that she was willing to see me married to a penniless gaijin? Or was it simply that she hoped that with me out of the way, Father would welcome my brothers back into the family?

"I will not marry Ian," I said firmly. "I don't believe that Father wants me to marry him. I will speak to him tonight, and he will agree with me."

Mother laughed. She laughed so long and so loudly that her eyes streamed with tears. She wiped them away with her hands, smearing her careful makeup. She looked a mess, I thought stonily. When she finally stopped laughing, she smiled at me. Unlike most younger women, Mother still blackened her teeth in the style that everybody adopted when she was young herself. I had never given them a thought before, but now it seemed to me that they resembled the bared teeth of a wolf who peels his lips back before he attacks his prey.

It was not a pleasant thought.

"Speak to him as much as you like, child. It will do you no good. He has already agreed to the match."

"I don't believe you," I said firmly. And I did not.

"I understand your distress, Mi. But the thing cannot be helped. I am sorry." Now she *was* lying, I was certain. "You do not understand your father as well as you think you do. But I understand him." She paused. Even though I knew I was walking into her trap, I had to speak.

"Father takes me to Edo with him. Introduces me to his important clients. I *work* with him," I added proudly. "Of course, I understand him, just as he understands me."

"You really believe that is so? You're wrong. He uses you. He has spoken to me about how valuable you have become to him. He has not replaced my dear sons because he says you are so clever and hardworking, you can do far more than both of them. And naturally, he is delighted that the gaijin like you so much."

I'd had enough. I bowed briefly and was about to turn when her voice stopped me.

"Don't you want to know the main reason why it is so important that you marry your gaijin?"

My gaijin? Had Mother not listened to a word I'd said?

"Ian-san is not *my* gaijin. He is—*was*—my doctor, nothing more. I hated him treating me. I only agreed because his uncle is such an important client of Father's." Mother was smiling serenely, a smile that mocked me. I took a firm grip on my temper and spoke coolly. "You may be sure that I will ask Father for his thoughts on the matter. I know he will speak honestly to me. But as you are obviously eager to tell me, go on. Why is it so important that I marry Ian-san? In your opinion, that is."

I rejoiced inwardly as her smile slipped. But my pleasure lasted only for a moment.

"When your Father told me that Ian had asked for permission to marry you, you may be surprised to know that I could not believe he was even considering allowing his clever, valuable daughter to marry a gaijin. And one without a bronze mon to his name at that. I protested. I said it was intolerable. That if he cared about nothing else, surely he would understand that it would ruin his business, that none of his clients would tolerate such a thing."

"What did he say?"

"He told me that I was completely wrong. I could hardly believe what he was saying. And for perhaps the first time in my married life, I did not give way to my husband. I told him that all his clients would turn away from him. That we would be ruined."

I was astonished. I had never heard Mother go against anything that Father said.

I breathed, "What did he say? Was he very angry with you?"

"Not at all. I guessed he had expected how I would react, and he wasn't concerned. He simply stared at me, his eyebrows raised as if he were bored and hoped I would hurry up with my questions. For once, I found the courage to tell him what I thought. I said, 'Husband, I do not understand. Ian-san is not only a gaijin, he has no money at all.

How will he support Mi? I am certain I could find a far more advantageous match for our daughter with a suitable Japanese boy, especially now that her leg is so much better. Would you like me to try?'

'"You don't understand, Emica." He spoke to me slowly, as if I was a stupid child. "It is because Ian-san is a gaijin that she must marry him."'

I was appalled. "I don't understand either," I whispered.

Mother shrugged. When she went on, she avoided my gaze. "I had gone so far in my defiance, I decided I might as well continue. As the saying has it, if one has tasted poison, one may as well eat the plate as well. I said, '"Such a match is unheard of, Husband. The whole of Edo will laugh at us. They will think that Ian-san has taken her and that she is pregnant."'

"Your Father was unmoved. He said, 'Time will prove them wrong. Although naturally one hopes that children will come along in due course.'

"Somehow, I found the courage to persevere. I said humbly, 'Husband. I must apologize for my stupidity, but I still do not understand why you wish Mi to marry Ian-san.'

'"Very well, I will explain to you. The gaijin are the future of our country, Emica. Even you, who rarely leaves the house, must be aware that the government is doing all it can to turn us toward Western ways.'"

"I know that," I interrupted and immediately wished I had not as Mother snapped at me angrily.

"I had no idea what he was talking about, but of course you do, my clever daughter."

"I seem to remember it being mentioned in Father's office," I murmured. "Please, do go on, Mother."

She paused as if gathering her thoughts. "Now, where

was I? Oh, yes. Your father was saying how important the gaijin were to our country. He told me, 'Already, many of my most important clients are gaijin. They spread the word that I am to be trusted, so their friends and business acquaintances also wish to use my services. In fact, I have been so successful in working with them that some of them borrow money from me not just for their own enterprises, but for the companies they work for. Although it has never been said outright, I am certain that some of the gaijin who borrow particularly large sums from me do so on the instructions of their own governments. From my point of view, they are excellent clients. They do not haggle over the terms of their loans, and the money is always repaid on time.'"

Mother frowned, her lips pursed as she contemplated the memory.

"It seemed to me that all this must be very good for us. If our government wants us to trade with the gaijin, and if they were making money for your father, then surely that must make him happy? Yet, he did not look at all happy. But what do I know? I am nothing more than a stupid wife, not a clever woman of business as you are."

She spoke the last words bitterly, as if she had suddenly recollected her anger with me. But I needed to know more, and I spoke to her as sweetly as I knew how, my voice soft and humble.

"At least Father confides in you. He has never said a word about these things to me, Mother. Then this is why he wants to me to marry Ian-san? Because it will please both the gaijin and our government?"

She glanced at me sharply. "It is part of the reason. But there is more. He went on, but almost as if he was talking to himself. 'Dickson-san is by far my most important client now. He has borrowed huge sums from me, and I cannot afford to lose him. He is the future of our prosperity. And remember, he dotes on his nephew, Ian-san. Dickson-san has told me that he intends to buy him a spacious house here in Edo that will give him room to live in comfort and also to use part of it as a clinic to treat poor people who cannot afford to pay a Japanese physician. He will pay all the expenses. Ian-san will want for nothing.'

"I thought I understood how things were, then. I assumed Dickson-san must be very pleased about the marriage. As your father said, he looks upon Ian-san as his son, and for some reason, it seems that he is also very fond of you. Knowing that Ian-san is deeply in love with you, he would think it a perfect union. And not only is Dickson-san your father's most important client and one who has intro-duced many other gaijin to him, but the government would be very pleased with the marriage. It can only mean great things for us in the future."

Clearly, Father had convinced her. For Mother, my marriage to Ian-san could only mean yet more Western-style furniture. More new kimonos and perhaps—should the gods truly smile on Father—admittance to social circles far above anything she could dream of. And at what cost? Why, nothing but the loss of a crippled daughter.

I spoke through a fog of misery. "I understand. I am… disposable. He is selling me to the highest bidder. The only bidder," I added bitterly.

"Selfish as ever." I heard the sneer in her voice and kept my eyes lowered. I would not give her the satisfaction of seeing my pain. "Do try to think how happy it will make your father that you are helping him in the very best way you possibly can. Far better than trying to take the place of my sons," she added spitefully.

My pain was so great, I thought my heart might stop. Yet I knew that I had no more arguments left.

I spoke calmly, determined she would not see the hurt she had inflicted on me. "Yes, Mother. I will try to remember that."

I stood, bowed politely, and walked away.

NINETEEN

The wind that whispers
In the night is your soft voice
When last I heard it

"The child is a burakumin, I suppose."

I bit back a sigh of annoyance; although he had heard the word often, Ian still seemed unable to pronounce "burakumin" properly. Was it that he found our beautiful language impossible to master, or did he simply not bother to even try? I suspected it was the latter. Why should he worry when I translated for him without giving it a second thought? I sometimes wondered if I should try to learn how to read and write English as well, but reluctantly decided I simply did not have the time.

Just as I had no longer had time to do many of the things I used to enjoy. My biwa sat forlorn, the joy of its music silent. Although I still had Gen's book of haiku, I rarely turned its pages. When I did, the poetry seemed to have lost its allure for me and I put it aside with a sigh of regret. My fingers flying on the abacus were no more than a pleasant memory.

"Mi, are you daydreaming? I've spoken to you twice now and you haven't answered me. I do wish the patients would wash their children before they brought them to me. They all seem to be filthy. Just look at this one."

Ian—my husband—sounded petulant. He was pointing at the child, seated uncomfortably on a Western-style chair. I winced at his rudeness and smiled at the obviously terrified little girl, trying to comfort her.

Although her face was dirty and her clothes were ragged, I knew she was not burakumin. The dirt was more dust than anything, and the rags were clean. It annoyed me that Ian could not understand why her parents had chosen to deliberately rub dirt on their child and dress her in rags before they visited him. Normally, I would have shrugged off his ignorance, but today I decided it was time I educated my gaijin husband.

"She is not burakumin. If you look at her parents, you will see they are quite well dressed and perfectly clean."

Ian frowned, his pale blue eyes puzzled. The child's face creased as if she were about to cry, and I went over to her quickly and crouched down so I was at her level, patting her hand. She still looked wary but less frightened.

"If she's not burakumin, why is she dressed like that? And she's dirty. I'm sure you're wrong."

"Ian, you said a moment ago that all the children who are brought to see you are filthy." It was, I thought, as if Ian was the child and had to have obvious things explained to him carefully. "Their parents smear dirt on their faces and dress them in old clothes deliberately before they visit you. It's a matter of face. They think that you will charge them a lot of money if you see a nicely dressed child with a clean face. I am sure they are poor people, so they dress their child in rags and smear dirt on their face to make them appear poorer still so you will understand they have no money and will not ask them to pay more than they can afford."

Rather like the parents who tried to avoid embarrassment, I smiled at Ian to soften the blow of having to explain something so very obvious to him.

I needn't have bothered.

"What nonsense. I don't charge anything for my services. You tell them that, don't you?"

"Of course."

I could have tried to explain that that made things even worse, but I knew there was no point. Ian would never believe the way things were done here in Japan.

I knew that his patients would mistrust anybody—not just a gaijin—who was willing to treat them for free. Everybody knew that physicians charged huge amounts for their services, as was only right. If he would not accept their money, then the gaijin must want something else in return. I had heard some of his patients talking amongst themselves and the consensus was that Ian was a cunning man. At best, they thought he was experimenting on them, trying to see if his strange gaijin medicine worked on Japanese people. At worse, they wondered if he was trying to steal their souls. It didn't help at all when Ian occasionally paused during a consultation and opened his holy book, tracing the words with his finger and murmuring out loud.

After a while, I understood that he only did this when he was unsure of his diagnosis. I thought that perhaps the book gave not only religious guidance but also practical advice, but when I mentioned this to Ian, he stared at me strangely.

"No, not at all. When I am unsure of a diagnosis, I open my bible at random and trust that God will guide me to a passage that will help me."

I struggled not to laugh at this obvious nonsense. "And does your god always help?"

Ian winced. I realized he was upset by my reference to "his" god, but it was too late to take the words back.

"His guidance is always there for me," he said firmly.

I was grateful the patients had no idea that Ian was healing them by divine guidance. He was the last resort for those who knew their children and parents and grandparents were seriously ill or in great pain, and who also knew that they could not afford ongoing treatment from a real doctor. If they thought magic was involved, they would scatter like leaves before the wind and word would spread quickly that the gaijin doctor was no doctor at all.

I did not tell him any of that. Suddenly, I was deeply weary of this new life of mine. And wearier still of my husband, who was somehow both extremely clever and extremely stupid at the same time.

My thoughts strayed absently as I waited for Ian's next command. I had no need to pay attention. Once Ian was intent on his patient, he expected that the right implement would be placed in his hand the moment he asked for it. Although he had never shouted, rarely even snapped at me when I hesitated in the early days, as a matter of my own pride I had quickly learned to anticipate what he wanted and to have it ready. Ian never showed any gratitude for my promptness. Rather, he seemed to take my skill for granted. Just, I thought bitterly, as Father had done when he learned of my ability to read and write.

Men, I decided, must be the same the world over. Takers, not givers.

The slip of wood was in Ian's hand before he could ask for it. I watched him slide it into the terrified child's mouth. I smiled at her, and—seeing that Ian was engrossed in his task and that I would not be needed for some time—for no reason at all, I found my thoughts drifting back to our wedding day.

CHAPTER

TWENTY

I understand that
Each grain of rice in my dish
Is nature's bounty

I knew, of course, what to expect of the day. As a child, I had attended a number of weddings. The Buddhist ceremony had been simple, and only close family and friends had attended the event. The bride had always been beautifully made up in the traditional palette of red, black, and white. Black hair and eyebrows; black lines around her eyes; lips bright red with safflower paste, all glowing against the dead white of her skin, masked with carefully applied cosmetics. The bride always wore a white kimono, which had puzzled me as white is the color of mourning, and surely this was a happy event? I had asked Anzu about that, and she had been delighted to explain.

"White is the color of mourning, but in a marriage, it is different. The bride wears white to show she is pure, but also because this is the day she will become the color of her husband's family and that is what the plain, white kimono represents."

I wasn't quite sure I grasped what Anzu was saying, but I nodded dutifully.

"And her headdress?"

I had never seen anything like it outside of weddings, and they had made me want to giggle, they were so odd—round, like a very large rice bowl, with a turned-up brim and golden decorations on top.

"That is to protect the bride," Anzu said solemnly. "It is called a tsunokasushi, and it will prevent her from being taken over by demons."

I didn't mind the idea of a white kimono. It suited my mood perfectly, as I could only look upon my wedding day as a day of mourning rather than joy. I was grateful for Mother making up my face for me, as it would help to hide my expression. And surprisingly, she seemed to be pleased with the effect.

"You are beautiful, Mi," she said quietly as she put down the lip brush. "Look."

She held a mirror up for me to look into, and I blinked in surprise as a stranger looked back at me. Hesitatingly, I turned my head from side to side, amazed at the difference the heavy makeup made. I thought I looked older than my eighteen years and very serious. I tried the effect of a smile, but Mother tutted at me at once.

"Keep your face still. I don't want your makeup to be disturbed."

I nodded. I felt more like crying than smiling, but I supposed that would be even worse. The thought that I might be given in marriage to Ian with black streaks of makeup soiling my cheeks gave me bitter satisfaction.

The white headdress came next. I thought that it sat on

my head like a bucket, and I was sure that if I so much as turned my head, it would fall down over my eyes, leaving me blind. So, I kept very still and looked straight forward. I remembered how every bride I had ever seen had kept her head rigid in just this way. Now I knew why.

But that was the last thing that happened as I had anticipated. As soon as we reached the temple where the ceremony was to be held, nothing was as I had expected at all.

Instead of a handful of close friends and family members, the temple garden was full, mainly with people I had never seen before. Father stepped forward and offered me his arm. Despite all he had forced on me, I was glad of his support. Keeping my head very still, I glanced around at the milling crowd. Were these people really here to watch me get married, or was it more likely that we were early and this crowd had just left the temple from an earlier service?

I soon realized I was wrong. I glimpsed my brothers, both with their wives at their sides. And Mikayo was present, beaming happily. I was amazed when both my brothers and their wives bustled over at once, bowing deeply to Father and smiling at me. Mikayo followed, and it seemed to me that Father was pleased to see them. I found it in my heart to hope that that was so. Mother was beaming and cooing happily over her "lost" sons. Although being Mother, she still spared the time to look carefully over their wives and I knew she was comparing their expensive, perfectly cut kimono adversely to her own colorful silks.

Apart from the sheer number of people present, something else was very strange. It took me a moment to understand, but when I did, I gasped out loud.

There were many gaijin in the crowd. To my astonished eyes, I thought they almost outnumbered my countrymen. I blushed beneath my makeup; surely, I should have expected this. My bridegroom was gaijin, so naturally, his countrymen would attend his wedding. Still, I was taken aback. Some of the gaijin had been courteous enough to wear robes rather than Western clothes, but polite as the gesture was, the effect was also almost comical. None of them seemed at all comfortable in their sumptuous robes. I saw several of them plucking the skirts from around their legs when they walked, and the rest stood with a deeply self-conscious air, their hands moving constantly as if looking for a place to rest.

I wondered if Ian would be wearing a robe, and almost laughed out loud at the thought. He was so tall and thin, he appeared clumsy even in Western clothes. The idea of him wearing a robe was unthinkable.

With no concern for protocol, a number of gaijin bustled over to us at once. Father obviously knew these men, as he bowed repeatedly and seemed delighted to see them all. I stood politely to one side. This might be my wedding day, but clearly, it was Father the gaijin wanted to talk to. Or perhaps I meant to be seen with—the conversation was one-sided, with Father's lack of English meaning that he contributed barely more than smiles and polite nods. To make it obvious that I was not trying to eavesdrop on the conversation, I glanced around the temple, ensuring that my expression was deeply impressed. That was not difficult. It was a very fine temple, and far bigger than the temple near our family estate where we worshipped on important occasions. Still, I wished we were at our temple. As large and well-appointed as this place was, it felt impersonal to me, as if

—as soon as I walked out of the doors—the priest would forget I ever existed.

My wandering gaze skimmed over the many guests who were standing around chattering. To my huge pleasure, I saw Tanaka standing next to a tiny woman, so very old it seemed to me that a slight breeze would cause her to sway. Tanaka had never mentioned his wife to me, but I assumed that this venerable lady must be her. Catching her gaze, I smiled at her, but she immediately looked nervous, so I switched my attention to Tanaka. I wanted to wave, perhaps even to go over and have a word with him, but I thought it would be discourteous, so I remained rooted to my spot. It should be sufficient for me to be standing next to my important father.

Following Father's gaze around the crowded temple, I saw yet more men that I did not recognize. Richly dressed Japanese men who held fans in their hands and glanced around languidly, as if they had been instructed to attend, rather than coming for their own pleasure, and were deeply bored. I knew from their bearing that these were important men. Not businessmen like Father, but high-ranking civil servants. And if they were important civil servants, then most, if not all, of them would also be high-caste aristocrats.

At that moment, I truly knew my fate was sealed, and that Mother had not been lying to me. My wedding was important. Although it puzzled me, I thought the gaijin guests were known to Father, but not to Ian. They were here out of respect for Father. If that was also so of the civil servants, then Father was more important than even I had ever comprehended. As I watched, one of the gaijin—one of those who was wearing robes—walked up to a civil servant and spoke to him. As he turned, I recognized it was

Tom. The important official he was speaking bowed deeply and assumed an expression of great interest, almost simpering in his pleasure at being spoken to by him.

I looked up at Father and saw he was smiling happily. Not at me, but at the dumb show we were both witnessing. He spoke softly.

"Mi-san, I am proud of you. This is a very happy day for our family. I thank you for your consideration. You have given me a greater gift than you could ever understand."

I wished he had never spoken. Did he know full well that his words would silence any rebellion in me? His hungry gaze was already fixed on the important civil servants, and it seemed to me that he had forgotten I was at his side. I was certain of it when he drifted away to speak to one of the guests without a further word.

TWENTY-ONE

Summer rain is light
On my face, but it still hides
The tears that I weep

I thought that Father had come back to my side, but I understood quickly that I was wrong. Ian had taken Father's place. The priest had come to stand in front of us, and I concentrated my gaze on him.

I held my breath, sure that one mouthful of Ian's stink would be my undoing, that I must move away from him in order to breathe. He stood very close, so close I could feel the heat of his body. Eventually, I had to breathe shallowly through my mouth. I was pleasantly surprised. His normal body odor was masked by a far sweeter smell. I took a cautious sniff and decided it was sandalwood with an undertone of lavender. Had Ian sprinkled scent on himself? If he had, then that must mean that he was aware of his own bodily odors.

I felt a flash of compassion for him. My deformity was terrible enough, but at least it was better than it had been, and I was determined that it would be better still in the future. Tom had told me that there was no cure for the smell Ian was forced to carry around with him like a shadow. How dreadful must it be for a physician to be unable to cure himself?

So great was my sympathy for him that I turned slightly and managed a shy smile. Ian was staring back at me with a curious expression. He looked puzzled and not a little surprised, as if he had never seen me before.

At that moment, the priest began to intone the first words of the ceremony and my attention snapped back to him. Still, I could barely believe that this was happening. I was so numb, I felt almost as if I was standing beside myself, watching some other woman being married. This was not me, not my body. It could not be so. I felt light-headed. The room was sweltering and I felt it begin to spin around me.

I did not faint. I clenched my fingernails hard into my palms and the small pain steadied me. I wanted to scream but did not. I wanted to turn and run—or at least stumble —out of the room, but I did not. My legs—in particular, my poor, deformed left leg—trembled so hard, I thought I might fall, but I did not.

Almost absently, I wondered how many other brides down all the long, lost centuries had stood on this spot and taken their marriage vows. And how many of them had felt just as I did now, knowing they had to go through with this, that it was their duty to do so? And at that moment, I felt instinctively that I was not suffering alone. That many of my predecessors had hated their new husbands or— possibly even worse—had never even met them before this day, so they had no idea at all what they were condemned to.

I felt sure that I could hear the whisper of all those long-gone women all around me, softly speaking their encouragement. I desperately wanted to explain to them that I did not want this. I did not want to marry any man, still less this gaijin who repulsed me. But instinct told me that I was shaming both them and me. They had been through this. They had married men they barely knew, men they did not love or even care for, and they had survived. Just as my own mother had survived, if living to hate her own daughter could even be described as survival.

It was not strength that held me here, I understood. It was the weight of tradition. All these women had submitted to the unthinkable because their parents believed it was the best thing for them, and one's parents knew best. Had they lived to enjoy great happiness, I wondered? Or did they spend the rest of their days trying to make the best of a bad situation, enduring a marriage that they could not escape from?

I shivered at the thought. In an attempt to distract myself, I glanced around at the temple. It was a mistake. Immediately, I connected the temple with Tengen, the Buddhist priest who had gone from being my teacher to my lover. The only lover I had ever had. I was conscious of the bitter irony of my situation. I had not been in love with Tengen, and with the unreasonable confidence of youth I had wondered what I would do if he were to ask me to run away with him, to become his wife in his new life. I had rejected the idea out of hand, and yet I had liked and respected Tengen greatly, as well as being physically attracted to him. Was it an ironic punishment from karma that I had stolen the soul of a priest and then rejected him, only to find myself about to marry a man who repulsed me?

The bitterness of the idea was oddly attractive, rather

like biting down on a bad tooth to find if it still hurt. Just as the tooth was still painful, then so was my situation now. Abruptly, I wondered what Tengen would advise me to do? He had insisted on training me—as far as my withered leg would allow—in the martial arts of hand-to-hand combat. One never knew what the future held, he had said, and it was always wise to be able to defend oneself.

But how was that to help me now? It could not. Nothing could. This situation was none of my making, and I had no defense against it. Refuse Ian, and my father would surely put me away from him just as he had my brothers. All I had ever done that was creditable—learning to use the abacus, to read and write—I had done to please him. If I had the courage to walk away now, before the thing was done, the loss of face would destroy everything he had worked for. I could not do that to him and continue my own life. *So, Tengen*, I mocked silently, *tell me what I can do to save myself from this situation?*

Perhaps Ian picked up on my thoughts. He swayed a little closer toward me, as if his balance was suddenly uncertain, and I turned fully toward him. I was startled by the thought that he was as nervous as I was, and I managed a weak smile. Ian looked startled and then smiled back, showing all his large teeth.

I heard myself mouth my responses to the priest calmly. My stomach was fermenting with horror, yet still I stayed in my place, outwardly calm. I thought that Tom must have tutored Ian in his replies; even so, his Japanese was terrible, almost unintelligible, even to me who was used to his rather high-pitched voice, but at least he was trying, and I appreciated his effort. I saw that the priest was straining to follow what he was saying. Perhaps the priest had performed the ritual so many times it barely mattered, for the ceremony flowed smoothly enough.

By the time we were handed the traditional three bowls of sake in turn—the san-san-kudo—I was back in my own mind again. I kept my eyes wide, daring the tears that had gathered to fall. I had done this thing. I had allowed myself to be subjugated, to be given in marriage to a man I hated. I had no one to blame but myself. The knowledge was cold comfort indeed.

My hand was shaking so much, I had to support it with my other hand as we each took a sip from the small, medium, and large cups. It was superb sake, and I had to stop myself from gulping down the entire contents in the hope that it would numb my senses. It was obvious that Ian did not enjoy the sake at all as he grimaced, and I saw that he was barely wetting his lips after the first sip.

There, the thing was done. I was a married lady. Even now, I could barely believe it. The crowd surged around us. Many of the gaijin in the congregation took Ian's hand in their own and pumped his arm up and down. I had never seen this done before and found it mildly alarming. I was deeply relieved when these strangers did not take my hand in the same way, but simply bowed formally to me. I smiled and smiled until my lips felt as if they were set in a rictus that would stay with me forever.

I bowed politely as a man I did not recognize pressed an elaborately decorated wedding money envelope into Ian's hands. He looked at it in puzzlement, so I took it from him gently, tucking it in my obi. This was only the first; there would be many more, far too many for Ian to stuff in the odd inserts in his clothes that I had learned were called pockets. What, I wondered, was wrong with putting valuable items in your sleeves or your obi? Safer, surely, than Ian's open pockets?

"What is that?" he whispered, watching as the envelope was concealed by my obi.

"Wedding money," I explained patiently. "All of the guests will give you an envelope. The amounts will differ, of course, depending on how wealthy the guests are."

"Really? How impersonal. In England, wedding guests give gifts—items for the house, that sort of thing—but never money."

Another guest advanced, holding out his flowery envelope, and I bowed and thanked him effusively. Ian looked disapproving and I reflected that I must make it a priority to improve his manners. I noticed that the Japanese guests were watching us both covertly, so I spoke through a smile.

"Here in Japan, the guests at a wedding give gifts of money. That is extremely sensible. How are they supposed to know what the couple wants or needs?" Ian's eyebrows rose superciliously, and I went on quickly, guessing that his reply was going to exasperate me yet again. "But Father will have a small gift ready for each guest as a memento of the occasion."

"Really? Backward way round, if you ask me. Like so much else in this country."

I glanced at him in astonishment, hardly able to believe that even such a clumsy, inept man as Ian could have spoken so rudely. But he was staring at the guests, shaking his head in apparent amusement, and I knew I was wrong.

TWENTY-TWO

The sickle of the
New moon is a dagger to
Plunge into my heart

There were so many good luck money envelopes that, finally, I was forced to trust Ian's pockets and hand some of them over to him. Some of them were very fat, and I guessed they must contain the new paper money that the government had introduced quite recently. The ordinary people greatly distrusted these notes, but the rich loved them. For the wealthy, using paper money was a sign of their prosperity, a subtle way of making the point that they had no need to worry if the money turned out to be as worthless as many thought it was.

In spite of my distress, I—just like any new bride—began to plan what to do with the money. There would surely be many things that our new home would need. I had never seen it, but as it had been bought and furnished by Tom, it would no doubt be lacking many essentials. Men were not to be trusted with such important matters.

I was brought back to earth as my bridegroom took my elbow and leaned toward me, so close that his forehead was only prevented from touching mine by my absurd headdress. His blue eyes, usually so cold, were glowing. I was sure I could see tears in them. When he spoke, his voice was a hoarse whisper.

"Mi-chan, you have made me the happiest man in the whole of Japan. No, more than that. In the whole of the world. From this day on, we will never be parted. I love you, Mi. I am such a lucky man. I do not deserve such a beautiful, good wife as you."

He meant it. I had no words to answer him, and I flinched as I saw bewilderment and hurt creep into his adoring expression at my silence.

"I am so sorry, Ian," I muttered. "A fly distracted me. I thought it was going to fly into my ear. You honor me, and I thank you for it."

It was the best I could do. I could not bring myself to lie and tell him I loved him in my turn. Perhaps he simply believed it had to be so; I had often read that those who are deeply in love can never bring themselves to believe that the object of their adoration does not return their feelings. In any event, he smiled happily and put his hand on my shoulder. Even through the silk of my kimono, I felt the moist heat of his palm and had to suppress a shudder.

Ian noticed nothing; he turned his head away, smiling, and raised his hand in greeting. Tom was pushing through the crowd, an envelope dangling casually from his fingers. He put it into my hand and wrapped my fingers around it.

"All brides are beautiful, but you surely outshine them all, Mi." He sounded as if he meant it. Oddly, the compliment was far more acceptable from him than it had been from Ian—from my husband. "You look a little tired. But of course you do. This must have been a long day for you."

I had no words to answer his sympathy but made a fluttering gesture with my hand that I hoped he would take to mean I was fine, that nothing was wrong.

Tom was obviously not fooled.

"Ian." His nephew jumped as if his thoughts had been far away. "Ian, your bride is tired, and you are ignoring her. Come, it is time we all moved to the ryokan to celebrate this occasion properly. I, for one, am famished, and I'm sure Mi has eaten nothing at all today."

He was right. I'd had no appetite for the morning meal. Mother, surprisingly, had not tried to force me to eat or drink, and Father had no more than poked his head around my shoji to smile at me and ask Mother if she knew where his new geta were.

Until this moment, I had thought that eating anything at all would make me ill, but Tom's words had been so kind that I thought that perhaps I might be able to eat a little, and tea would be very welcome; my throat was parched. I smiled at Tom, grateful for his consideration.

Ian looked at me with that odd expression I had noticed earlier, as if I were a stranger to him. I thought his smile was strained, but perhaps I was wrong, as his voice was very gentle.

"Of course. Come, Mi. I understand there is a jinrikisha waiting outside for us. That will be exciting—I've never traveled in one before." He put his hand on the small of my back and propelled me through the crowd that parted before us.

Like Ian, I had never traveled in one of the newly fashionable jinrikishas either. I eyed the flimsy-looking cart suspiciously. It might have been ample for a single person, but for two of us—especially given Ian's height and long legs—I thought we would be dangerously cramped.

Tom and Ian helped me into the seat, then Ian squeezed in beside me. I was right, there was barely room for both of us, and I bit back a grimace of distaste as Ian wriggled against me. At a word from Tom, the man pulling our jinrikisha picked up the shafts and set off at a brisk trot.

I couldn't help but gasp with fear. Ian promptly put his arm around my shoulders. I was very grateful that I could turn my attention to the crowd of wedding guests that were walking briskly around us, although I was far less pleased as I saw the normal crowds that thronged Edo's crowded streets part to allow us through so quickly, I knew intuitively that they wanted no contact at all with us.

I glanced back and saw that a sea of faces sour with distaste was turning to watch us.

CHAPTER
TWENTY-THREE

The first shoots of spring
Are always green, just as green
Is hope's sweet color

"M i." Ian's irritated voice cut across my thoughts. I jerked with surprise. I had been so lost in my remembrances that I had almost forgotten where I was. "I have asked you to pass me a swab twice, and you ignored me." His voice softened as he added. "Are you tired, dear? If you would like to rest, I'm sure I can manage on my own."

In spite of his kind words, I heard the petulance beneath them and shook my head quickly as I passed him the clean swab.

"No, I'm not tired. Is this child very ill? Her parents told me they lost a child last year to the strangling demon of children, and they are very worried that this child might have it as well."

Ian laughed. He didn't laugh often, and I thought it

sounded rusty. He wiped around the child's mouth carefully before he answered me.

"No, it's not diphtheria. That is the correct name for the disease, Mi. Please try and remember it. This little girl just has a very sore throat. Can you tell her parents that she is not in any danger, but that she should have plenty to drink for the next few days. Tea with honey will be soothing for her."

He turned his back to write himself a note on the case, and I took the opportunity to pull a funny face at the little girl, who smiled back at me uncertainly. Her parents were overjoyed when I gave them the good news and tried to push cash into my hand.

As always, I did my best to explain that Ian did not want their money. At first, I had stumbled in my explanations and knew I often caused great offense to his patients. Although it was never said out loud, clearly most of them believed that Ian thought their money was not good enough for him and were insulted. Finally, I hit upon the idea of telling them that amongst the gaijin, it was traditional for doctors to give their time for free. In fact, their religion insisted that it must be so. The patients were astonished, but as it was widely known that the gaijin were not only strange but capable of anything, they believed me, for which I was thankful.

"I think we will call it a day, Mi."

Ian laid his pen down carefully, exactly in line with his notebook. I had been fascinated with the pen when I first saw it, and when Ian was not present, I had tried to use it in place of a brush. My attempts were so ugly, and the pen felt so awkward in my hand, that I thew it away in disgust, although I had to admit it looked quite elegant when Ian used it.

"There are another two children waiting, Ian."

"Tell them to come back tomorrow. You might not be tired, Mi, but I am."

I lowered my head at the mild rebuke and went to apologize to the families squatting on the tatami in the waiting room. It was furnished with Western-style chairs, but the patients regarded them suspiciously and refused to sit on them, preferring to kneel on the tatami. Ian seemed not to notice. I was grateful that he was not a perceptive sort of man; if he had been, then he would surely have noticed my simmering resentment of the way he spoke to me.

The patients nodded when I spoke to them. They would come back in the morning, I knew. Or the day after. Or as long as it took for their precious children to receive the help they needed. I could not share their stoicism. I was sure Ian was not in the least bit tired. Rather, he was turning it against me that I had dared to appear tired when it was he who did all the work. He who cured the endless patients who would wait and wait for his time.

I bristled at the unfairness of it all.

"Ah, Mi." How was it possible that Ian managed to sound surprised that I had returned? Had he expected somebody else? I stared at him incredulously. "I believe I forgot to mention it to you, but a messenger brought me a note from Uncle Tom. He wishes to see me on a matter of business. I doubt I will be back for supper. Will you be all right on your own?"

He had never intended to see the last two patients, then. He had used my non-existent tiredness as an excuse to send his patients away disappointed when all along he had known about his appointment with Tom. Ian turned away silently, but I was certain he felt my empathy for his unseen patients, and that my distress pleased him.

I knew that I should be grateful that my husband did not beat me, as many men did. Yet, in a way, his was a far more subtle cruelty. Had I tried to explain it to Mother—assuming she had the time or inclination to listen to her mewling daughter—she would have looked at me in astonished disbelief and demanded to know what I thought I had to complain about.

The belittlement had begun from the first afternoon we arrived at our new home. I had entered hesitantly, unsure what to expect but determined to praise whatever I found, whether it was to my taste or not. As it was, I was too bewildered to say anything.

"Do you like it, Mi? Tom ordered everything. He has excellent taste in matters such as furnishing, whereas I have never been interested in such things."

Ian broke off, humming softly to himself. He strode through the entrance hall, calling over his shoulder for me to follow him. He did not, I noticed, take off his shoes. I slipped off my geta and limped behind him.

The textiles of the house were pure Japanese, with wood floors and sliding silk shoji to separate the rooms. Apart from that, it looked like no Japanese home I had ever seen.

The hallway was bare, apart from a curious wrought iron stand. I learned later that this was to hold Ian's walking sticks and umbrellas. I had never heard of an umbrella and was slightly disappointed when Ian explained that it was just a type of parasol, but one designed to keep off the rain rather than protect the skin from the sun.

If the hallway was plain, then the rest of the house made up for it. Every room was so cluttered with furniture and ornaments that I gathered my skirts carefully toward me for fear I would knock something precious to the floor.

Ian seemed delighted. He pointed out the features of each room to me as we passed through.

"This will be the waiting room for patients." I nodded dumbly; did he and Tom really expect them to sit on chairs rather than the floor? "This room beyond it is my consulting room."

It was a spacious room but appeared smaller as it was crowded with a large chair set before something that looked remarkably like a very high chabudai table, except that this table had drawers at each end. There was also a long, padded piece of furniture and—odd against the Western furniture—a rather lovely Japanese screen, decorated with cranes in flight.

"The screen is lovely," I said lamely.

Ian beamed at my praise. "Tom said the cranes were traditional Japanese symbols of good luck, so it would reassure the patients when I asked them to undress behind it."

Undress? I felt quite faint. Our family doctor had seen my naked legs when he treated me for paralysis of the morning, but that was the same trusted doctor who had brought me into this world. I thought that Tom was certainly right; any patients who were asked to disrobe so that a strange gaijin could examine them would need all the reassurance they could get.

And so it went on. There was a reception room in the wrong place and crammed full of little, round tables, padded chairs, and a sofa. The sofa was very like the one Mother had in her apartment. How she would love this house!

A moment later, I realized that Ian had saved the ultimate horror until last.

"This is our bedroom."

He slid back the shoji and stepped back courteously to allow me to enter. I thought I must have misheard him, that surely he had said our "rooms," not room. Even at home, I'd had a room to myself. As was tradition, Mother and Father had separate apartments. Neither of them would have dreamed of entering the other's space without clapping their hands and waiting to be invited in.

I turned my head toward Ian, smiling uncertainly as I waited for him to show me my apartment. He smiled back and waved his hand in a clear invitation for me to look around the large room.

The truth hit me like a blow. I had not misunderstood. This was unmistakably *our* bedroom. My kimonos were neatly hung to one side of a huge piece of wooden furniture with two doors that were hanging open as if inviting me to look inside. Immediately, I wanted to run to them and bury my nose in my clothes, to inhale the subtle odor of jako that would hang about them, and rub the familiar silk between my fingers. Take reassurance from my old acquaintances.

More bedroom furniture contained what had to be Ian's clothes. A chest with drawers stood at the side of the hanging wardrobe. A screen—just like the one in the waiting room—white and decorated with flying cranes, stood proud against the wall. I assumed it must be hiding a prayer alcove and was pleased to see it, although I did wonder why two strips of very ugly, coarse material had been flung over the top of the screen. I dismissed the thought. Surely it was some strange gaijin custom I was not aware of.

There were two, much smaller chests with drawers, one on each side of what seemed to me to be a huge futon on legs. Forgetting my manners entirely in my panic, I pointed at it and asked, "Where are the futons?"

Miserably, I knew that I had acknowledged that we were to share this room with my question, but surely I would at least have the respite of a futon to myself.

"There are no futons." Ian had stuffed his hands in his pockets and was looking around with a pleased smile. I could smell his odor even through the scent he had sprinkled on himself. "I did try to sleep on one of the wretched things when I first came to Japan, but I have never had a worse night's sleep in my entire life. This—" He patted the enormous piece of furniture, clearly pleased. "—is a proper bed. This is where we will sleep. You will soon become accustomed to it, Mi, and you will find it very comfortable."

We were to sleep in it. I had been right. I felt the blood drain from my face. If Ian saw my horror, he made no comment. As he was clearly waiting for me to respond, I managed to whisper, "It is very big."

"And very, very comfortable," Ian reassured me. "So, this is our new home, Mi. I haven't shown you the kitchen and storerooms, but I see no reason why you need to concern yourself with them. Uncle Tom has hired a servant for us to clean the house, do the laundry, and cook. You will meet her tomorrow."

"Yes."

I felt as helpless as a netted fish. I had been captured and taken from my own world, and there was no help for me. I could barely hear Ian's voice; the blood was pounding in my ears so noisily, it drowned out everything else. My husband was frowning at me, and I realized he expected an answer from me. Dazed, I shook my head. He spoke loudly and slowly, obviously irritated.

"Mi, will you do something for me, please?"

CHAPTER
TWENTY-FOUR

Weeds are easily
Plucked from their shallow roots. A
Flower needs more care

My mouth was so dry with fear, I could not speak. Panicked thoughts shrieked in my head as I wondered frantically what Ian wanted from me. Whatever strange desires he wanted to inflict on me, I was sure of one thing—I would not let him take me more than once.

My fluttering thoughts came to rest abruptly, and I felt my entire body fill with determination. I would kill myself after he took me. I knew it would be the ultimate betrayal. I would be the cause of Father's downfall, and I knew myself to be the most ungrateful of daughters, but even for Father, I could not allow myself to let Ian make love to me and live with myself afterward. Wildly, I thought that perhaps I had no need to worry about the means of my death. Surely, if Ian laid his hands on me, his smell would choke me and take the breath from my body forever.

In a sane corner of my mind, I knew I was wrong. Ian was my husband. He had every right to do what he wanted to me. Nobody—not my Father, not my Mother—would either understand or forgive me if I refused him.

The knowledge sobered me. I wondered fleetingly how many other brides had suffered as I was suffering now yet had somehow survived. Perhaps, against all the odds, they had even found happiness of a sort with the men they thought they despised. Oddly, the bleak reflection soothed my churning mind to the extent that I was able to lift my face and meet Ian's gaze. I thought I was prepared for anything he might ask of me.

Except for what he actually demanded.

He pointed toward the bathroom. "There is a jug full of water and a basin in the bathroom. Please, wash all that paint off your face. I barely recognize you. I do not want to see you wearing makeup ever again." He frowned and then added in a rush, "It makes you look like a yujo, not my own sweet Mi."

I walked away without replying. So much for all my fears! Suddenly, I was filled with a huge apathy. My courage fled, leaving me exhausted. I had been lying to myself all day, I acknowledged sadly. I could not kill myself. Karma had led me to Ian, and I could do nothing to change my fate. This was to be my life from now until the day either I or Ian died. His stink would not kill me. In time, I might even come to accept it. But at this moment, I shuddered at the horror of what was to come—a shared bed, all my privacy gone forever.

I splashed water on my face and lathered the soap. A pristine, white towel hung beside me, and I dried my face on it. Absurdly, when I saw the streaks of makeup defiling its purity, I wanted to cry.

My reflection stared back at me from the mirror on the wall before me. I had never seen such a large mirror before, and I guessed it must have been very expensive. I traced the outline of my naked face in its reflection. I widened my eyes, daring the tears to fall.

I would not cry. I would not give Ian the satisfaction of making me cry. Not now. Not ever. Deep in my mind, I remembered Tengen saying that he was certain that he would hear my name spoken of with awe in the years to come. I sighed and spoke very softly to my reflection.

"You were wrong, Tengen."

The thought of my lover ignited a new fear. Where I had been cold before, now I flushed with heat. Tengen. My lover. Surely Ian would expect his bride to be a virgin. What would he say, what would he do, when he found out I was not whole?

I caught my breath. Had I found the answer to my prayers? Had Ian been Japanese, I would have known what his reaction would be. He would be horrified. He had married damaged goods and would have put me aside instantly. No one would blame him, not even Father. I would be forced to return home in shame. I doubted that either of my parents would be able to forgive me. I would be packed off to a nunnery to atone for my sins. But surely even that would be better by far than waking every morning next to Ian!

I examined the idea carefully and my spirits began to rise. Surely, even a gaijin would not be able to accept the dishonor of a bride who had already been taken by another man. It had only been the once, a small voice in my mind protested, but I shrugged the thought aside. One or many, what was the difference?

"Mi? Are you finished?"

"Yes, Ian. I am done," I called back without a tremor in my voice as I walked back to our bedroom. The huge bed no longer held any terror for me. After all, I would be spending hardly any time in it.

"Ah, but that is better. Much better." Ian was rubbing his hands together. They made a dry noise, and immediately I wondered what those hands would feel like roaming over my body. Some of my courage began to seep away.

"Yes, Ian." It was all I could find to say, and even the two words cost me a great effort.

"Well, it has been an exhausting day, Mi. I don't know about you, but I found it difficult to sleep last night." I nodded; I hadn't dared try to sleep for fear of the dreams that might come to me. "It is a little early to retire, but a good night's sleep will do us both good. I see the servant has put out our night dresses, good." He inclined his head toward the screen and I followed his gaze. I could see nothing but the two strips of coarse material I had noticed earlier. By now, I was too dull, too exhausted to ask what he meant. "I will leave you to get changed, dear. I will join you when you are ready."

Ian smiled at me in what I guessed he thought was a roguish manner. I watched in bewilderment as he closed the shoji gently behind him.

What did he expect of me? I had no idea. This was my wedding night. And my husband had left me while I changed. Changed into what? I thought of Tengen, and my thoughts were bitter. We had made love in the open air, ripping and tugging at each other's clothes until we were naked. Our lovemaking had been sweet. I closed my eyes and recalled the whisper of my lover's breath, soft and insistent on my naked skin.

I almost cried out loud at the cruel contrast with this

moment. Perhaps I did make some sound, as Ian called out to me, "Are you all right, Mi? Have you found your night dress? It is next to mine, hanging over the screen. Naturally, yours is the smaller one. I hope you like the color. I thought pale pink would suit you very well."

Pale pink, like the sprigs on the new kimono I had changed into at the ryokan. I called out something—I had no idea what I was saying—and walked unsteadily to the crane screen. I peeped behind it timidly, almost as if I was afraid something that meant to do me harm might be hiding behind it. I told myself firmly that that was nonsense. How could a prayer alcove contain anything that was not pure and good?

Alas, I was disappointed yet again. There was barely room to turn around behind the screen, and it hid nothing but an outside wall. I paused, confusion making my head whirl. Where was the altar scroll? The plinth bearing an exquisitely bare ikebana arrangement, twigs and flowers carefully grouped to suggest the season of the year?

I folded my arms across my breasts, hugging myself in a gesture that failed entirely to give me any comfort. I reached up and tugged down the nearest strip of cloth in a daze. It unfolded as it fell, and I realized it was actually a garment of some sort. It had a row of buttons from neck to hem and long sleeves. It was colored a very pale pink.

This...this coarse, enveloping *thing* was what I was to wear for my wedding night? I held it unwillingly in front of me and found it covered me from the nape of my neck to my ankles. It was made of cotton and the feel of it made me itch at once. I wanted to weep for the loss of my lovely, silken sleeping robes.

Did I have any choice? I thought not. Unwillingly, I undid my obi and unwound my kimono. My underthings followed. The evening was cold and when I pulled what Ian had called a nightgown over my head, for a moment, I was grateful for the warmth of the strange garment. But then the coarse cotton started to itch terribly, and I longed to tear it off.

I supposed I would have to wear it. Ian had chosen it for me. Courtesy demanded that I should at least pretend to like the hideous thing. I walked from behind the screen and sat on the edge of the bed carefully. I was deeply grateful that it felt far more comfortable than I had expected. I shifted my weight and almost squealed with shock as the bed bounced beneath me like a living thing. I might have given in and allowed hysterics to have their way with me at that moment if Ian hadn't called again.

"Are you changed, Mi? May I come in?"

What nonsense was this? This house was Ian's. Everything in it—including me—was his property. Was he making fun of me? The thought vanished as soon as it came to me. I doubted that Ian knew what a joke was. I called out softly, "I am changed."

He had not had time to bathe, but I guessed that he had washed while he was waiting for me. His hair was wetly sleek and his skin looked pink, as if he had bathed in very hot water. Would it be sufficient to get rid of his bodily odor? I hoped so.

"I will help you to take off your brace if you wouldn't mind waiting for a moment while I get changed myself?"

He didn't wait for an answer but vanished behind the screen. I wondered what he was doing behind there. As it clearly did not conceal a prayer alcove, what was taking him so long? I found my answer as a curious assortment of garments was flung over the screen. Trousers, a jacket, and a shirt did not surprise me, but what was I to make of the curious, almost bodily-shaped garment made of some nasty reddish material that flapped over the screen and hung limply? It appeared to have arms and legs, and I almost screamed in terror. Tales of the strangeness of the gaijin abounded, but I had never heard of them taking off their skin before they slept.

I was so terrified, I could barely breathe. A moment later, the twin night garment to mine was whisked out of sight and Ian emerged. Like mine, his night dress enveloped him from neck to ankle and covered his arms to his wrists. I examined what little flesh I could see anxiously, but it appeared to me that the skin on his hands, face, and neck was still intact. What lay underneath, I dreaded to imagine.

"You haven't got into bed yet. Good. Could you put your leg flat on the bed for me? I will remove your brace."

I did as I was instructed, but it was an effort to lift my leg, hampered by the heavy brace, to the surface of the bed. Ian bent over the brace, manipulating the screws that held it in place deftly. He had large hands and I had often wondered at the skill he showed when he manipulated the delicate screws.

While his head was bowed, I took the opportunity to peer down the back of his night dress. The relief when I saw nothing but pale skin, dotted here and there with moles, was immense. Was it possible that the body-shaped thing that still hung over the screen was some sort of peculiar undergarment? I hoped so, fervently.

The final screw was unloosened, and Ian slid the brace off my leg. I gave a sigh of relief and wiggled my leg, stretching it out and bending my knee. Immediately, Ian grabbed the hem of my robe and tugged it down so that it covered my entire leg. I was bewildered. Ian had seen my naked legs more times than I could remember. He had even touched my black moss. I recalled the occasion when he had touched my private parts on purpose and had given in to his lust and howled strange words like a madman. Then, he had been my doctor. Now, he was my husband. How was it possible for him to be suddenly shy of seeing my nakedness?

Before I could make any comment, Ian rose abruptly from the bed. His movement was so sudden that I almost bounced off. The whole situation was becoming so very silly that my hysterical laughter threatened to return, so I hid my mouth behind my hand to smother it.

"All done." Ian spoke briskly, just as he had done when I was his patient. He was not looking at my face, but at some point over my shoulder. "Before I sleep, it is my custom to pray. Will you join me, Mi?"

As he spoke, he slid from the bed and sank to his knees on the pretty mat that covered the woodblock floor. I looked at his bowed head and wondered if I had truly married a madman. Surely, it would account for so very much of his strangeness. He raised his head fractionally, his eyebrows raised in question, and I felt I had to say something.

"I am sorry. I cannot kneel. My leg will not allow me to do that."

It was as if I had slapped him across the face. Ian closed his eyes and, for a moment, his expression was contorted as if he was in pain.

"Naturally not. How remiss of me not to realize. It is traditional in my religion for one to kneel in prayer, so if you will forgive me, that is what I will do. Perhaps you could join your thoughts to mine, even if it is not physically possible for you to join me?"

This was obviously what gaijin did before they retired for the night. Clearly, I had much to learn about my new husband. I wondered if he would also make an effort to understand me. I doubted it.

I watched Ian bury his face in his hands and begin to murmur, apparently to himself. I waited in respectful silence until he had finished and then, in response to his gesture. climbed off the bed to allow him to throw the coverings aside.

"Would you like me to help you get into bed?" His tone was courteous, but I was having none of it and climbed into the bed as smoothly as I could. Ian did the same at his side and instantly drew the coverings up to our necks.

The light had faded whilst Ian was at his prayers. I was grateful, as I knew my face was contorted with anxiety. What would my husband's reaction be when he discovered I wasn't whole? Was it possible that he might truly love me enough to forgive me? I trembled, I couldn't help it, yet at the same time, the irony of the situation was not lost on me. Only this morning, I had made plans to kill myself rather than spend a single night with him. Now, I was terrified that he would put me aside and bring unthinkable shame and disgrace to my family.

I thought of Tengen yet again. I had not loved him, yet he had been my lover. I did not love Ian, yet I had married him. So intense were my reflections that I thought I might have spoken my lover's name out loud.

TWENTY-FIVE

Time flies forward like
An arrow. Would that I could
Reverse its smooth flight!

"There is no need for you to be nervous, Mi." Ian spoke abruptly into the darkness. His tone was tender, and a very little of my fear calmed as I realized I had not revealed my thoughts.

"Thank you," I whispered. My voice was hoarse. I could not bring myself to regret making love to Tengen. I would not have undone our precious time together even if I could. But I was sorry beyond anything that I had allowed myself to be forced into marriage with Ian, not just for my own sake, but for his. Ian was a good man, I realized belatedly. He deserved better than a wife who did not love him, who would never even be happy with him. I struggled to put my thoughts into words that he would understand, words that would not leave him hurt and distressed, but I could not.

Ian broke into my thoughts, speaking quickly and briskly without any emotion. I was grateful. Tenderness would have undone me entirely. "I understand that this must be a difficult moment for you. Naturally, that must be so. All brides are nervous on their wedding night, it is only to be expected. But there is something that I must explain to you. Something very important."

His voice trailed off, and I wondered with amazement if he was finding it just as difficult as me to search for the right words. Whatever he had to tell me, I wanted him to get on with it. I broke into his silence and was proud and not a little astonished to find that my voice was steady.

"I am very nervous, Ian. Thank you for understanding that. Please, what is it you want to tell me?"

In spite of the perfume he was wearing, Ian's bodily odor was overwhelming, much worse than usual. I tried to breathe through my mouth to avoid the worst of it. Without warning, an idea came to me. Was Ian going to tell me that he was a virgin? That he had no idea what part he should play in the drama of his own wedding night? The thought filled me with amazement. Surely, it would not be me who was the teacher and Ian the pupil? Oh, Tengen, if only it were you who was beside me and not this man! I reminded myself sadly that it was I who had turned Tengen away. Had I hurt him, I wondered. If so, then surely I was being punished for my error now.

"We are not married, Mi."

I heard what Ian said, but I could make no sense of it. What was he talking about? Had I imagined my wedding ceremony? Had it been some other man who had taken his vows at my side? Or perhaps it had simply been a bad dream. If so, then surely I was still asleep, and that I could not believe.

"Of course we are married." I did not trouble to hide the disbelief in my voice. I propped myself up on my elbow, peering at the vague outline of Ian's face, barely visible in the falling dark. "Oh, I know you have to complete the papers and register with the authorities, but that is nothing, just a formality. Is that what you mean?"

I supposed it was. Although, I was hardly likely to forget that Ian was a gaijin, I was perhaps overlooking the fact that he knew so very little about what any Japanese person would take for granted. I felt a huge sense of anticlimax. Was that all that was worrying him?

He shook his head. I felt the movement in the darkness.

"No. I understand that, and I will take care of it as soon as I can. When I say we are not married, I mean we are not married in the eyes of God. My God." He took a deep breath and began to speak very quickly. "The ceremony we went through this morning was a Buddhist ceremony. I know that is your religion, but it is not mine. Until we take our vows in front of a Christian priest, then we are not married."

What nonsense was this? What did it matter who officiated at our wedding? We were married, whether I liked it or not.

"I don't understand," I said warily.

"I know that this must be difficult for you to understand. I am sorry." I felt him knot his hands together on his chest. It seemed to me that the gesture was intended to ward me off and—absurdly—I was hurt. "But you know that I am a devout Christian. My religion is important to me, too important to allow me to simply follow my own wishes and desires. My conscience would not allow me to live with you as man and wife until we are correctly married in a Christian ceremony. Do you follow what I am saying?"

I considered for a moment, and then shrugged. I had no

idea why he was so worried, nor did I see that there was any real difficulty.

"I think I understand. If it is important to you, then naturally, we must repeat our vows in front of one of your priests. Will you arrange that for us?"

"No." The single word was abrupt. My head reeled. How could he insist that the thing had to be done with one breath only to retract it with the next? "I cannot do that. You do not understand, Mi. We cannot take our vows before a Christian priest. There is not a single Catholic priest in the whole of Edo. I have asked Tom to make inquiries of his Japanese colleagues, but he assures me that, at the moment, there is no priest to be found anywhere on Honshu. If there is no priest here on the main island, I cannot believe that we will find one anywhere else. Until one arrives and conducts the appropriate ceremony, we are not married in the eyes of God, and there is nothing I can do to change that."

I thought about his words carefully. It mattered not at all to me, but it was clearly very important to my husband. Not that he was my husband, it appeared.

"So, I am married, but you are not." The silliness of what I had said made me want to laugh, but Ian seemed to take my words seriously.

"Exactly so. As soon as a priest arrives, we will take our vows in front of him, and then we will truly be man and wife."

Man and wife? Not husband and wife? He had lost me again, and I was suddenly weary of all this nonsense. As far as I was concerned, I was lying next to my husband. Above all else, I needed to confront my fears. I could not stand the anguish of not knowing what my fate was to be a moment longer. I took a deep breath and then wished I had not, as it stuck in my throat and made me want to cough. So instead of speaking, I put my hand over Ian's clenched fingers and squeezed them gently.

"From what you say, that day may be a very long time in coming. Tonight is our wedding night, Ian. That is all that matters."

I took my hand away and ran it lightly down his ribs. I was torn. I was supposed to be an innocent virgin, yet it was quite clear that if I did not take the lead, then Ian would not. If I was fortunate, he might think that any boldness on my part was a Japanese tradition. If he was as inexperienced as I thought he was, it was surely possible that he might not even realize that I was not a virgin. No matter. I had to get the moment over, had to know how he would react to my body. Tentatively, I allowed my fingers to wander slowly down to his tree of flesh.

Certainly, that particular part of Ian was not worried about whether we were truly married or not. His tree was poking his ridiculous nightgown into a tent, and a substantial one at that. I closed my fingers around his cloth-shrouded tree cautiously, deciding that undoing the buttons could wait until later. The cloth hampered me, but I decided briskly that that was no bad thing. I had no wish to betray the fact that I knew exactly what I was doing. I gripped a little more firmly, at the same time rolling toward my husband, intending to kiss his cheek. Tengen had taken me by surprise when he kissed me, but I had loved it. The gaijin had so many strange habits, I thought it likely that kissing would be something that they did, so Ian would hardly find it surprising. I hoped so.

His hand clenched over mine so fiercely, my knuckles cracked. I thought he must want me to grip his tree harder, so that is what I did. I flinched as he howled suddenly. He sounded as if he was in pain, great pain, and immediately I worried that I had hurt him.

"Ian? What is it? Have I hurt you?"

His fingers pried my hand away from him. He held my wrist tightly, forcing my hand down onto the bed. He was panting, clearly aroused. I was astonished and not a little bewildered. I knew instinctively that he wanted me to touch him and, clearly, he was very aroused, yet at the same time, he was holding me away from him.

"I am not hurt." His voice was very hoarse, and I knew I was right. I could feel the heat of his body. He was squirming as if he could not get himself comfortable—of course he could not when his tree was screaming for my attention. He might not be hurt, but his grip on my wrist was so tight that I was in pain.

"*You* are hurting *me,* Ian." I twitched my hand as a hint, and he let go abruptly, literally throwing my hand away from him. I rubbed my wrist, trying to ease the feeling back into my hand.

"I am sorry, Mi. I did not mean to hurt you. I would never want to cause you harm." He was controlling his voice, but not very well. I heard the tremor. "I thought you understood what I was telling you. The fault is mine that you did not, and I am sorry. When I said that we were not married in the eyes of my God, I meant that we can live together. Clearly, that will be expected by everybody, and it would be very wrong of me to send you home. I doubt even your parents would understand, so I have no intention of doing that."

I let my breath go in a sigh of relief. Ian obviously had no idea of how important his words were to me! I was shaking with relief and had to force myself to concentrate as he went on earnestly.

"I realize tonight must come as a great disappointment to you, but when I say we will live together, it will not be as man and wife. Rather, until we can exchange our wedding vows correctly, we will be together as friends. Or perhaps it would be better to say we will live as devoted brother and sister. But we cannot lie together."

He was clearly mad, I thought judiciously. What did he think we were doing at this moment if not lying together? Mad persons had to be humored, I knew, otherwise they might be dangerous. So, I spoke cautiously.

"But we are together now, Ian."

He sighed deeply, whether in exasperation or anger at my slowness, I had no idea. I waited and waited for his answer for so long that I thought he might have fallen asleep. When he finally spoke, I jerked with surprise.

"We are together. We will live together, here in this house that Uncle Tom has kindly bought for us. But we will not be joined as man and wife until it is before my God." He paused, and I guessed I was supposed to say something in reply, but as I still had no idea what he was talking about, I stayed silent. I could feel a great urgency gathering in his body; he was trembling even though the night was not cold and his nightgown—as I knew only too well—was thick. "Mi, our marriage cannot be consummated. We cannot make love until we are married properly. It would not be right, and I could not dishonor you in that way. Do you understand?"

My mouth opened and closed, opened again, and finally snapped shut. At last, I understood what my husband was talking about.

And I had no idea whether I wanted to laugh or cry.

Ian waited a moment and then sighed. He turned away

from me and settled into the bed with a grunt, finally pulling the bed coverings up around his ears.

I lay beside him until dawn lightened the sky, praying that it would be a very, very long time before his God's representative arrived in Edo. Long enough, at least, for it to be too late for him to put me away from him when the moment arrived when we did make love.

TWENTY-SIX

The winter birds are
Migrating to find cold. Spring
Must be on its way

There was a clock in each room of our house, except for the bathhouse, or bathroom, as I supposed I must learn to call it. I hated every one of the clocks with consummate loathing.

The first time I went into our bedroom, I was intrigued by the strange object that hung on the wall there. I thought it must be some sort of gaijin ornament made for decoration. Perhaps it was the gaijin equivalent of a scroll? I would have asked Ian what it was, but he rose as soon as it was light, gathered his clothes from the cupboard, and dressed behind the screen. I was too embarrassed to speak to him and pretended to be asleep. I heard him pause by the shoji for a moment, and then he was gone, and he did not return until evening.

I walked through my new home cautiously, afraid that I might be clumsy and sweep some of the many objects from the tables and chests that cluttered the rooms. I knew I was ungrateful, that the house—near the center of Edo—must have cost Tom a great deal of money. And given the price of Mother's simple, western-style chairs and sofa, the furniture must also have been very costly indeed. Although I recognized that I should be deeply thankful for his generosity toward us, but instead, it rankled with me. Father had earned his place in the world. I had hoped that I would follow in his footsteps. Alas, it appeared that that was not to be so.

There was so much furniture, so many ornaments! I felt as if each piece was watching me, gathering around me, and restricting my movements. I longed for Japanese simplicity and space around me.

I stopped in the middle of the reception room, my arms tightly by my sides in case I knocked against anything, as I heard a strange noise. Something was clicking rhythmically and constantly. I cocked my head to one side, wondering which of the many decorative things might make such a noise. I lifted a vase—empty of flowers—and shook it cautiously. Nothing. Nor could I rouse a noise from any of the many figurines dotted about the room. Finally, I realized the noise was coming from a fairly large wooden case pinned to the wall, very similar to the one fixed to our bedroom wall. Both things must be heavy, I thought, and probably very valuable, as they were attached not to the flimsy shoji but to an external wall. I approached the case cautiously and watched a strange attachment at the bottom of the case swing back and forth endlessly. Greatly daring, I put my finger on it. The noise ceased at once and I jumped back, alarmed that I might have broken it. But no, once freed, the weighted arm began to swing rhythmically again and the endless clicking noise began anew.

Wandering around the house, I found similar cases in each room. My new maid found me in what Ian called his surgery, staring at the wooden case in there.

The maid was a plump, middle-aged woman, and at once I ached for Anzu. Had she been there, how much simpler everything would have been. We could have sat down and chatted. She would have been as bewildered by her new surroundings as I was. We could have explored together. But my new maid looked surly, although she was flawlessly polite as she asked me if I would like anything to eat.

I smiled at her pleasantly but was met by a stone face. "Thank you. I would like tea and some rice. What is your name?"

She looked so surprised, I thought I had somehow been impolite. But she answered quickly enough.

"My name is Shig, Mi-san." The name meant plenty or luxurious. It had no doubt been bestowed on her by her parents in the hope that her life would be blessed with riches. In spite of that, I thought it ugly. "Shall I serve your meal in here, Mi-san?"

Shig glanced at the cluttered tables doubtfully, but I nodded. This was the only room that seemed meant to be lived in; I had no choice. A thought struck me and I asked, "Shig, do you know what that is?" I nodded toward the wooden case that had fascinated me earlier.

Shig's face brightened and she nodded. "Oh, yes. I have seen them often. I have worked for gaijin before and they all have them." She blushed suddenly, realizing her dreadful error. I pretended not to have noticed her reference to gaijin, and she rushed on quickly, obviously intent on trying to hide her rudeness. "It is called a clock, Mi-san."

I turned the word over in my mind. *Clock.* Yes, that

made sense. The sound the case made sounded rather like "clock" to me.

"Why does it make a noise?"

"The gaijin... I mean, it is used as a means of telling the time, Mi-san."

My eyes widened in amazement. Why did anybody need an ornament to tell the time, I wondered. On most days, the sun shone, and it was easy to tell the time from its position in the sky. In any event, the temple bells always rang out for sunrise and sunset, and the time in between was divided into six periods, beginning with the hour of the dragon in the morning and ending with the hour of the rooster at sunset. What could be simpler? The night was similarly divided, but few people—except for the militia and those who had no business to be on the streets at night —cared greatly about that.

When it was around the middle hour of the day, one's stomach said it was time to eat. In the evening, it became dark and all work ceased for the day. That was perfectly sensible, as naturally the actual periods of the day changed from summer to winter. That had to be the case. It was not possible to work the paddy fields in the dark, and nobody wanted to go to sleep in summer when the sun was still high in the sky.

Was Shig making fun of me? I asked, "Are you sure? Why would anybody need an ornament to let them know the time? How does it work?"

"I don't quite know how it works, Mi-san," Shig said humbly. "My last master saw me looking at his clock. He spoke quite good Japanese and was kind enough to explain to me how it told the hours."

"Do you mean it speaks?" I interrupted. I was alarmed by the idea of an ornament speaking.

"No, no. Nothing like that." Shig nodded briskly at the clock. "The white circle is called a dial. The symbols around the edge of it represent half a time period. For the gaijin, the daylight hours are divided into twelve, not six, as is the night."

"Then why does the clock show only twelve symbols?"

"I don't know," Shig said humbly.

"Never mind. Tell me how it works."

"The little pointer moves on one symbol for each half time period that passes." She looked at me hopefully, obviously thinking that her explanation was complete.

"And the other pointer?" As if it had heard my question, the longer pointer jumped suddenly. I jerked back in alarm.

"I'm not quite sure," Shig admitted. "It has something to do with the way the other pointer works, but I don't know what."

I murmured my thanks and dismissed her. As I waited for my tea and food, I watched the clock intently. I had not been deceived. The longer pointer jumped forward regularly. I glanced at the shorter pointer and saw that it, too, had moved forward when I was not looking at it. And constantly there was the soft noise, *click, click, click,* over and over and over again.

By the time Shig came back, I had decided I did not like the clock. By the time I had finished my meal, I had decided I hated it. It was stealing my time, I knew it was. It was measuring every breath I took, watching and recording my every movement. Did it store all the time it stole from me? I had no idea, but the thought terrified me. This strange thing was stealing my life, and I could do nothing about it at all.

I mentioned the clocks to Ian when he finally came back home quite late that evening. Shig had asked me doubtfully if she should cook a meal for him. She was really asking if my husband could eat Japanese food, but she was too polite to ask outright. At least I knew I was safe there. I had seen him eat, rapidly but with apparent enjoyment, at my Father's house many times. But I had no idea what time he would return, so told Shig to prepare food, but not cook it until he returned.

Ian looked surprised when I greeted him calmly. Like any new wife, I was feeling my way carefully and watched his face to make sure I was correct. I had intended to wait until he had eaten and taken some sake, but I could not restrain myself and asked him about the clocks almost at once. The clocks had stolen a whole day from my life and I wanted it back.

"Good evening, Ian. Are you hungry? Have you eaten already?" When he shook his head, I said, "I will ask Shig to prepare our evening meal at once. Once we have eaten, can you make the clock give me my time back?" I smiled—I hoped charmingly—and added, "It—all of them—have eaten every moment of my day. If they carry on like this, I will be an old woman before the year is out."

He stared at me and then began to laugh loudly. He laughed until the tears ran down his cheeks. I could not take the terrible insult and ran from the room to instruct Shig to begin cooking our meal and put the sake into a warming flask.

"The sake is ready." I was sure she was looking at me curiously, as if my shame was written on my face. "Shall I bring it through at once?"

"No," I said quickly. "Ian-san will wish to wash and change. I will clap when I want you to bring it in."

I took a deep breath before I went back to the reception room. Nobody had ever laughed at me in such a manner before. I felt both humiliated and hurt. I had done nothing to deserve such treatment, I was sure of that.

Ian was sitting, apparently comfortably, on one of the padded chairs when I went back to the reception room. I thought he was trying not to laugh, and I stiffened.

"I am sorry, Mi. That was very rude of me. Please, sit down and let me explain to you."

"Would you like some sake while the meal is prepared?" I spoke as rigidly courteously as I would have to a guest in my house. I hoped my coldness was not lost on my husband.

"I do not drink alcohol, and I would prefer that you do not, but as this is our first day in our new home, it is surely a cause for celebration. I will not object to you taking a bowl of sake on this occasion."

I would hardly have thought it possible, but as I clapped my hands for Shig, my spirits sank even lower. I had married a man who would not—or could not—make love to me, nor did he drink. Was he truly a man? Was it possible that a spirit of something cold and less than human, a snake, perhaps, had taken possession of his body? Or was it simply that all gaijin were like this? I doubted it. Tom was nothing like his nephew. He was kind and pleasant, as warm as Ian was cold.

I sighed. The conundrum was beyond my comprehension. All I knew was that I was condemned to a lifetime with this humorless man. I almost smiled to myself as I thought that perhaps I should be grateful to the dreadful clocks. The sooner they stole my time on earth, the better. Surely, my next reincarnation had to be more favorable than this one.

I poured a bowl of sake for myself. I had filled the bowl rather full and concentrated on not spilling the contents when I lifted it. Because I was distracted, I did not turn my head away from Ian.

Because of that, it took me a moment to realize he had none of his usual spoiled-pork odor. I sniffed as discreetly as I could, and it was undoubtedly absent. But there was a smell hanging about him, something clingingly sweet, not exactly unpleasant, but odd. I was certain I had never smelled anything like it before. In any event, it was much better than his normal odor. I was wrong, I supposed, to define my husband in terms of how he smelled, but I could not help it.

"Our food will be some time," I said formally. "I asked Shig not to cook it until you came home."

"Thank you. Mi, I am sorry I laughed at you about the clocks."

His voice sounded genuinely apologetic. I looked at him suspiciously. Surely, this was some sort of trick. Men did not apologize to their wives. What was the point? I was as much his possession as the chairs we were sitting on. Would he apologize to one of them for inflicting his weight on them? I stared at his feet and flinched as I saw he was still wearing his outdoor shoes. This was too much! I put down my sake bowl and stood, wincing as my left leg twinged with pain.

"May I take your shoes off for you, husband?"

I did not wait for an answer but tugged them off and carried them to the entrance hall, laying them next to my geta.

"I am sorry," he said again. "I completely forgot I am supposed to take my shoes off when I come indoors. I have much to learn, don't I?"

He was smiling, and I decided that now was a good time to ask him about the clocks after all.

"Tell me about the clocks. I have never seen them before. Do they really not steal time?"

"Not at all. They just record the passing of time, no more. I promise, they cannot take a single moment of your day."

I supposed I would have to take his word for it about the clocks, but I still hated them. The endless *click, click, click* set my nerves on edge and made me want to glance at them constantly.

When we had eaten our meal and gone to bed—Ian waiting to enter our bedroom until I had changed into my night dress before he changed behind the screen—I lay awake at his side, listening to that endless sound of time being counted until sleep finally claimed me. Even then, I was sure the sound haunted my dreams.

TWENTY-SEVEN

The night is for sleep,
But also for dreams. May all
Your slumber be sweet

I have no idea how he found us, but the next morning, Shig answered the jangling of the house bell and came—wide-eyed—to tell us we had a visitor.

"There is a man at the door who says he wants to see the doctor," she said breathlessly. "I think he means you, master. He does not have an appointment. Shall I send him away, Ian-san?"

Ian turned to me with raised eyebrows, and I translated for him quickly. I barely had any need to wait for his answer; I was certain he would tell Shig to tell the man to make an appointment. It was unheard of for even close friends and relatives to visit uninvited, and judging by Shig's disdainful expression, this man was probably low caste.

"No, certainly not. He must be a patient." Ian sounded

delighted. "Ask Shig to show him to the consulting room. We will both attend him at once."

I kept a stone face as I told Shig. Her astonishment was obvious. I hoped that mine was not.

The man was clearly a laborer of some sort. His robe was old and shabby, his skin weather-worn. I knew at once what was the matter with him—his shoulder hung at an unnatural angle and he was clearly in pain, just as I had been when I had dislocated my shoulder when I was a child. He looked terrified and spoke quickly as soon as he saw us.

"Please, I am a poor man and cannot afford much. But if my shoulder is not put right, I cannot work. Someone told me that the gaijin doctor would put me right and would not charge as much as a real doctor. Can you ask him if he will help me?" He held out a handful of small coins pathetically. Ian spoke before I could translate for him.

"Explain to this man that I do not want his money. My services are free. Tell him to take his robe off," he instructed crisply.

He walked around his bewildered patient, inspecting the crooked shoulder from all angles. Even I could see what the problem was. Why was Ian taking so long to put it right? Finally satisfied, he put his long fingers on the man's arm and shoulders and gave the arm a sharp wrench.

The man cried out with the pain, and I winced with him. Ian appeared not to notice. He opened a drawer and pulled out bandages and padding.

"Now, watch what I do carefully, Mi. This is a dislocated shoulder and is a very common injury. It is important that it be bandaged correctly to keep the joint still. We will no doubt see more of this kind of thing. Next time, I will expect you to act as my nurse and apply the padding and bandages just as I am doing now. When I have finished, please tell him that it is very important that he keep the arm still for as long as possible, and certainly until he has no more pain."

I was fascinated by the nimbleness of Ian's fingers. He worked quickly but neatly, with none of his usual hesitation. If I could work with the same degree of skill, I would be proud. When he had finished, I explained to the man what he had said and added—from my own experience—that it would probably be at least twelve days before he could use the arm with care, and probably four times as long again before he could use it to do any heavy work. He looked appalled.

"But I am a carpenter, mistress! I am halfway through building a house for an important client. If I do not do the work, he will turn me away and employ somebody else."

"What did he say?" Ian demanded. I explained and he shrugged. "Well, that is up to him. I have put the joint back in place. I can do no more."

He turned away and began to make notes in his tiny, gaijin handwriting. I was confused. How was it possible for him to take such care over healing this stranger only to apparently forget him immediately after finishing his treatment?

"I am sorry. The doctor says you must rest it. If you do not, it will be very painful for you and will not heal properly."

The man stared at me, and when I said nothing more, he bowed abruptly and walked out. Later, I found the handful of coins neatly lined up on the stand in the entrance.

The man was but the first of many. After the mid-day

meal, a couple brought in a child who was consumed with fever. Ian examined the little boy carefully and then handed the mother a screw of paper containing small, white pills. The boy would be fine in a few days, Ian said. He was to take one of the pills three times a day and drink plenty of water. When I translated, I changed the water to tea—the weather had turned and it was already beginning to be hot; one could no longer be sure that well water was wholesome. Just as the man had earlier, the father held out coins. I folded his hand gently over them and told him that the gaijin doctor did not charge. He looked at me in alarm and was obviously prepared to argue, but his wife had more sense. She held her son in one arm and pulled on her husband's wrist with the other, hustling him out before the mad gaijin could change his mind.

Word of the doctor who treated his patients for nothing obviously flew around Edo. Day by day, the amount of people wanting Ian to treat them increased until poor Shig began to roll her eyes and sigh theatrically as the bell jangled yet again.

Unexpectedly, I discovered that I was beginning to take great pleasure in helping Ian treat his patients. As time passed, I learned to bandage wounds and apply poultices to abscesses, to smooth ointment on burns and lance painful boils. Once, when Ian was absent, I even dared to stitch a terrible gash where a man had bit into his own leg with a scythe.

I was proud when I realized that most of our patients treated me with the same awed reverence that they showed to Ian. They even seemed to overlook the fact that I was a woman. I began to wonder if Tengen had been right all along. Was I truly to become known as a healer of the sick, a woman who was unique in the whole of Edo? The thought filled me with pride.

Ian was clearly happy. I noticed that when he was treating his patients, he did not smell at all. Or at least, smelled no worse than any other gaijin. Even at the end of the day, when he was busy in his consulting room, his smell did not come back. Oddly, if I awoke in the night—as I did often as I could never get used to the soft bed—the stink was back. But by morning, it had almost always gone again.

Although I had never expected it, I was happy. It was a quiet happiness, marred only when I reflected that I was still married but not married. Occasionally, I asked Ian if a suitable priest had arrived in Edo yet, but he always said no.

As time passed, I found to my astonishment that I began to long for our mock marriage to become a real one. I had become used to Ian and, to my own amazement, proud of him. His patients were clearly in awe of his skill, as was I. He was surely a good man.

When I did wake in the night, my first thoughts were always of the memory of Tengen's touch, of the sublime pleasures of our lovemaking. I longed to find that joy again. Greatly daring, now and then I reached across the vast space that lay between us and touched Ian gently, trailing my fingertips over his nightgown in the hope of finding some naked flesh. Alas, the all-enveloping gown defeated my probing touch. Even when I pressed harder, Ian never awoke, never moved, and I was forced to turn away from him, my desires unquenched.

Each morning when we woke, Ian fastened me into my brace. At first, I protested. My leg was much better in appearance and was barely even painful. I felt sure the brace was no longer necessary. Ian shook his head firmly at my reluctance.

"I told you long ago that the brace would work. You did not believe me, but now you can see I was right." I opened my mouth to argue, but Ian silenced me with a sharply lifted hand. "If you stop wearing it now, then the muscles will weaken again. Your limp will get worse and you will have increased pain and fatigue. I know that you hate it, but I promise you it is in your best interests to keep wearing it. Surely you trust me in this matter, Mi?"

He looked so hurt, I gave in. I did trust him. But I loathed the heavy, clumsy brace that anchored my leg to the floor and made it obvious that I was still a cripple. Thankfully, I was almost able to forget I was wearing it in the bustle of surgery. But on some days, there was no surgery. On those days, Ian simply told me that he would not be available. That he had business in Edo and had no idea what time he would be back in the evening.

I quickly learned to recognize when that was going to happen. On those days, Ian did not hurry his morning meal; I am a very slow eater, but on the days when he was going to be absent, I would finish my meal before he did. Inevitably, when he had downed his last bowl of tea, he would pull out the miniature clock he wore on a length of chain across his stomach and consult it gravely.

"Ah, yes. Time I was off." He would tuck the watch back in its small pocket carefully and stretch his arms, clicking his shoulder joints. I hated it when he did that. "I have business today, Mi. Please tell any patients that they must come back tomorrow."

When he first did it, I was appalled. "But they will be so disappointed!" I protested. "Some of them will have walked a long distance to see you. They will not be able to afford a ryokan for the night."

Ian shrugged. "I can't help that. I told you I have important business. If the patients' needs are that great, they will be happy to wait. Tell them I will be here tomorrow."

He rose and left before I could say anything further.

That first day he was absent, my stomach knotted with pain as I was forced to tell the waiting patients that the doctor was not there. He had, I lied, been called away on urgent business. Could they come back tomorrow when he would be there for certain?

Worse still were their reactions. Inevitably, they looked at me with eyes that told of mute suffering and turned away after thanking me courteously. I hated that. Even more did I hate my husband at that moment.

With no patients to attend to, the day stretched endlessly before me. Shig did everything that was needed in the house. It was immaculately clean, as were our clothes. The food she produced was delicious.

I pulled out my biwa, but somehow the music that my fingers plucked from it sounded lifeless, so I put it down in disgust. Even Gen's beloved book of haiku failed to rouse any interest. The joy of the poetry had left me entirely. I rubbed the soft, leather cover between my fingers and tried to remember what Gen looked like. Oddly, although I could recall his individual features quite well, it did nothing to help me remember what he actually looked like. Just as my biwa no longer had any emotion, my recollections of Gen were as cold as a statue. The thought filled me with great sadness.

Gen had been kind to me, and I had returned his kindness by turning my face away from him. I had been younger then, and careless of others, but it was no excuse.

Would I ever get the chance to both return his book and apologize to him for my nastiness? I doubted it, and my sadness increased.

Above all, the clocks in each room drove me almost to madness. Each tick they made mimicked my heartbeat. I put my hands over my ears to block out the sound, but I could still hear it. In desperation, I wandered through each room, trying to escape from the subtle torture. Still, the clocks measured every moment of my life until I wanted to scream to block them out.

We had no garden—that would surely have been a luxury in the center of Edo—so even on sunny days, I could not sit out and enjoy nature.

Had it not been for Ian's abandoned patients, I think I might truly have gone mad.

TWENTY-EIGHT

Winter grass whispers
In the breeze. If I listen,
It calls out my name

There is a proverb that says that if you do not enter the tiger's cave, you will not catch its cub. When I first explained it to Ian, he laughed and said that in English, one would say, "Nothing ventured, nothing gained." I told him that I preferred the Japanese version, and he agreed with me.

"Far more romantic," he said, although he still sounded amused.

I repeated the proverb firmly to myself on the day I knew I could no longer turn aside his patients.

The child and his parents were standing outside our door before Ian left. He must have walked past them without saying a word because almost as soon as he had gone, I heard the bell jangle timidly. I could have left it to Shig to deal with them—I was often tempted to do just that—but I never could. It seemed to me that they deserved an explanation from somebody other than a servant, and that left me. I rose wearily, feeling my morning rice heavy in my stomach.

These patients really were burakumin, I saw that at a glance. Their robes were ragged, their feet bare, and they were dirty. Dirt was under their fingernails, ingrained in their skin. I guessed the father was one of those unfortunates employed to empty richer people's night soil.

Before I could explain that the doctor was not present, the man held out a dirty bundle of rags to me in mute appeal. The bundle made a soft, sad, mewing noise and I realized the rags concealed a child.

The hope in their faces shriveled my own pain into nothing. Even if I could do nothing for the child, I could not bear to turn them away. They looked hungry, the sort of hungry I had never known. They made me feel guilty for all I took for granted.

I stood back and gestured for them to come in. "The doctor is not here today," I explained gently, and the man looked puzzled.

"But you are here." He looked at me hopefully. "We have heard that there are two doctors here who will treat the poor, and that one of them is a woman. You are here, so you must be the other doctor."

I had no words to answer him. Tears sprang to my eyes as I wondered how I could explain to him that I was not a doctor. That—as much as I wished it was not so—I could not help his child.

But I had no chance to explain.

The man glanced at his wife, and she immediately began to strip the filthy rags from the bundle. Beneath them, the child—a boy, I thought perhaps two or three years old—was naked. I almost cried out loud at the sight of his poor, thin body.

I had to do what I could for this pitiful child. Turning them away was unthinkable. I was shaking with nerves as I forced myself to recall Ian insisting that one must look carefully before touching. With enormous pity, I saw how emaciated the little boy was. His arms and legs were swollen, and all his limbs were purpled with bruises.

Satisfied with my inspection, I took the child from his father's arms and laid him gently on the couch. I heard his mother gasp with horror and knew instinctively that she was worried that her filthy son would dirty the fabric. I smiled at her reassuringly.

"Please don't worry. The fabric is tough. What is his name?"

"Katsu," she whispered. I knew the name meant victory and wondered if she had lost many children before this one had survived. She answered my unspoken question shyly. "I had many miscarriages before Katsu was born. I am no longer young, and I was beginning to worry that I would never bear my poor husband a child."

I felt her pain. I gave thanks as I realized with a rush of confidence that I was sure that I knew what little Katsu's problem was. And even better, I knew how to cure him.

"Katsu-chan, will you open your mouth for me? Please?"

I smiled at the obviously terrified child and opened my own mouth wide to show him what I wanted. Katsu glanced at his mother, and when she nodded, he opened his mouth far enough for me to see all his baby teeth. As I had anticipated, his gums were blackened and bleeding.

"Does he seem tired all the time?"

I addressed my question to his mother. Katsu's father

was staring at the tatami in awed silence, and I guessed he would say whatever he thought I wanted to hear, as was only polite. Polite, but totally useless.

"Yes. Yes, he does. He has always been an active child. He used to love to play with his friends, but now, it's as if all the life has been sucked out of him by some vengeful spirit. He just sits wherever I put him, as if it's too much effort for him to move."

"And the bruises?" I asked. I touched Katsu's arm gently and he flinched. "Has he perhaps fallen over and injured himself?"

"No, not at all. The purple started to come a few days ago, and it's just gotten worse and worse. If he knocks against something, even very softly, he bleeds. And—" She turned her head in appeal to her husband. He hesitated and then nodded. "Please, look at his eyes, doctor-san. The whites have turned yellow."

I was annoyed with myself. I had missed that. How wise Ian was when he told me to look and look again!

"Katsu has kaiketsubyo." Both parents looked at me aghast.

"Is it a very bad disease, doctor-san?" his mother asked.

I knew she was really asking me; is he going to die? And I answered reassuringly. At the same time, I felt a huge pride fill me. These simple people had called me "doctor." Even though I was nothing of the sort, I knew I could help them. That I could save their precious son's life. The knowledge filled me with such happiness, I wanted to laugh out loud with my joy.

Ian had seen two patients—both of them men rather than children—who showed symptoms of kaiketsubyo. The disease had not been as far advanced as this in either man, but I was certain that it was what Katsu was suffering from. Ian had asked me what the disease was called in Japanese. I had to think carefully about the symptoms the men were displaying before I answered hesitantly, and in return Ian told me in English it was called "scorbutus." I reflected wryly that the only time my husband appeared interested in learning Japanese was when it had to do with illness. But that hardly surprised me.

Katsu's father spoke suddenly but very quietly. So quietly that I had to bend my head toward him to hear what he was saying.

"Is there anything that can be done for him, doctor-san? Is...is my poor son going to die?" Before I could answer, he blurted, "We are poor people, doctor-san. I work hard, but I earn very little. When we have bought food and paid the rent, there is nothing left. But if you can save my son, we will go hungry to pay your fee. I must work, but my wife can clean and wash and cooks very well. She could help you keep your house clean and wash for you in payment."

As he spoke, he glanced around furtively, and I knew he was marveling at the furniture in the consulting room. To him, I must have appeared a very rich woman. I took a breath, knowing that if I dismissed his offer out of hand, I would be insulting him deeply.

"You are most kind. I greatly appreciate your offer. But I do not want your money." The man stared at me, his expression stone, and I went on quickly. "My husband is a very skilled doctor, but he is also a gaijin. His religion instructs him to help everybody who comes to him at no cost. If the shogun himself asked him for help, my husband would not charge him a bronze mon. Although I do not share my husband's religion, naturally I must take my lead from him. He would be very angry with me if I took any sort of payment from a patient."

I could see the two burakumin were digesting this. Finally, the wife spoke.

"The ways of the gaijin are strange to us simple people. If you will not accept any payment from us, then please accept our gratitude for even seeing us. Can you help my poor son?" Her last words were anguished.

I put my hand on her arm in reassurance. "Yes. Yes, I can help him. He will not die. I will not let him die."

Katsu wailed thinly. I thought he must be very frightened, and I gestured to his mother to wrap him up again.

"There is some gaijin magic that will save him?" Katsu's mother sounded as if she barely dared to ask. "My husband's mother says she has seen this illness before, and that nobody has ever recovered from it."

"Katsu will not die," I repeated firmly. "My husband has cured many people of this disease, I promise you."

An exaggeration, I knew, but also did I know that these burakumin were simple people who needed all the reassurance I could give them.

"What must we do?" Katsu's father was still staring at me doubtfully. I spoke to his mother, knowing that she would do anything I told her without question.

"There are no potions or pills that will cure kaiketsubyo on their own." The mother's eyes widened with fear, and I went on quickly. "It is a strange condition. Even the wisest of the gaijin do not understand quite what causes it. Tell me, do you eat much fruit? Many green vegetables? Salad greens?"

The parents exchanged bewildered looks. It was the woman who spoke, hesitatingly, as if she was ashamed of being poor.

"We eat mainly rice. We cannot afford to buy anything else. Now and then, the people my husband works for give him a little fruit if they have bought too much and it is getting past its best, but naturally, he eats that."

It was clear she was aching to know why I had asked. I was about to explain that Katsu's condition was caused by a lack of fruit and vegetables in his diet, but caution laid a finger on my lips. If I told them that, they would not believe me. To them, it would be nonsense. And—inevitably—Katsu's mother would take it as a criticism of the way she cared for her precious son.

Had I not seen the amazing difference eating fruit every day had made to Ian's patients, I would never have believed it either. I had to tread very carefully. I knew Ian would never have lied to his patients, but equally I knew if I did not, then little Katsu would die a lingering, painful death. I spoke firmly, hoping to impress my patients with my confidence.

"I told you that kaiketsubyo is a very strange disease." Both parents nodded warily. "But there is a cure for it. I will give you the correct pills today. It is very important that you give Katsu one pill first thing in the morning and one at night until you can see that his bruises have faded and that his eyes are no longer yellow. But it is also as important that Katsu has at least one piece of fruit every day. More would be better."

The wariness was back in their eyes again. I understood how much it must have tested their courage to bring their only son to a gaijin doctor. I knew Ian would have given them the same advice as me, although he would never have prescribed the pills. They were no more than very mild soothing tablets that would help to calm Katsu's pain. Useless to cure kaiketsubyo, but I knew these burakumin would believe it was the pills that were working, not the fruit.

I smiled reassuringly and added, "It is very strange, but the gaijin wise men have discovered that it is essential to eat fruit and green vegetables every day as well as take the pills to cure this disease. There is some unknown thing in the fresh food that combines with the pills. As I am not a gaijin, I do not understand such things. But I promise you, I have seen it work like magic many times."

I was rather proud of my fiction, and I was disappointed when Katsu's parents refused to look at me. They fixed their eyes on the tatami and the father spoke dully.

"Thank you, doctor-san." He took the pills I had put into a small envelope, and both he and his wife rose and bowed politely. "We will give Katsu the pills, twice each day. Thank you," he repeated.

They were almost at the shoji before I understood how foolish I was. The pills had cost them nothing. But fruit and vegetables were simply too expensive for them to buy.

"Wait a moment, please." My thoughts were racing, and I spoke quickly. "You said that you would be pleased to help me in any way you could. One of my husband's patients very kindly gave him a large quantity of mikan in gratitude for his successful treatment. It was very thoughtful of him, but we have far more than we can use. Would you take some of them with you? It would be such a shame for them to go bad. I would be very grateful, and they would help little Katsu recover much quicker."

Katsu's mother took a sharp breath. I knew how delighted she was when she spoke before her husband. "Thank you, doctor-san. We would be very pleased to accept your mikan."

I asked them to wait a moment and frightened Shig

almost out of her wits when I appeared in her kitchen. I knew we had plenty of mikan. Shig knew I liked the tart, orange fruit and she had told me only yesterday that she had bought a large amount at a good price in the market.

The mikan rested in a pile on the table. I guessed Shig was about to prepare some for the mid-day meal. The coarse, cotton furoshiki that she had carried them home from market in was neatly folded next to them. Shig must have thought I had gone mad when I grabbed the cotton square and began tipping mikan into it.

"I have a patient who needs these," I babbled. "You can always buy some more for us."

I was gone before she could reply. Was there enough fruit to cure Katsu? I thought so, but what about the future? I forced myself to think clearly.

As I passed the bundle to Katsu's mother, I added casually, "By the way, it would be very good for Katsu—and both of you—if you had time to gather wild cresses and sorrel for your table. If you eat them every day when Katsu has finished his tablets, the green stuff will ensure that they keep on working and his disease will not come back."

I sounded authoritative. Katsu's parents clearly believed me. His mother said, "There is a field quite close to where we live." They lived right on the outskirts of Edo, then. I marveled at the distance they had traveled to get to us; it must have meant walking for most of the night. "It has a stream running through it. That is where I get our water. I will make sure to gather watercress every day. Thank you, doctor-san."

I barely saw them leave through the tears that blurred my vision. That day, I had surely saved a child's life.

In the quiet, I heard the clock tick the seconds away. Suddenly, it held no fear for me at all.

TWENTY-NINE

The crane may live for
A hundred years. The tiny
Wren for only one

After the day I treated Katsu, whenever Ian left the house after the morning meal, I did not turn away his patients.

At first, I worried that if I did not have the knowledge to treat them, then the patients would have to return and Ian would find out what I was doing. I was not afraid of his anger if that happened. Rather, I felt that what I was doing was my own secret joy, and I did not want anybody else to know about it. I laughed to myself when it occurred to me that it didn't matter if some patients did have to return. Ian still spoke barely a word of Japanese. He knew only what I translated for him. If I chose not to tell him this was a second visit, he would never know.

It was about this time that it began to irritate me that Ian did not even attempt to learn to speak Japanese. He was an intelligent man, so it should not have been so very difficult for him. His uncle had mastered Japanese. Everybody knew that learning new skills became more difficult when one was older. If Tom could manage it, then surely Ian could at least try.

The more I thought about it, the more annoyed I became. Not only did Ian speak no Japanese, neither did he try to understand our culture. Even now, I often had to remind him that he had not taken his shoes off in the house. He often pointed at his patients and appeared not to notice that they were horrified by his rudeness. He even showed impatience with old people when I had to repeat things to them. Even though he spoke in English, I was sure they understood his tone and were offended.

Tom visited us now and then, courteously arriving after the evening meal so we would not have to feed him. Tom, I knew, would be well aware that it was unknown for a guest to arrive without making prior arrangements to visit. As Ian never seemed surprised to see him, I assumed that arrangements had been made, but Ian never got around to mentioning it to me.

That exasperated me as well. Perhaps if I mentioned the problem to Tom, he might have a word with Ian. But perversely, good manners forbade me from making any comment that might be taken as criticism of my husband, so I stayed silent.

Anyway, I was always pleased to see Tom. He was a ray of unexpected sunlight on a dull day, a breath of breeze from the outside world. A world I missed so very greatly.

I had loved traveling to Edo with Father. Enjoyed every moment I spent in his bustling office. Now, I had no need to venture out of the house. I had more clothes than I could ever need. Shig did all the shopping. Although I saw patients every day, I could hardly demand that they give me news of the outside world. Had Anzu been with me, I would have enjoyed a chat with her. Sadly, I remembered how often she had driven me mad with her incessant gossip about what was happening on the estate; now, I would have loved it.

So, I welcomed Tom's visits like a thirsty man who is given abundant water. I hung onto his every word.

"Mi, how radiant you look!" Tom smiled widely at me and then glanced down discreetly. "Do you perhaps have some welcome news for me?"

I was baffled for a moment and then colored deeply as I understood that he was asking tactfully if I was pregnant.

"No. I am afraid not."

For once, Ian seemed to have picked up on the fact that something was amiss. He looked enquiringly between us, and Tom immediately switched to English.

"I was just telling Mi-chan how beautiful she looks."

"Indeed. I am a lucky man."

Ian sounded so sincere, I blinked in surprise. Fortunately, I had no need to hide my amazement as Tom spoke quickly.

"I am glad to hear you appreciate your good fortune, nephew. Mi, I have a little something for you."

He handed me a flat package wrapped in paper that told me it was from one of Edo's most sought-after merchants. I knew what it was at once from the shape and the feel—a slab of bean curd jam. I accepted it with a murmur of pleasure and clapped my hands for Shig. When she appeared, I gestured at the bean curd and asked her to bring me a sliver of bamboo to eat it with and to make us tea.

I had liked Tom from the day he had given me a gold Victoria coin as a keepsake. I still had the shiny coin, wrapped in a scrap of silk, nestled next to the good luck money envelopes we had been given at our wedding ceremony.

It was a constant puzzle to me why Ian appeared so indifferent to money. He never mentioned our finances, although I assumed we were reasonably well off as we never went short of food and a messenger arrived with expensive medical supplies regularly. My curiosity became too great eventually, and I asked him tentatively if we had enough money. His reply was so sharp that I felt as if he was astounded by my impertinence.

"I have no money at all."

I gasped with horror; I couldn't help it. Father's favorite saying had been, "Prosperity grows on the tree of perseverance," and I had always thought it a very wise saying. Father had earned every coin he had by his own work. And now my husband was telling me we had nothing, and—given his refusal to charge for his services—were never likely to have anything. I was appalled.

"But how can we survive without money? How do the bills get paid? Does Shig work for us for nothing? I don't understand."

I trailed off helplessly. Ian stared over my shoulder, drumming his fingers on the arm of his chair. I remained silent, determined not to speak until he answered me. He finally spoke reluctantly.

"My parents are missionaries. They have no money at all, except what the church, and one or two very kind benefactors, gives to them. They have never found it a problem, so why should we?"

He seemed to feel that this nonsense was a sufficient answer. I was having none of it.

"We do not receive any money from your church, and

you ask no payment from the patients," I pointed out. "Yet we live in this house and we eat the food Shig cooks for us. How does that come about, husband?"

"Tom sees to all our needs."

His body odor was growing stronger. I knew he was squirming with anger and embarrassment at my questions, but I was so worried I felt I had to persist.

"Why?" I demanded. I knew that Tom had said he would pay for the surgery expenses, but it appeared his charity went far beyond that. It made no sense to me at all.

"Because he is my uncle. He is a very rich man and has no children of his own. He looks upon me as the son he never had. He knows that I am doing very worthwhile work here, and he is happy to give me a regular allowance so I do not want for anything."

I wished I had never asked. We—or rather, Ian—I noticed he had said "I" and not "we" in his explanation. We were no better than beggars. I was appalled. Did Father know, I wondered? Surely, he could not. He would never countenance his daughter receiving charity from a man who was not even a blood relative. Yet, Ian seemed to feel it was only right and proper that Tom should pay for all his—our—needs.

Even knowing that, I was still pleased to see Tom.

THIRTY

The sound of a night
Bell recalls your voice when you
Said farewell to me

I could not find it in my heart to be angry with Tom for his charity. No doubt, he thought it was the correct thing to do; perhaps in his society, it was. Tom, I could forgive. I was less certain that I could feel the same way about my husband, who appeared to simply think it was his right to take all that Tom wanted to give without questioning it.

So, I was happy to see Tom in our—or rather, I supposed bitterly—*his* house. Especially when he brought with him all the gossip of Edo. I did not join in the conversation greatly. How could I when I no longer knew anything of the outside world? Instead, I listened and stored away each morsel for consideration later.

I was especially alert when the conversation turned to politics. Tanaka had often discussed the state of our country with me, and I missed our fascinating conversations dearly. Unlike me, it was clear that Ian was not particularly interested in much of what Tom spoke about, but his uncle appeared not to notice.

"The Satsuma Rebellion shows no sign of abating," Tom said thoughtfully.

Ian grunted absently in reply, but my interest was caught. I had never heard of any rebellion, not in the province of Satsuma or elsewhere.

"If things get any worse, will it be a step back for us?"

I was quite surprised that Ian was interested enough to comment, and also was I puzzled. By "we" did he mean he and Tom, or all the gaijin in Edo?

I leaned forward in my eagerness to listen to Tom's response. Ian glanced at me and frowned.

"Mi-chan, do you still have your biwa?"

I was startled by the change in subject but nodded anyway. "Of course."

"Why don't you bring it in here? I'm certain Tom would love to hear you play."

I was confused, but since Tom was smiling at me approvingly, I rose as graciously as I could and obeyed Ian's instructions.

When I returned, both men were deep in conversation. I paused, waiting for them to stop talking and listen, as was only polite. I waited and waited, and finally realized that they had no intention of ceasing their conversation. I could barely believe it. Surely Tom, if not Ian, understood that having asked me to play, they should listen. I reflected bitterly that it was just as well I had not asked Tom to speak to Ian about his manners. Clearly, Tom was just as discourteous as his nephew.

Defiantly, I began to play. At first, I was very nervous, but gradually the music swept aside my nerves and I played with growing confidence. After a while, I stopped concentrating on the music and began to listen to what the men were discussing. I guessed that, for some reason, Ian had not wanted me to hear their conversation, so I was careful to keep my eyes on the strings, as if they required my whole attention.

"I don't understand why Takamori is leading this rebellion against the government. I thought he was one of the senior men in the government?" Ian commented.

"He was." Tom paused to take a sip of his tea. "But I believe he's come to be very concerned about the growing evidence of political corruption at the highest levels of government."

"And the government takes him seriously?"

"Indeed, they do. Don't forget, it's not just Takamori who is taking a stand. He's established what amounts to a private army in his home area of Kagoshima. He calls it a military academy—the Shi-gakko—but it's already so popular that it has over a hundred branches. And it's not only disaffected samurai and members of the police forces who are supporting him. The brightest and the best young men in the area are flocking to join his academy. Takamori trains them in the use of weapons and military tactics, and even artillery."

"But surely it's not enough to worry the government here in Edo?"

Ian sounded incredulous. I was so interested in the conversation, I played a whole series of false notes. Ian clearly didn't notice, but Tom glanced at me, his lips twitching with amusement, and I knew he had heard my mistakes.

"They are worried, and with good cause. Satsuma Province has effectively cut itself adrift from the central government. If you remember your military history, Ian, divide and conquer has always been a successful strategy."

Ian shrugged sulkily, hunching his shoulders around his ears. I had to choke back amusement. He looked just like a schoolboy who had been scolded by his teacher for inattention.

"I suppose so. But still, it's just an isolated incident, surely?"

"No, it isn't. And that's part of why it's being taken so seriously. The government has dealt with a number of small, but very violent, samurai revolts in Kyushu recently. I know all about those, and I also know that they were resolved successfully and very efficiently. But this rebellion in Satsuma is different entirely. Apart from anything else, it's led by Takamori, who is already a popular hero. And don't forget, he's backed by many of the Satsuma samurai, who have a reputation for extreme fierceness and loyalty. Add all that to the fact that many ordinary Japanese—as well as daimyo and samurai—still deeply resent that we gaijin are here in Japan, and the situation becomes a potential powder keg."

"I can see it's worrying," Ian acknowledged. "So, what are you doing about it?"

What was *Tom* doing about it? What did it have to do with him, a mere gaijin? I was so startled, I was very grateful that my fingers continued to pluck the strings of my biwa automatically. This was both exciting and intriguing; I tilted my head as if listening to the music, all the time paying attention to Ian and Tom.

"That, dear nephew, is the problem. I know no more about the situation than the man on the street does. Nobody will talk to me about it. As you know, I have always been a great believer in the proverb that knowledge is power, but at the moment, I have neither knowledge nor power. A situation I intend to remedy very quickly."

"Nobody will speak to you about the rebellion?" Ian's face was sly. "Not even..." Tom raised his hand abruptly and Ian coughed, and I knew he was changing his words before he spoke. "Not even our mutual friend?"

"Not even him. He claims to know nothing about what is happening in Satsuma. I don't believe him, but no amount of threat will make him speak. How beautifully you play, Mi!"

I was so startled by being spoken to directly that I almost dropped my biwa. I managed to smile as I accepted the praise modestly.

Tom left us shortly afterward. Ian stretched and yawned and said he was going straight to bed. He reared back as if I had bitten him when I said I was not tired and would follow him shortly. Even his retreating back looked injured.

I was not lying. I was not at all tired. Rather, I was excited by the conversation I had overheard. Even if Ian could not understand how important the Satsuma rebellion was, I could. If the samurai Takamori succeeded in overthrowing the government, then our lives would change dramatically. It appeared to me that he and his men wanted to turn the clock back; perhaps not to turn Japan into the casket sealed against the rest of the world it had once been, but certainly to limit the power of the gaijin, and probably even expel many of them.

And if that happened, what would it mean for Ian and me? Ian was, of course, doing good work here in Edo. He treated those who were too poor to seek help from a Japanese doctor. But would Takamori see that as a good thing? Might he take the opposite view and decide that he did not want Japanese people being treated by a gaijin doctor? I could quite see that happening. He was a proud samurai warrior. He had a thousand years of tradition behind him, and I thought it unlikely that he would understand the needs of the poorest of the poor.

And what of Tom? Even though I still had no idea what his business was here in Japan, he was obviously a man of influence and power. A rich man. It had to be so or Father would not do business with him. Surely, it would be men such as him who would be the first to be expelled. And if that happened, what would become of us? I shuddered at the thought. Without Tom's support, we would be penniless. Would we be forced to join Ian's parents, wherever they were? Would Ian follow in their footsteps and become a missionary?

Bleakly, I thought that if that was our future, then at least we could be properly married. If Ian's father was not a priest, then he would surely know one.

Without me touching it, my biwa slipped suddenly to the floor. I shivered with superstitious awe. Was it possible that my lovely instrument had heard my thoughts and disapproved? I picked the biwa up and set it carefully on a relatively clear table. Superstitious nonsense or not, the trivial incident had cleared my thoughts.

I would not leave Japan, no matter what happened. This was my home, my country. I would not allow myself to be shipped to somewhere I had never heard of. Nor would I lose dependence on one gaijin only to have it replaced by complete and total reliance on another. Even if the other gaijin was my father-in-law.

If Ian and Tom had to leave Japan, then I would not go with them. I had cash of my own—the gold Victoria Tom had given me so long ago, and also the contents of my wedding envelopes. As Ian had never shown any interest in them, I had finally given in to my curiosity and counted the contents of the flowery envelopes.

Many of the envelopes contained a single coin, but that coin was gold. Some had two or more valuable silver coins in them. One—the one that Tom had given to us—I remembered the remarkably pretty flower pattern on the envelope—had another gold Victoria in it. A few of the envelopes contained large denomination paper notes. I sat back—my brace dug in cruelly, but I was so delighted I ignored it—and counted the cash. I calculated that there was easily enough to support a large, quite prosperous family for at least a year. For a woman on her own, even assuming I kept Shig? Three years, perhaps more.

Certainly, long enough for me to establish myself as a healer. I would have to charge, naturally, but nowhere near as much as any traditional Japanese doctor. Perhaps it was even possible that Tom might be persuaded to give me some money. Or, even better, introduce me to the person who supplied Ian with his drugs. Although, as soon as the thought came to me, I dismissed it. The man would no doubt be gaijin; if Tom were cast out, so surely would all his contacts.

I could do it. I would do it, given the smallest chance. A woman doctor was unheard of, but if everything else in my homeland was changing and changing again, why not? Of course, I would not have anything like Ian's great knowl-edge, but I certainly knew enough to treat most of the day-to-day ailments that the majority of our patients had. Even Ian had his limitations.

I recalled the day that an elderly woman had come to us, unusually, on her own. She was pitiably thin, and her skin was the color of ashes. I guessed that she was very ill when I saw that Ian was reluctant to examine her. I gasped when she undressed. She had a lump in her left breast that was not only nearly as large as the right breast, but was leaking pus. It stank.

Ian looked but did not touch. His voice was cold when he asked me to tell the woman he could do nothing for her. I understood. She had advanced gan in her breast. What Ian called cancer.

The words stuck in my mouth, but quite clearly the woman had expected the diagnosis. She thanked me with great dignity and walked out with her head held high. I thought she was wonderful and wished with all my heart that we could help her.

That night, I was still awake in the early hours of the morning, my thoughts wandering from the poor woman with gan to our strange existence. Perhaps it was the juxtaposition of Ian and Tom that called it to mind, but for some reason, I began to wonder who Ian and Tom's mysterious "mutual friend" was.

THIRTY-ONE

If I awoke blind,
Deaf, and dumb, I would still know
You by your sweet touch

I would have guessed that something was happening even if I had never heard of the Satsuma Rebellion. Suddenly, our flow of patients slowed to a trickle. And those that did come were clearly worried; Ian might not have noticed, but I saw that the patients were nervous, far more so than usual. They could barely keep still whilst Ian was examining them, and they snatched their medicine from my hand and nearly ran out of the surgery. When I mentioned it to Ian, he shrugged my concerns away.

"We are seeing fewer patients, but I daresay that's down to the weather. It's quite cool for the time of year. Summer's the time for fevers. You just watch. When it gets warmer, we'll have more patients than we can handle. Anyway, if there's nobody waiting for me—" *For us,* I corrected silently. "—I'll take the opportunity to go into Edo. Tell anybody who turns up to come back tomorrow."

Shig brought me tea and I sipped it with enjoyment. Everything had suddenly acquired a sharp brightness that I was sure had not been there before today. I was happy. Happier than I had been since the day I married Ian. I had made my mind up and was excited by my new vision of the future. *My* future.

No matter if the Satsuma Rebellion failed, I would not stay as Ian's wife. Not that, in his eyes, and the eyes of his god, I was his wife. That being so, then surely he would not be greatly unhappy to lose me.

I had money. I had learned to heal. I knew that it was unlikely that I would have the clever medicines that Ian offered to his patients, but I knew what they were called and what they were used for. Surely, a good apothecary could offer me something similar. I would not let that deter me. Now that my mind was made up, I would not turn back.

But nor would I rush headlong into my new life. As the proverb says, victory belongs to those who wait a moment longer than their opponent. I decided that I would be wise to wait for the outcome of the rebellion. If it succeeded, then I would have no need to do anything. I was sure that both Ian and Tom would be expelled from Japan, along with the rest of the gaijin. I had always been fond of Tom, and in spite of his newly revealed bad manners, I would miss him, a little at least. And my so-called husband? I reminded myself that if it had not been for Ian, I would have neither money nor skill, and grudgingly decided that I should be grateful to him for that.

And if the rebellion was suppressed by the government? I would still leave Ian, there was no question of that. And if he remained in Edo, then he would find he had far more problems than I did.

All of Edo loved to gossip. The news that his Japanese wife had left him would spread like wildfire, and the loss of face for Ian would be insupportable. I knew that the patients—already reluctant to be treated by a gaijin—would never allow themselves to be touched by a man who had been humiliated by his own wife. I felt sorry for Ian but hardened my heart. I had tried to be a good wife to him. Tried my hardest. But it seemed to me that he cared nothing at all for me, perhaps never had.

Father would be appalled. He would disown me, I knew that. The knowledge was painful, but I had not even heard from him since the day of my marriage. Did he ever think of me? I had no idea. I would surely be dead to him when I left the husband he had selected for me. But in practice, would it make any difference to my life? I told myself firmly that it would not.

Ian had once told me an English proverb about a fly in the ointment. I had told him that the Japanese equivalent was "a single fart in the temple ruins a hundred days of sermons by the priest." I had thought it very funny, but Ian had turned a stone face to me. I decided now that I would not let anything deter me. I would force myself to regard my love for my dear father as either a fly or a fart.

Once I had decided that, my thoughts wandered back to the unknown "mutual friend," and I became fascinated by who he could be. It seemed to me that Ian had been about to name the man—for surely, it must be a man—and had caught his tongue at the signal from Tom. That had to mean it was somebody I knew.

I nagged at the question almost obsessively. Was he one of Father's clients? I had seen many obviously impor-tant men being ushered into Father's private office—Tanaka had told me proudly who they all were and what their histories were. I remembered the samurai that Tanaka had told me was so reduced in his circumstances that he was forced to borrow money from Father. Was it possible that Tom could be paying this man to give him information? It seemed likely to me.

The samurai would have contacts in high places, places that even Tom could never hope to reach. I wondered again what Tom was actually doing in Japan. It must be trade of some sort, I thought, and so it would be important to him to be aware of what the future held.

Tom had spoken of threatening his informant. That had puzzled me at the time, but now it made perfect sense. If it were ever found out that the samurai was in Tom's power, he would be ruined. He would probably have to go into exile. Yes, it was all perfectly logical. The only slight puzzle was Tom had not named him. How could he know that the samurai's name would mean anything to me?

The doorbell jangled briskly, breaking rudely into my reverie. Patients after all. I expected Shig to come to ask me to attend them, but instead, she tapped on the shoji and stood back to let someone in.

I knew it was Tom before I saw him. He was the only man—gaijin or Japanese—who had any effect at all on the stolid Shig. She actually smiled when he arrived, and when he spoke kindly to her, she blushed. Her whole aura changed. I could almost see the pink glow of pleasure that surrounded her.

"Tom." I rose and smiled. "Have you come to see Ian? I'm afraid he's not here. He's gone into Edo on business." I lied awkwardly. I hoped Tom would not question what Ian's business was. I would feel intensely foolish if he did, as I had no idea.

"I hoped Ian would not be here." Tom smiled, but his

tone sounded odd. Stern rather than his normal lightness. "It was you I've come to see, Mi-chan."

I was astonished but remembered my manners. "It is very good to see you, Tom. Would you like some tea?"

Shig was still hovering and was visibly disappointed when Tom refused. I nodded to her to leave and gestured to Tom to sit in one of the deeply upholstered and deeply uncomfortable chairs.

"I would really prefer to sit on the tatami. I have lived here in Japan for so long that an armchair is no longer comfortable."

He folded gracefully to the floor as he spoke, and I followed him, although far less gracefully. My brace made it difficult to bend my left leg easily, and as always, I cursed it.

As if he had read my thoughts, Tom said thoughtfully, "Your brace has obviously helped your leg greatly. If I did not know you'd had paralysis of the morning, I don't believe I would even notice your limp these days. Do you still have pain in the leg?"

"It aches a little sometimes. And I still have very little feeling in it, but compared to how it was, it is nothing. But the brace is very heavy and clumsy. I will be delighted when I no longer have to wear it." I sounded ungrateful and so added quickly, "Of course, I am very thankful for all Ian has done to help me."

"Naturally you are. But if you feel the brace has done its work—and it certainly seems to me that it has done so—then perhaps it is time that you no longer wear it. Of course, I am not a doctor, and Ian knows best, but perhaps he is being a little over-cautious. Would you like me to have a word with him, to see if he can be persuaded that you can do without it?"

"Oh, yes. Yes, please." I spoke from my heart. To no longer have to wear the clumsy, heavy thing that chained me to the earth would make me feel like a prisoner being loosed from his shackles. I am not, generally, a superstitious person, but it seemed to me that Tom's words were an indication that fate had heard my plans and approved of them. I was sure that Ian would agree with Tom—as he always did—so already I was a little further toward gaining my independence.

"Consider it done."

Tom leaned forward and held my gaze. I had noticed before that when he spoke to me, even when Ian was present, he had the ability to make me feel as if I was the only person in the whole world who was of interest to him. It would have been flattering if I had not seen him do the same thing to Shig.

"Thank you. What did you want to see me about, Tom?"

"This is a little difficult, Mi. I may be wrong, but it seemed to me last night that you were perhaps a little bored. It must be very restrictive for an intelligent young woman such as you to be inside the house day after day, seeing nobody but Ian and his patients?"

How very perceptive Tom was! I felt a rush of gratitude so deep that I spoke without considering how ungrateful my words must seem. "It *is* very difficult for me. I loved it when Father took me to his office with him. I saw so many different people, and I knew I was able to help him in his business. Every day was different. And it was wonderful going into Edo. The crowds! The shops! I loved it."

I stopped abruptly, almost panting with my emotion. Tom's expression was grave, and I knew I had spoken out of turn.

"It is only natural that you must be bored, being tied to the house as you are. I believe that your mother does not leave your estate often, so she will not have visited you here." I nodded, watching his expression hungrily for a clue as to what was to come. "And you are not acquainted with your sisters-in-law." He frowned and then clapped his hands so suddenly it made me jump. "I have the answer! For today, at least. I am actually on my way to see your father. He asks after you often." I hoped Tom meant that Father asked him how I was, if I was happy with my new husband, and I listened with rising joy. "And I am sure he would be delighted to see you. Would you like to come with me?"

I hesitated. Tom might be sure Father would be pleased to see me, but I was far less certain. Had he invited me, that would have been different. But for me to arrive without notice? And presumably Tom was seeing Father to discuss business. Did he intend that I should sit and listen to private—and no doubt important—matters that no longer concerned me?

"It would give me great pleasure." I paused and added delicately, "If you are certain that Father would not find me intrusive."

"Of course not," Tom said heartily. "He will be over the moon to see his only daughter."

I had no idea what his words meant, but I judged from his tone that he thought Father would be happy.

Truly, today was a fortunate one! If I had thought it a lucky omen that I was to lose my brace, then how much better still was the chance to see Father one last time.

THIRTY-TWO

The cherry blossom
Is beautiful, yet still it
Must fall from the tree

The closer we got to the center of Edo, the more nervous I became.

Tom had left me while he hired a jinrikisha. He said he had passed a jinrikisha stand on his way to our house and it would not take him a moment to return with one. I was impressed by his consideration. A Japanese man would have instructed Shig to go out and direct the jinrik-isha puller to our house. She would have been expected to follow on foot.

Although our home was in a quiet area, in a fairly short time, we were engulfed by the sights and sounds of central Edo. Particularly the sounds. I had forgotten how noisy the streets were. Voices were raised all around us—street food vendors crying out the merits of their wares, merchants calling out to attract housewives to their shops, and everybody talking loudly just to make themselves heard. Our puller shouted constantly, warning people to get out of his way and calling greetings to other jinrikishas as he passed them. I was astonished by how many jinrikishas there were and reflected that on the day of my marriage, they had still been quite a novelty. I began to be seized by a nervous melancholy. It seemed that the world was changing around me while I continued as I always did, cut off from what was happening in the rest of the world. That would not always be so, I told myself firmly. Soon, I would be part of this world again.

Tom did not attempt to talk over the noise, and that pleased me. I wanted to be left alone to compose myself. It would not do to allow my delight at seeing Father again to be too obvious. It would be far better that I was simply polite at first and took my cue from his behavior.

Our puller clipped along at a fine pace, and I wondered if he was anxious to get rid of his gaijin passenger. In any event, we arrived at Father's office far too quickly for my liking. I'd had barely had time to collect my thoughts.

I noticed that Tom did not bother to ring the bell, but pulled the shoji aside briskly, gesturing to me to walk before him. I wanted to explain to him that this was all wrong, that my place was in his shadow, but it would have been even more impolite for me to leave him standing waiting for me, so I walked in front of him with as much confidence as I could summon.

At first glance, little appeared to have changed. A number of the clerks raised their heads as we entered. At sight of Tom, all of them bowed—it struck me as rather amusing. As they all bowed at the same moment, I thought they resembled carefully orchestrated puppets—and then immediately went back to their brushes and abacus, clearly intent on showing how busy they were. A messenger approached us quickly, almost kowtowing, his bow was so deep.

"Dickson-san, Kono-san is expecting you."

I did not know the messenger. He must have arrived since I had last been here. He glanced at me curiously and wet his lips with his tongue, clearly bewildered as to who I was and how he should treat me. Tom spoke calmly but with great authority in his voice.

"Thank you. This is Mi-san, Kono-san's daughter. She is here to visit her father."

Consternation at his gaffe made the messenger turn pale. He bowed deeply to me and then stood aside, gesturing for both of us to walk in front of him. His dismay did nothing to calm my jumping nerves.

I glanced around quickly, hoping to see a familiar face. Was it possible that Gen might have returned to my father's employment? I would have been delighted to see him, but there was no sign of him. Nor could I see my old friend Tanaka. I was disappointed and whispered to Tom,

"Is Tanaka-san still here? He was always very kind to me, and I would like to speak to him."

I spoke in English, and the messenger blinked at me in obvious surprise. His amazement was complete when Tom replied in English.

"I'm afraid not. He retired some time ago. He and his wife have gone to live with his eldest son, on the outskirts of Edo. I believe he is very happy."

I was deeply disappointed but had no time to dwell on it. The messenger was already tapping softly on the shoji frame before pulling it smoothly back and ushering us forward into Father's inner sanctum.

"Kono-san, how good to see you again," Tom boomed cheerfully. "I have a surprise for you. I know you will be pleased to see Mi-chan again. And here she is."

Father had half risen. I hesitated, unsure whether to wait for him to beckon me forward or—as I dearly wanted to do—run to him. A moment later, I was relieved I had not moved as Father simply stared at me, his expression horrified.

I wanted to cry. After all my daydreams of how he must be missing me, this was the cruelest blow fate could bestow on me. Clearly, he had been glad to get rid of me. Not only had he not missed me, but far worse, he appeared appalled that I had returned uninvited and unexpected.

If Tom had not been standing directly behind me, I would have turned and ran—or at least, walked as fast as my brace would allow. As it was, Tom had his hand on the small of my back and was pushing me forward, gently but insistently.

I walked straight-backed as close to Father as courtesy dictated, and then bowed deeply.

"Mi, this is most unexpected." Father's voice was as stiff as my bow. "How kind of Dickson-san to think of bringing you to see me."

His voice was flat, and I noticed at once that he had not said a single word to indicate he was pleased to see me.

"I knew you would be delighted to see Mi," Tom said cheerfully. "I am afraid she is becoming bored with only my nephew for company. Shall we sit down, Kono-san?"

I stifled a gasp of amazement. Tom's voice made it clear it was hardly a question, and the discourtesy made me shiver with alarm. This was Father's office. Tom and I were visitors. No matter how long Father left us standing, Tom should never have taken it upon himself to suggest we make ourselves comfortable. I was even more confused when Father flushed. He spoke almost humbly.

"But of course. I will send for tea." He clapped his hands, and the messenger was there at once. I thought he must have been hovering outside the shoji.

Silence fell with the arrival of the tea. The messenger poured and I sipped from my bowl eagerly, pleased to have something to occupy myself with.

"Thank you." Tom spoke courteously to the clerk then fell silent until he had closed the shoji behind him. "You are obviously busy, Kono-san. Business is good, I hope, in spite of the current difficult political situation?"

I saw Father stiffen. It seemed to me that he thought carefully before he answered Tom's harmless question.

"I am nothing but a lowly businessman, Dickson-san. Politics mean nothing to me, as you know."

"Really? But surely, the unrest must affect everybody. I know my nephew is concerned that if the Satsuma Rebellion is successful, it will mean that he—and Mi, naturally—will have to leave Japan for good. He feels, no doubt rightly, that if they remained, they would both be in danger."

I had not heard Ian say that. I glanced at Tom sharply. He was smiling, his head slightly to one side as he waited for Father's reply.

The silence went on for so long, I was becoming uneasy. There was something going on behind the exchange of words, something I could not understand. I felt as if the very air was vibrating, and I jumped when Father finally replied.

"That would be a very sad day indeed. As I said, I know little about politics, but if the situation is as difficult as you seem to think, then perhaps it is time I concerned myself with such things."

"I think that would be very wise. Very wise indeed."

Tom was smiling broadly. Something had clearly passed between him and Father, but I had no idea at all what had happened. I stared at my empty tea bowl rather than look at either of them.

"Would you like some more tea, Mi-chan?"

Father's voice was suddenly very kind. Although I had longed to hear tenderness in his voice, now that I had my wish, I would rather he had remained distant. It would have made my imminent betrayal so much easier.

Tengen's voice whispered softly in my thoughts. *Be careful what you wish for. You may get it.*

Tom answered for me. In spite of the discourtesy, I was grateful.

"That is most kind, Kono-san. But I am afraid I have urgent business elsewhere, and I have to take Mi back home before I move on."

Tom stood, clearly ready to take his leave. I got to my feet as gracefully as I could.

"Dickson-san." Father's voice was soft, but his tone was the crack of a whip. Tom stopped and turned to face him. He was still smiling, but the smile did not reach his eyes. "As a matter of interest, if the Satsuma Rebellion was to be successful in overthrowing the government, would you also be forced to leave Japan?"

"Oh, yes. I think that would definitely be the case."

"Then I can see that the outcome will be of deep concern for you. I will most certainly see if I can get any information that may clarify the situation."

"You are most kind, Kono-san." Tom bowed briefly and

turned to go. I could not look back because his hand was tight on my shoulder, urging me forward.

Father said nothing at all as the shoji slid shut behind us.

THIRTY-THREE

The river flows in
Only one direction. It
Cannot change its course

I was shocked to find that the jinrikisha was waiting outside for us. Such extravagance, and so unnecessary. One of Father's messengers would have found us another in a few moments. Not that we even needed it. Tom told the puller to take us to a teahouse that I knew was only a short distance away. Even with my brace, it would have been an easy walk. Father, I knew, would have been appalled at such a waste of money. Not that Father's opinion mattered to me any longer, I conceded sadly. Clearly, I no longer played any part in his life.

Perhaps Tom read my thoughts. He said cheerfully, "There is a saying in my country—time is money. I am hungry. The sooner we arrive at the teahouse, the sooner we can eat."

"I thought you had urgent business, Tom," I said dully.

"I most certainly do. It is sitting beside me."

It took me a heartbeat to understand what he meant. I smiled dutifully, even as I thought sourly that the flattery was far from subtle. Nor was I in the least hungry. I wanted nothing more than to be left alone with my sadness, but clearly Tom did not see my sadness.

The teahouse was not one I had visited with Father, but there were similarities. Most of the tables were taken even though I guessed that such elegance would be very expensive. And just as had been the case when Father entered his preferred teahouse, we were greeted effusively and ushered to a pleasant table, as secluded as was possible despite the crowd.

Although I protested that I was not at all hungry, Tom ordered food for me. I had expected tea. In spite of the bowl I had drunk earlier, I was thirsty and would have welcomed it. But to my surprise, Tom ordered sake instead.

When the food arrived, the savory steam awakened a small miracle of appetite and I ate rice and vegetables with relish. Tom poured sake for me and nudged the bowl toward me.

"Don't tell me that you have adopted Ian's bad habits and you don't drink," he said slyly.

"I don't, normally." I shrugged. "I had sake occasionally at home to celebrate special occasions, but as you say, Ian doesn't drink alcohol, so we don't keep it in the house."

"But you will take a bowl with me? I hate drinking alone."

I could hardly refuse. I sipped my sake slowly. It was excellent and had been heated to the perfect temperature. I was thirsty, and my bowl was empty quickly. Tom refilled it at once and gestured to the server to bring us another flask.

Tom raised his sake bowl to me in a polite toast and I drank automatically. I was suddenly feeling quite cheerful.

Tom smiled at me and gestured at my plate. "Are you still hungry? Would you like something sweet to finish your meal? Or perhaps a little more sake?"

"No. Nothing, thank you. If you would be kind enough to ask for a jinrikisha to be fetched for me, I will leave you to get on with your business."

Tom's smile slid into soft laughter. It was so very good to see and hear genuine amusement after Ian's surly manner that I laughed with him.

"But I told you, Mi-chan. Today, you are the whole of my business."

He raised a hand and when the server came at a trot, he asked him to find a jinrikisha for us. I noticed that Tom made no effort to pay the bill, and I thought that he must truly be an important man for an exclusive teahouse such as this one to trust him to pay his account later. I found the knowledge that I was of such interest to him oddly exhilarating.

Tom kept up a flow of chatter on the short journey home. He seemed not to expect an answer, and I was grateful for that as I wanted to see and hear everything central Edo had to offer. I had been gone a long time. I had no way of knowing how much longer it would be before I could return.

The journey was short. I called out cheerfully to Shig to tell her we were back. There was no reply and I called again, becoming slightly anxious.

"Shig is not here." Tom's voice was very close to my ear. "She happened to mention to me when I arrived that her sister was ill and that she was concerned that her family would be finding it difficult to cope without her, so I told Shig to take the rest of the day to herself. I doubt she will return until it's time for the evening meal at the earliest, possibly not until tomorrow morning if she finds things are difficult."

I was mortified. Tom—who barely knew Shig—somehow knew more about her personal life than I did. I was angry with myself, and even angrier with his presumption. Before I could speak, I saw that Tom was gazing around the reception room with an obviously proprietorial glance and the words died on my tongue. Of course, he had every right to give orders to Shig. His cash paid her wages, just as he had paid for everything in my home. Even the roof over our head depended on his charity.

My light mood darkened. I watched Tom bend down to take off his elegant setta sandals. I was about to kick off my own geta when, shockingly, Tom knelt at my feet. He took my right foot in his hand and slid off the geta. He put my foot down carefully, and then lifted my left foot even more gently before pulling off the geta and setting it next to its companion.

"Can you walk in comfort without your geta?" He sounded deeply concerned for my welfare and I was overwhelmed by his kindness.

Ian had never spoken to me in such a way. He had never offered to help me get dressed or undressed, even on bad days when my leg was stiff and refused to bend at all. The nearest he had ever come to caring for me was for the few moments each day when he fitted my brace, making minute adjustments to the screws that fastened it in place. Even then, when he spoke, it seemed to me that all his concern was centered on the workings of the brace rather than my comfort.

I felt a flash of self-pity and was appalled. Was I prepared to trade my spirit, my very essence, for the sake of a few kind words? I stood straight—ignoring Tom's outstretched hand—and bowed formally.

"Thank you, Tom." My voice was firm. I was pleased. "I can walk very well without help. I have enjoyed my day very much. But I am sure you have better things to do with your time than stay here and chat with me." I stared pointedly at his discarded shoes.

"There is nothing I would like better than to stay here with you, Mi-chan."

His answer left me uneasy. He sounded sincere, and I was flattered, but I put the thought from me at once. It didn't matter. Politeness dictated that I must welcome Tom to what was, essentially, his own home. I spoke neutrally.

"In that case, please sit down. As Shig is not here, I will make us some tea." I sounded cross, like a spoiled child who has had her plans overturned. I cringed inwardly. I was sure Tom was laughing at me, and I turned abruptly, for once forgetting about my weak left leg.

Alas, my leg did not forgive me for my neglect. I put my foot down wrongly and felt my brace twist abruptly. Horrified, I flailed my arms, but my balance was stolen from me by the rigid brace and I tumbled to the floor and landed with a grunt as the air was knocked out of my lungs.

"Mi!" Tom kneeled by my side instantly. "Are you hurt? Has your leg twisted?"

"I am not hurt." I managed a stiff smile. "Only my dignity has suffered."

I tried to stand, planting my hands on each side of me on the floor. I found at once that I could not move. The brace— unyielding at the best of times—appeared to have locked in place. My knee was twisted to one side and, with a flash of horror, I wondered if the damage would be permanent. I sat back down again, willing Tom to leave me alone. To go. If I had to sit on the floor until Ian came back home this evening, it would be far preferable to Tom fussing over me.

"Is it your leg? Do you have pain there?"

Tom was running his hand carefully down the brace as he spoke. His touch was so briskly impersonal that I wasn't embarrassed. In fact, it was very similar to the way Ian touched me when he was fitting my brace each day. I twitched my knee fractionally and was relieved to find I had no pain.

"No. I am fine. Please, go away." I spoke so bluntly I surprised myself. I was even more surprised when Tom laughed, a rich, deep sound full of real amusement.

"Leave you sitting here? And what would my nephew say when he arrived home and found his dear uncle had deserted you?"

The answer was, I knew, that he would be angry with me. He would insist that I had fallen because I was clumsy and that I had embarrassed myself in front of Tom, our benefactor.

"Mi? Are you sure you are all right? I don't think you heard a word I just said to you."

I collected my scattered wits quickly. "I'm all right. I promise you I am."

The lie came fluently. True, I had no pain, but I could not move my left leg, no matter how I tried. I was so terrified that my own clumsiness might have left me crippled once more that I found it difficult to breathe.

Wryly, I reflected that I had no need to worry. Tom was here. He would help me. I hated the thought that I would be dependent on him—to depend on him to help me get up, as with everything else in my life—but I had no option. If I had to lie on the floor, unable to move and wracked by my worries, I would be mad by the time Ian finally came home. I spoke as calmly as I could, but even to my own ears my voice sounded fluttery and unsure.

"To be honest, I think my brace must have twisted when I fell. I can't feel my leg at all. If you could help me into the bedroom before you go, I will take the brace off. Ian can look at my leg when he gets back."

I thought I had phrased that very nicely. I had accepted Tom's help politely while at the same time making it clear that he was to leave me in peace once I was comfortable. I had no idea how I was to get the brace off unaided, but I was not about to tell him that. I was so busy concentrating on appearing unconcerned that I was taken completely by surprise when Tom bent down and slid his arms beneath my legs and back and lifted me with no apparent effort at all.

THIRTY-FOUR

A snake may bend and
Fold, but it is still a meal
For the hungry fox

I could have protested. I could have told Tom firmly to put me down. I could have tried to wriggle out of his arms. I could have told him I did not, after all, need his help. If none of those had any effect, I could try one of the physical retaliations Tengen had taught me. I could ram my elbow into his ribs, or—if that had no effect—grab his kintama and squeeze hard.

I chose to do none of those things. Instead, I rationalized the situation to myself calmly. This was no unknown man, intent on causing me harm. This was Tom, my uncle by marriage and our benefactor. A man who had never shown anything but great kindness to me.

And also a man I liked. On the heel of that thought was another that startled me more than a little. He was a man I found attractive.

In any event, I was sure he thought he was acting in my best interests. Despite all I had said to him, I knew I could not take the brace off unaided. I had tried before, when Ian had been back very late and my leg ached. The screws that released the device were at a difficult angle and were so small that I could not grip them tightly enough to turn them.

Tom wanted to help me and I clearly needed his help. In that case, where was the argument? Once he had left, I would have time to consider all that had happened today. I could dwell on the hurt Father had inflicted on me so casually. Gather my anger at Ian's absence when I needed him. Rehearse the words that would leave Shig in no doubt that she took her orders from me—not Tom. But for the moment, the only thing that mattered was the state of my leg.

Tom put me down on the bed with what felt like exaggerated care. He inspected the tiny screws that held my brace in place, and I watched curiously as he began to turn the first of the many screws, holding them delicately in his fingernails. I noticed absently that they were cut very short and were very clean.

As the first screw came out, I knew that nothing at all mattered to me other than that I had done no damage to my leg. If my leg was twisted out of shape again, then all my plans were ash. If I could not even walk without people staring at me in sympathy—or worse, turning their heads politely away at the sight of my deformity—I was tied to Ian. Probably forever. My life could have no other purpose. I knew that nobody would trust an obviously deformed woman to heal them. Why should they? Who would ever believe they could be helped by somebody who could not even heal themselves?

I groaned aloud at the thought, and Tom raised his head and looked at me anxiously.

"Am I hurting you? I'm sorry, but I must get all these screws undone before I can attempt to take this thing off your leg. It's my fault. I should have spoken to Ian earlier, told him to allow you to walk without it. It could always go back on if it was still needed."

I shook my head wordlessly. If the brace left my leg other than for sleeping and bathing, I would never allow it to restrict me again. No matter how difficult I found it to walk without it, I would never be able to face dragging its weight around, being enveloped by its cold, uncaring embrace day in and day out. It made me ugly. It tied me to the earth. I could not believe that Tom would understand that, so I shrugged and tried to make light of the situation.

"It's not your fault. Not at all. It was an accident. I turned too quickly."

"Fortunate that I was here, then. That's the last screw out. Keep still while I pull the brace off for you."

I held my breath as the clumsy, heavy brace slid off my leg. Tom threw it on the floor with contempt, almost as if he hated it as much as I did.

Now that the moment had come, I was almost petrified with fear. I tried to move my leg but could not so much as wiggle a toe. I felt my face contort as I did my best to hold back tears. I was paralyzed again. I had endured so much already; to be struck down again was too much for me to bear. My spirit died within me.

I whimpered at the unfairness of it. Just one small step and I was once more doomed to be a helpless cripple.

Tom's whole attention appeared to be on my leg. I was grateful he had not seen me giving way to despair.

"I don't think there is any major damage."

I stared at the top of his bowed head incredulously. Was he lying to be kind? I would much prefer it if he told me the truth.

"I can't feel my leg," I choked out.

Tom put his hands on each side of my knee. His body shielded my leg from my sight, but I could feel his touch. A moment later, hope spurted into my thoughts. I could feel him touching me! Surely, that must mean something.

"Your knee is quite straight. Your father told me how badly disfigured it was after your illness. I guess it must be far, far better now than it was then." Tom raised his head and smiled. "I do not have Ian's skill in healing, but when I was younger, I was quite athletic. We had no doctor on hand to cure our injuries in those days, so my friends and I learned how to help each other. I certainly have enough skill to massage your leg for you. I think you may have trapped a nerve when you fell. A massage will help. Will you allow me?"

Without waiting for a response, Tom put his thumbs on each side of my knee and pressed firmly. I gasped as his touch caused me intense pain. He ignored my cry and circled his thumbs carefully down my leg and then back up again, pausing to rub his palms on my knee.

Warmth flooded into my leg wherever his hands touched. I was trembling with anticipatory fear as I tried to force my leg to move. The leg stayed where it was, but at least I was able to jerk my foot. Tom paused and nodded at me encouragingly. I cried out loud with joy when I finally managed to raise my leg slightly from the bed.

Without warning, a sensation as if ants were crawling under my skin erupted all over my leg. At the same time, my flesh tingled unpleasantly. I pushed Tom aside to rub frantically at my thighs, where the sensation was the most painful.

Tom sat back and watched me with a smile of satisfaction on his face. It took some time for the pain to subside, but after what felt like a very long time, I lied back on the bed and took enormous pleasure in cautiously swinging my foot back and forth. I could move my leg. I was not crippled.

My joy was so great I wanted to sing. Instead, I spoke softly.

"Thank you." Two, simple words that I must have used a thousand times before, but never had I meant them so truly. "I thought my leg was paralyzed again. I thought I would never be able to walk properly again."

I reacted impulsively, throwing my arms around Tom's shoulders and pulling myself up to him, burrowing my head into his shoulders. I felt him stiffen and at once I was appalled at my own actions. What must he think of me? Even a yujo, a woman of pleasure, would surely have been more restrained. I pulled away.

Before I could apologize, Tom grabbed my wrists. He held me in place effortlessly, a hand's width away from him. He stared at me intently. I was as transfixed by his gaze as a rabbit caught by a snake and could not look away. Hard as I tried, I could not understand the expression in his eyes.

"Do you believe in fate, Mi? That there is something that rules all our destinies?"

"Of course," I agreed promptly.

I am a Buddhist, if not a very devoted adherent. Naturally, I am aware of the teaching of karma, the law of cause and effect that can only be altered by an individual's adherence to the eightfold path taught by Buddha. Yet, even as I thought it, I knew instinctively that this was not what Tom was talking about.

"Then you must know that some things are meant to be. That we foolish humans cannot argue with fate."

I wet my lips with my tongue. My joy at discovering my leg was not crippled again was beginning to be tempered by common sense. I was not frightened. This man was Tom, our benefactor, not some stranger who meant me harm. But I was troubled. I was alone in the house with him—not just in the house, but in my own bedroom. Despite that, I was oddly reluctant to tell Tom to leave.

His massage had been deep. It had left me stimulated and relaxed at the same time. I reflected that I had never experienced as much enjoyment as this all the times I had laid beside my husband's rigid form, our ridiculous night-shirts forming an impenetrable barrier between our bodies.

Tom's hands had been warm and strong on my skin. So close, his clothes smelled faintly of jako. Unlike most gaijin, the odor of his flesh was sweet and fresh, as if he had just bathed. I could feel desire for me rising from him. I closed my eyes, reveling in the knowledge that he found me attractive. I wondered what his body would be like beneath his robe.

He was as tall as Ian, but where my husband was lanky to the extent that his arms and legs never seemed to be fully under his control, when I had hugged Tom, I had felt strong muscles beneath my touch. This was a man who had control of himself. Could I vanquish that control? I found the idea quite exciting.

I spoke softly. "Unless you are an adept of the eightfold path, it is not possible to change karma."

His response puzzled me. It seemed to me that he was talking to himself rather than to me. "I should have known better. Right at the beginning, it was impressed on us time after time. Never ever get involved with anybody who has anything to do with your mission. That was why I was approached, of course. My masters knew my history, that I had neglected my betrothed in favor of business to the extent that she married somebody else, and that I had never been close to a woman after that. They saw me as a cold man. A man who could be trusted to follow orders rather than any personal inclination. Do you follow me, dear one?"

I could make no sense of anything he said except for the last two words. He had called me dear one; that was the only thing that mattered.

Without warning, I was overwhelmed with the knowledge of all that was wrong with my marriage to Ian. He did not love me, just as I did not love him. Oh, I had not expected love. Few Japanese brides would, and those that did were mostly disappointed. But to be ignored in my own marriage bed! To be told we were not married and that I was untouchable. Suddenly, I wondered if Ian spent his days in Edo with a yujo, a paid woman of pleasure, rather than making love to me.

The thought was so hurtful I felt as if I had been punched in the stomach. Tom raised his hand to my hair and stroked it gently. The small tenderness was my undoing. Ian cared nothing for me. I was sure he was lying about the need for a priest to bless our union; it was an excuse. The reality was that he found me so unattractive that he could not bear to even touch me.

But Tom did not find me ugly. He wanted me. I could hear his breathing rasping hoarsely in his throat. The hand that caressed my hair was trembling. I remembered the pleasure Tengen had given to me so freely when we had made love, and I ached to feel wanted like that once more. Tom was staring at me intently, his expression questioning.

I did not want to lose him, to throw away this moment. But there was something I had to know first.

"Tom, are there any Christian priests in Edo?"

CHAPTER
THIRTY-FIVE

Sand tickles my palm
As it trickles back to the
Earth. All else is lost.

I had expected Tom to be amused, or perhaps puzzled, by my question. To my astonishment, he answered me seriously.

"A Christian priest? You mean a Catholic priest?" I nodded. "Why? Why do you want to know?"

There was something so urgent in his voice that I blurted my answer without thinking. I looked away from Tom's face so I would not see the pity in his expression when he heard my pathetic confession.

"Ian says we are not married in the eyes of his god, not until we are married by a Catholic priest. He tells me that there are no such priests here in Edo, or on the whole of Honshu for that matter. Because of that, he says we cannot come together as husband and wife."

"Ian said that?"

I nodded, reluctant to speak, as I knew that my voice would betray my shame.

"Oh, Mi! What have I done to you? I am so very, very sorry. I had no idea." Tom's words amazed me. His voice shook, not with amusement, but deep concern. I risked a glance at his face and saw that it was contorted with what looked like pain. In spite of my own distress, I reached up and smoothed my fingertips across his lips, as if I could heal his hurt with my touch, just as he had done for me a few moments ago.

"You are sorry, Tom? But you have nothing to be sorry about."

He took my fingers from his lips and kissed the tips. My hand tingled at his touch.

"It's all my fault. Ian told me that he had fallen in love with you from the moment he first saw you. I told myself I should be delighted, that the match was perfect. I managed to put aside my own emotions, and when Ian finally said he wished to marry you, I brokered the match with your father."

I thought he was about to say more, but when he simply stared at me, his expression imploring, I repeated my question. I knew something was very wrong here, but I would think about that later. Much later. First, I had to know if my husband had been lying to me, either by his words or his actions, for each and every day of my marriage.

"Tom, please tell me. Was Ian lying to me when he said we were not really married? And if that is so, is it true that there is not a single priest here in Edo—on the whole of Honshu Island—that could make us husband and wife in Ian's eyes?"

"I will not lie to you, Mi. Ian is a deeply religious man.

To him, no marriage service would be binding unless it was officiated by a Catholic priest."

I closed my eyes as a dagger of pain slid into my heart. Ian had not lied to me, then. The pain increased as I understood that to my husband, his principles were far more important than how he felt about me.

"I see. Thank you for telling me that." How dull my voice was. It showed none of my pain. I heard Tom speak as if from a long distance.

"But you asked me something more, and I must tell you that Ian is not telling you the whole truth. There have been a number of Catholic priests in Japan for some years. I am acquainted with two here in Edo, and I know of several more. The intention is to establish a Catholic church in Edo —in fact, building work has already begun. Out of the two priests I know, one would insist that you converted from Buddhism to Christianity before he would marry you and Ian. The other is far more liberal in his outlook—a decent donation for the new church would be more than enough to convince him that the marriage was an excellent idea."

I felt as if I had been punched in the gut. I tried to breathe, but the air would not reach my lungs. I tried again and made a curious whistling noise. I held my hands out, palms up, in an attempt to show my bewilderment. Tom said nothing, and eventually I managed to whisper, "Why? Why has he lied to me? You said he loved me. I don't believe that. If he loved me, then he would want me as his wife."

"Whenever I asked him about you," Tom looked as if he had bitten into a ripe orange only to find it sour, "he insisted that you were both very happy. I had no reason to doubt him. Is it possible that you are happy, Mi-chan?"

I almost laughed in his face. "Would you be happy with

a wife who was not your wife?" I demanded bitterly. "A wife who lay at your side every night, refusing to be touched? Would that make you happy, Tom?"

"I am sorry. So very sorry." Tom sounded helpless. My frustration boiled over finally. What use was regret to me?

"Thank you for your sympathy," I said levelly. "But I do not want it. Ian obviously does not find me attractive. Do you, Tom?" I leaned away from him deliberately. If he lied, I would see it in his eyes.

"I should never have allowed Ian to marry you." Tom's voice was the harsh caw of a raven. "I should have married you myself. If Ian is a fool, then I am a worse one for letting you go."

He was telling me the truth. I saw it in his eyes, heard it in his voice. I had no idea what he was talking about. Nor did I care.

Triumph surged in my belly. I closed the small space that separated us and kissed Tom softly, lingeringly, on his lips. I felt rather than heard the groan that rose from his throat.

As I parted his lips with my tongue, his arms slid around my shoulders. His fingers dug into my flesh so hard that it hurt, but the pain was delicious. I bit his lip in return, and Tom pulled away, throwing his head back with a wolf's howl.

I ran my fingers beneath his robe, following the line of his breastbone. His chest was hairy, and I almost laughed in surprise. Tengen's body and—from what I had seen of it—Ian's were as bald as a bird's egg. Did I like this? I decided that I did.

Tom obviously liked what I was doing. He grabbed my hand and pressed the palm hard against his chest, rubbing it back and forth. I took my hand away and traced it down toward his tree of flesh. I hesitated, wondering if Tom would stop me. When he made no move, I carried on until my fingers found the rearing head of his tree.

I was astonished by what my fingers discovered. I had seen men's trees in my brothers' shunga that were so monstrously large that they had made me giggle in disbelief. I had been relieved to find that Tengen's tree was far more manageable. I had never seen Ian's private parts. When, on our wedding night, I had dared to grope through the thick material of his nightgown, his tree had reared joyfully at my touch, but he had shaken off my hand in apparent horror, and I had been too hurt by his reaction ever to try and repeat my cautious fumblings. Even so, I was certain that Ian's tree was a mere twig compared to what lay in my hand now.

Tom rolled over, holding me firmly at his side. "Where did you learn to kiss, dearest?" he murmured. "Not from Ian, I know that."

"I had a lover."

There had been too many lies already. I would not lie to Tom now. Absurdly, I blushed. Tengen and I had made love once; did that merit the grand title of "lover?"

"Who? Who was he?" Could it be possible that Tom was jealous? He sounded as if he was.

"He was my tutor. He taught me to read and write. He was also a Buddhist priest." I would hold nothing back. I added, "We made love only once, but it was wonderful."

"It must have been, for you to remember it so fondly. I can only hope that I will not prove to be a disappointment to you."

I had no idea how I was supposed to respond to that, so instead, I rubbed my face against Tom's cheek. It seemed to me that if he truly found me attractive, then it was time he lived up to his words. I felt him draw a shuddering breath.

He leaned over me and I thrust up against him, all thoughts of right and wrong flying away. He kissed my lips, then trailed his mouth down my neck. He pushed my kimono aside. I moaned with frustration as he fumbled with the knots that anchored my hadajuban in place. I tried to help, tugging at the knots myself, but Tom pushed my hand away and attacked the cords with his teeth. When they finally loosened, he snatched the silk aside and I lay naked and exposed to his gaze.

I wanted, desperately, for him to tell me he found me beautiful.

He did not.

Instead, he gave a quiet sigh and bent down to lick my nipple. The cool evening air made it pucker with delightful pain. I must have made a noise as Tom raised his head and looked at me for a long moment.

"I thought this day would never come, Mi," he said huskily. "I was certain I had lost you when you married Ian. If it takes a fool to repeat their mistakes, then surely I am the world's greatest idiot."

I heard his words and rejoiced. But I wanted far more than words. They could come later when all questions could be asked and answered. I linked my hands behind Tom's neck and pulled his head down to my breasts.

He blew softly between them. It tickled, but I had no desire to laugh at all. His head moved down my stomach, his tongue trailing wetly on my flesh. He paused as he reached my black moss and I arched against him, urging him to go on, not to stop. Not now.

I shivered as his tongue flicked against my moss. I almost screamed with delight when he parted me and his tongue licked lightly inside me. But I wanted more. Much more.

All modesty fled as I grabbed Tom's head and forced him further into me. He nibbled and lapped until I thought I could take no more pleasure. I guessed he felt my delight —I hoped he shared in it—as he raised his head and pushed me onto my back.

If I had had any doubts that I would find it possible to take his tree, they were instantly set aside. Tom rubbed himself none too gently against me and parted my black moss with his fingers. He paused for a moment; if he was silently asking me if I was ready for him, then he was to be disappointed. I could barely breathe for my excitement and could not speak.

Tom seemed to understand. He took a deep breath, and I felt the head of his tree probing me. Suddenly, he was inside me, and almost at once I felt my yonaki beginning to build.

I gripped Tom's arms so hard I could feel bone beath the muscle. I arched against him, trying to force even more of him inside me. I heard him whisper my name over and over and over again, and then the waves of my yonaki were upon me and all else faded away.

When I found myself again, we were lying side by side, touching along our entire bodies. I exulted in the feel of his nakedness, loving the way he kissed my neck and stroked my shoulder.

"I must leave you, Mi."

Even though I knew it had to be so, I sighed. "Will you come back?"

How languid I sounded. Tom laughed and buried his head in my shoulder, just where it joined my neck. It was a very sensitive spot and I shivered with the pleasure of his touch.

"Now that I know the truth, do you really think I could ever leave you again?"

It took me a moment to understand what he had said.

THIRTY-SIX

Spilled water cannot
Return to the tray. Nor can
My tears be recalled

"I cannot change the past, Mi. I did what I thought was right at the time. Now, I know it was completely wrong. I have condemned you to a marriage that is no more than a sham. I always knew Ian was a weak man, but I had no idea that he was so..." He paused, searching for the right words, and finally said, "That he was so flawed."

Perhaps it was my own guilt, but absurdly, I felt the need to defend Ian. "He is a good man. He has helped many people who are too poor to go to a Japanese doctor."

"He can only do it because I pay for everything for him," Tom said brutally. "Without me, he would have nothing. It would have been better if I had not stepped in. Without me, he would have been forced to become a missionary like his parents."

"If that is how you feel, why do you support him? Us?"

I was satiated bodily. But my curiosity was not. After making love, Japanese men often enter a state called kenjataimu. During this time, they claim to be completely relaxed and able to think clearly. Tom was gaijin; would he enter this state? I hoped so, as I intended to find answers to all my questions, and it seemed to me that this was the best chance I would have.

I expected Tom to say he looked upon Ian as a son. That he felt it was his duty to support him.

He did not.

"Because it suits my needs. I am well-established as a rich, gaijin trader here in Japan. But that does not mean that I am trusted. I was delighted when Ian told me he wanted to work with the poor here in Japan. I knew he was an excellent doctor—he was one of the top pupils at his medical school. I let it be known—subtly, naturally—that it was I who encouraged Ian to come to Japan and that I supported him. It gave me great kudos."

That made sense to me. Anything that helped a person gain face in the world of business was good. But it did not explain why Tom had been pleased when Ian told him he wanted to marry me.

"But why was it so important that Ian married me? I mean, me rather than any other Japanese girl?" I demanded bluntly.

"Because it made you family."

I shook my head in confusion. Tom stared at the ceiling, and I wondered if he was about to lie to me. I put my hand on the side of his face and turned his head toward me. If he lied, I would see it in his eyes.

"Why does that matter? Tell me, Tom."

"It was essential. Or so I thought at the time." He sounded bitter. "I knew of the unrest that was spreading throughout Japan. It was becoming obvious even before the Satsuma Rebellion began. Not everybody supports your government in strengthening links with us gaijin. I was beginning to be worried. If things developed, then it seemed to me that it was entirely possible that most of the gaijin would be expelled from the country. But if I was related by marriage to a Japanese girl, especially one who was the daughter of a man who was as well respected as your father, then it had to work in my favor. And, of course, I was already an important client of your father's, so I knew he would listen to me when I supported Ian's cause. And Ian was mad for you. I thought he would make you an excellent husband."

Tom was…not lying, I knew that intuitively. But neither was he telling me the whole truth. I was suddenly deeply uncertain. I had allowed him—no, rather, I had encouraged him—to make love to me. I liked him a great deal, and I had thought I could trust him.

Now, I was no longer sure.

I gathered my thoughts and spoke precisely. "I see. So, I am no more than a pawn in your business plans."

"No!" Tom's voice was hoarse. He raised himself on one elbow and stared down at me. His eyes were unblinking, as if he was trying to force me to believe him. "You were never that, Mi. I was entranced by you when we first met, even though you were no more than a child. I saw something very special in you. It seemed to me that you were deter-mined that you were going to make your own destiny. Unlike Ian, I am not a religious man. But when your father told me how gravely ill you were, I prayed for your recov-ery. When he told me of your brothers' stupidity, it was I who suggested to him that you should be allowed the chance to take their place."

I shook my head. I could not believe what he was saying. "Why? Why would you do that?"

"I thought that you would be far more valuable to him than your wastrel brothers could ever be. And I had a personal interest. I wanted to see you again. To find out if you had really grown into the woman I'd hoped for. I knew that you had as soon as I saw you. You were so alert, so interested in everything. And so very beautiful."

"I was a cripple," I said brutally. I added grudgingly, "Without Ian's help, I would still be a cripple. I owe him a great deal."

"You have paid him back a thousand times," Tom said. "Ian has told me how you have helped him. He has even said that he believes you can treat the patients almost as well as he does now. He is a fool, but a fool who loves you."

"Then why is he lying to me?" I burst out. "He told me that he asked you if there were any suitable priests in Edo, and you said there was nobody. If he loves me so much, why does he insist that we're not married? Why doesn't he make love to me?"

"I don't know. That, you must ask him yourself. Do you love him, Mi?"

I was oddly reluctant to answer him. I did not want to discuss my husband with a man who had just made love to me. Tom watched me closely. The silence stretched until I became deeply uncomfortable, and I answered him with a sigh.

"No. I do not love him. I never have."

"Then there is hope for me. My time here in Edo will be up soon, whether the gaijin are expelled or not. I have just had word that I am to return to England. I imagine I will be sent somewhere else quite quickly, but I will never return to Japan. Will you miss me?"

"Of course."

I was sincere in my answer. I liked Tom greatly. His visits meant a great deal to me. Without him, I would have known nothing at all of the outside world. And I had certainly greatly enjoyed our lovemaking. I assumed he would continue to support Ian, even if Tom was forced to leave Japan. If Ian was allowed to stay, of course. Not that that mattered to me greatly. I would no longer be living my sham marriage with Ian, no matter what happened. I wondered if I should tell Tom of my plans, but he cut across my thoughts and spoke urgently before I could make my mind up.

"Listen to me, Mi. Please. I doubt Ian has registered your marriage with the authorities. I'm sure he would have mentioned it to me if he had. If that is so, then in truth you are not legally married. You are not bound to him. Will you leave him, Mi? Come with me to England? Marry me?"

I felt my mouth opening and closing. I was so shocked I could not speak. Tom wrapped his hands around mine and stared at me imploringly. I cleared my throat and said the first thing that came into my head.

"You are very kind, Tom. But…" I ground to a halt. What could I say that would not offend this kind man?

"Please, don't rush into an answer. I have some time before I go. I will wait. I am not Ian, Mi. I love you. I have shown you that today. I promise you, life with me would be very different for you. If you agreed to marry me, I would tell my masters that my time with them is over. I will stay in England. I have plenty of money. It was never about that. I was just bored; I needed the excitement. If you are at my side, I will want nothing more. I would never seek to tie you down. Women in the West have far more freedom than Japanese women, you must have seen that for yourself. We could travel if you would like that. If you wanted to put the skills you have learned to good use, then I assure you that there are as many poor people who need medical help in London as there are here in Edo. You could have your own clinic if that would make you happy."

My thoughts scattered like doves put to flight by a sudden noise. Some of what he had said meant nothing at all to me, but the lure of freedom? That tempted me more than anything else he could have offered me.

I guessed Tom read the indecision in my expression. Wise man that he was, he did not push, but immediately rose.

"I will leave you to think it over." He was dressing as he spoke. When he had tied his sash, he turned to me and smiled. "I don't want to force you into a decision. Whatever you decide, I will accept. Unlike Ian, I have no wish for an unwilling bride. I will leave you to think about what I have said. May I come back tomorrow after the mid-day meal for your answer? Is that too soon?"

"Tomorrow." I repeated the word simply for something to say. I was so shocked, my thoughts flew like shattered glass. I simply could not think coherently.

As Tom reached the shoji, he paused and spoke without turning toward me. "Might I suggest one very small thing, Mi-chan? When Ian comes home this evening, ask him where he has been. Where does he go every day that he leaves you here alone."

THIRTY-SEVEN

Birds flock together
For friendship or protection?
Only a bird knows

I was sitting cross-legged on the bed, wearing one of my long-neglected silk sleeping robes, when Ian finally came home even later than usual.

Shig normally filled the bath for me with cans of water heated in the kitchen. As she had not appeared yet, I assumed she was going to spend the night with her family and I knew I could not manage to heat the water and fill the bath on my own, so I had been forced to be content with a cloth wash in cold water. Did I still smell of Tom? I sniffed my flesh carefully and decided I did not.

I was uncomfortable sitting cross-legged. My left leg was reluctant to bend and began to ache badly, but I did not move. I knew I was being stubborn. As Ian would have phrased it, I was cutting off my own nose to spite my face. I didn't care.

The evening was fully dark when Ian finally came

home. I listened, following his progress by the sounds he made. He kicked his shoes off in the hall—ironic that he had finally remembered!—and I heard the scrape of a match and then the smell of the wick catching light in the oil lamp that stood by the entrance. As the rest of the house was dark, I assumed he must be guiding his way with the lamp, but his progress sounded clumsy. I heard him bump into a table and mutter something under his breath.

When he finally slid our shoji open, I was collected and as calm as I could be.

"Mi?" He sounded deeply puzzled rather than angry, as I had expected. "Mi? You're still awake."

He held the lamp aloft. The movement puffed a cloud of a peculiarly sweet odor toward me. I watched him intently and saw him catch his breath as he saw my brace, propped defiantly at the bottom of the bed.

"I have been waiting for you, *husband.*" I hissed the last word and saw, even in the yellow light of the lamp, that Ian had flushed deeply.

"What's happened? Why are you dressed in that...that thing? How did you get your brace off yourself? Tell me, Mi."

His voice, calm to begin, had risen to a howl. The sound sent shivers down my spine. I had never seen Ian display anger, or any other strong emotion for that matter, and I was suddenly afraid. He was head and shoulders taller than I was, and although he was thin, I had seen him move patients effortlessly who must have weighed half as much again as he did.

If he was so angry that he was moved to strike me, could I stop him? I took a deep breath and decided that I could. Barely a day had passed that I did not practice the exercises that Tengen had taught me. My body was supple, and now that my deformed leg was almost straight, I knew I had more strength than Ian realized.

I met his gaze and spoke without a tremor in my voice. "Tom thought I must be bored. He came here and took me to Father's office. When we got back here, I slipped and hurt my crippled leg. He helped me take that thing off." I gestured at the brace. "Later, we talked. He told me many things, Ian. He told me that you were lying when you said that there were no Catholic priests in Edo. He said that at least one of them would be pleased to perform the marriage ceremony for us."

Ian's face sagged like hot candle wax. Despite everything that I now knew, I felt a surge of pity for him. I reminded myself that Tom had called him a weak man, which he surely was. I was not weak. I would be strong— for myself.

"He's lying."

I shook my head. "I don't think so. Tell me, Ian. Have you even registered our marriage with the officials?"

I watched as my husband crumpled. As if his legs could no longer support him, he collapsed on the edge of the bed. I noticed cynically that he had the presence of mind to set the lamp down on the bedside table before he put his head in his hands and began to sob.

"Mi, I am so sorry." He gulped the words. "I have wronged you, I know it. Can you forgive me?"

So close, the sweet odor had an undertone of rottenness. It seemed to be coming from Ian's clothes and his hair. I remembered Tom telling me to ask Ian where he had been, and suddenly that seemed to be more important than anything.

I was certain he had spent the day at a brothel, amusing himself with some cheap yujo. No higher-class woman of pleasure would ever smother herself in such cheap scent.

"Where have you been all day, Ian?"

My question seemed to surprise him. His sobs ceased for a moment, and he took his hands from his face to stare at me. "Does it matter?"

"It matters to me. Where have you been all day? Today and every other day you are away from home?"

He shrugged, his face sulky. "If you must know, I've been to an opium house. My work is very stressful. I need the opium to relax. I suppose Tom told you that, as well?"

Opium. Not a yujo. I almost laughed. Most men took opium from time to time. It was almost as acceptable as drinking sake. Then I remembered that Ian's absences had become more and more frequent recently. When Tom had called him a weak man, had he been trying to tell me that my "husband" was addicted to opium?

"No, Tom did not tell me that." I spoke evenly. "Why didn't you tell me, Ian?"

"I thought you would despise me," he said simply. "You never need anything. Not opium. Not alcohol. Certainly not me," He added bitterly. "When we first met, I thought you were a sweet, timid girl. Somebody who would look up to me. Somebody who would follow my lead and think I was wonderful. I thought our marriage would make my life complete, that I would find happiness with you. But I was completely wrong about everything. You're strong. Far stronger than I am. You're just like she was."

His face was working. I sat very still, wondering if he had gone mad. Everybody knew that madmen had immense strength. I began to breathe deeply, preparing to ready my body for the struggle that was surely to come.

Despite my worries, I was intensely curious. I needed to know what he was talking about. Who *she* was.

"I don't understand." I spoke gently, as if trying to calm an aggressive dog. "You must have cared for me when we married. Why did you lie to me? Why have you never made love to me? And who is this woman you're talking about? Tell me, Ian. Please."

"I didn't lie to you." Ian sounded and looked sulky. This was so much more like the Ian I knew that I relaxed fractionally. "Or at least, I didn't mean to. I intended to ask a priest to marry us as soon as possible. But the one I knew who would be happy to perform the ceremony was out of Edo, and nobody could tell me when he was to return. Not even Tom," he added spitefully. "You were not my wife. I could not make love to you. I couldn't do that to you; it would not have been right."

He broke off and stared at me, his expression that of a child who has been accused unjustly of stealing food.

"But when the priest came back, why didn't you ask him to marry us then?"

"I couldn't. I was caught between a rock and a hard place. I knew by then that I had made a terrible mistake, that you were not the girl I thought I had found. But both you and the world thought we were married. I knew nobody would understand the truth. It seemed to me that the best thing I could do was leave things as they were. I prayed, Mi. Prayed to my God every day. Asked him to make things better. To give me back the girl I married. But it never happened. I knew that you saw the weakness in me. That you despised me. That you had all the strength that I lacked. Even my patients, the people I healed for nothing, they preferred you to attend them. When I found out you were treating them when I wasn't here, it was the final straw. I had nothing left, not even my self-respect."

"How did you know? About the patients?"

"I guessed. There should have been many more of them the day after I was absent. And I noticed that some of my medical supplies were gone. I hoped I was wrong, but I knew I was not. You were so good with them, it had got to the stage where I didn't even have to tell you what to do. You just did it. Oh, Mi. Why did you have to betray me?"

He was clearly close to tears, but I could feel no pity for him. I had betrayed him? I, who had tried and tried to be a good wife to him, to help support him in all he did, I had betrayed him? I spoke stonily.

"I have never betrayed you. How dare you say that when you have been living a lie since the day I thought we were married?"

"You don't care, do you? You are hard, Mi. Hard as stone. Just the same as Judith was. What a fool I was to think you would be different."

"Judith? Who is Judith, Ian?" He stared at me silently, his face working. I spoke as gently as I could, guessing that if I pushed too hard, he would never tell me. "Did you love her? What happened?"

A fat tear leaked from his right eye and rolled down his face. He brushed it away and stared at the moisture on the back of his hand as if he was astonished to find it there.

I knew that the unknown Judith was the key to every-thing. For a moment, I wondered if it would be better that I never knew. But only for a moment. I needed to know so I could understand. Understand, and move on.

"Please, tell me, Ian." I put my hand gently on his sleeve. He looked at it for a long moment and then put his hand on my fingers and looked at me imploringly, like a child searching for comfort from its mother.

"She was my lover. I loved her. But she never loved me. Never."

"Tell me," I repeated.

Ian looked at his hand, not me, as he began to speak.

CHAPTER

THIRTY-EIGHT

The owl flies by night.
His beauty is enhanced by
The glow of the moon

"Do you remember me asking you about those envelopes that the guests gave us at our wedding ceremony?"

I wondered if Ian was trying to evade the issue, but his expression was so anxious, I decided to give him the benefit of the doubt.

"I remember. What about them?"

"They reminded me of the envelopes Father used to send me at the beginning of each school year. There was generally a handsome amount of pocket money in each one. Although I never gave it a thought at the time, now I suppose Tom provided it, as he did everything else."

Ian sounded bitter, but I was too bewildered to really notice.

"I don't understand. Why would your father send you money rather than just giving it to you?"

"My parents were missionaries when I was born. My very earliest memories were of living in Africa." He glanced at me, and I shrugged helplessly. I thought Africa must be a country, but I knew nothing of it. "It was very hot, I remember. I had nobody to play with, as my parents were the only English people in the area, and they said it wasn't right that I should play with the native children. I liked it there, all the same. When I was seven, my father told me I was going back to England, to boarding school."

Something else I didn't understand. School, naturally, but what was a boarding school? Ian obviously saw my puzzlement. He smiled thinly and explained.

"You don't have anything similar here in Japan. In England, high-caste families often send their sons off to stay at a school a long way from their home. If the parents live in England, then the children go home when the school closes for the holidays. But it's not unusual for some parents to live a long way from England. At my school, some of the pupils' fathers were diplomats, who were posted all over the world. So they, like me, were not able to join their parents at all. But unlike me, they all had relatives in England and went to stay with them during the school holidays. Do you understand that?"

"It's barbaric!" I was appalled and couldn't hide my indignation. "Your parents sent you away when you were only seven? Why?"

"Because I was a nuisance. I got in the way," Ian said calmly. "I was like any other young boy. Always up to mischief, wanting to explore. And worst of all, I kept trying to make friends with the native children. Father tried beating me to make me behave, but I was lonely, Mi. I wanted to have friends. Somebody to play with. So, Father decided I would be better off at a good boarding school in

England. He gave me an envelope with money in it when he and Mother put me on board the ship that would take me to England, and another arrived in the post at the beginning of each year.

"I rather liked it at boarding school. I was quite clever, and very good at sports, so the teachers were kind to me. Despite the fact that I was very shy and quiet, I even made a few friends amongst the other boys. Once, one of them invited me to his home for a long holiday. I loved it, but perhaps I did something wrong, as I was never invited again."

"You must have been very lonely," I said softly. It wasn't quite what I meant. To me, Ian had been betrayed by the people who should have loved him, but I could not use the word. I sensed it would have opened many wounds that had long ago healed beneath mental scars. But I thought I was beginning to understand him, at least a little. And with the knowledge came a great sense of pity.

"Not really." Ian shrugged. "Not most of the time, anyway. The holidays were difficult. I was generally on my own with the teachers, and of course they weren't interested in keeping me amused. But I was fed, and I kept myself occupied well enough. I had the library all to myself, and I loved reading. I spent many happy days just sitting in the quiet, reading anything I fancied."

It sounded dreadful to me. I asked, "Couldn't you have gone to stay with Tom?"

"I might have, I suppose. But he never asked me to stay with him. Now and then, he would come and take me out for the day, but of course, he was often out of England for long periods himself. He was always very generous to me. His envelopes always had far more cash in them than Father's."

It seemed to me that Tom was no better than Ian's parents. The thought was disturbing.

"Tell me about Judith. How did you meet her?"

"Ah." Ian's expression was far away. "When I was thirteen, I changed schools. The first school was what is called a preparatory school. Children went on from there to finish their school education at another boarding school." He had lost me again, but rather than interrupt his flow, I stayed silent. "I was very unhappy at first. The new school was in a different part of the country, and I knew nobody at all. At my last school, I had found the lessons very easy, but at the new school, everything was a great deal harder. Most of the pupils were expected to go to university, and I was terrified that they would think I was stupid, so I didn't even try and make friends. Most of the boys came from very rich families, and when they found out my parents were missionaries, they teased me about it. I hated it. I wrote to my father and told him I wanted to go back to living in Africa. He didn't reply to me, but Tom came to see me and talked to me for a long time. He told me I couldn't go to live back in Africa. He never said why, just that I couldn't go. I started crying and he told me to stop being such a baby. I remember that, even now.

"Did I want to be a missionary like my parents? he asked me. I had always attended church regularly. I loved the rhythm of the services, and the priest at my school was very kind to me. I knew I didn't want to be a missionary, but I had begun to consider seriously the thought that I might take religious vows and become a priest. Tom shook his head when I said that."

"'No, that's not for you, Ian. I can't see you as a contemplative. Is there anything else you think you might enjoy as a profession?'

"I had always obeyed Uncle Tom. I would have done that even if Father hadn't told me how important it was. He had always been kind to me, and I was grateful to him for that. Apart from my priest at school, it often seemed to me that nobody else in the world cared for me at all. So, if he were telling me that the priesthood was not for me, then I would listen and no doubt agree with him.

"But other than taking the cloth and becoming a priest, I had given no thought at all as to what I might do when I left school. I had to do something to earn a living, I knew. Unlike most of my schoolmates, who came from well-off families, I had no hope of marrying a rich bride. Although, if I did become a priest, there would never be any question of marriage for me.

"Uncle Tom was drumming his fingers impatiently, so I spoke quickly.

"'I don't really know.' His face darkened with exasperation, so I said, without really thinking about it, 'I enjoy helping people. Perhaps I might train as a doctor.'

"'That would do very well.'

"I was deeply relieved. Even more important than his kindness to me, I had always known that Tom held the purse strings. Father's letters were full of warnings to obey him and assurances that I do as he told me without argument. Tom himself had told me candidly that my grandfather—who had died before I was born—had not approved of Father's decision to become a missionary and had left all the family fortune to Tom as a result. He was rich. We had nothing except what Tom chose to give us.

"So, I spent barely a year at my new school. Just before my fifteenth birthday, Uncle Tom told me I was to move to another school, one that specialized in ensuring boys who wished to become doctors were accepted at a decent university."

Ian smiled softly to himself. I wondered what memories he had recalled. I was beginning to feel his pain and was pleased that the move had been good for him. But still, I wondered. There had been no mention of Judith so far. Who was she? What had she done that had hurt Ian so very badly?

"You were happier at the new school?" I prompted gently.

"Oh, yes. I was happy. So very happy. Judith was there. How could I not be happy?"

THIRTY-NINE

Evening is not the
Close of day. It is the start
Of the joy of night

Judith. We were there at last. I leaned forward slightly in my eagerness and then stiffened, worried that I might distract him. I saw at once that I had no need to be concerned. Ian was looking at me, but it was obvious from the far-away look in his eyes that he saw not me, but Judith.

"She was beautiful. Flawless. Tiny, almost like a doll. Black hair and the darkest eyes. Skin the color of a tea rose in bloom. So fragile, it seemed impossible that she could cope with everyday life." My skin crawled as Ian said dreamily, "As soon as I saw you, Mi, I thought you were my Judith come back to me."

I supposed he meant it as a compliment, and I managed a small smile.

"Who was she, Ian?"

"She was the headmaster's wife. Much younger than

him, of course," he said dismissively. "All of us boys thought she was wonderful. She knew all our names, and she always had a kind word for everybody.

"Just as it was at my first school, I was the only pupil who stayed on during the holidays. It didn't bother me—I was determined that I would get excellent grades, so I haunted the library. It was there that Judith found me. I was engrossed in a textbook, and she came in so quietly I didn't hear her. When she spoke, I was so nervous I dropped my book. She smiled at me and picked it up, putting it back on the desk."

"'Good morning, Ian.' She glanced at my textbook and raised her eyebrows. 'Now, what on earth are you doing studying on a lovely day like this? Put your books away and come for a walk with me.'

"I stood and followed her like an obedient dog. Any of us boys would have done the same, but I felt a moment of absolute triumph. She had not chosen any other boy, just me. Naturally, I chose to forget that I was the only boy left in the whole school.

"That first day, we walked in the garden. Judith handed me a pair of scissors and told me which roses she wanted me to pick. I not only plucked the blooms, but I also carefully took off all the thorns in case she pricked her finger on them. Being clumsy, one of the thorns lodged in my finger. Judith looked at the bead of blood oozing from the tiny wound and to my amazement raised my finger to her lips and sucked the blood away. From that moment, I was her slave. I loved her in a way I had never even known existed."

"And Judith? Did she care for you?"

There was something wrong with Ian's tale. Even though I had never met Judith—never would, I hoped—I felt that her behavior was more like a yujo enticing a client than a respectable married woman offering friendship to a young boy.

"Of course," Ian responded sharply. "It was the long summer holiday, and after that day, she sought me out constantly. We walked in the sunshine, at first in the garden and then on the school grounds. I was ecstatic, but still, I worried about her husband. If he found out I was spending so much time with his young, beautiful, wife, surely he would be angry. He might even expel me, and then what would Uncle Tom say? Finally, I shared my concerns with Judith.

"She laughed, but there was no humor in the sound.

"'Patrick? You need have no fear of him, Ian. His only loves in life are riding to the hunt and drinking with his cronies. At this time of the year, I don't even see him until evening.'"

I had no idea what he was talking about. I asked, "Riding to the hunt? What is that?"

"Ah, here in Japan, you are far too civilized to contemplate fox hunting. In England, it is a sport for the rich. Men —and some women—ride on horseback with a pack of well-trained hounds to accompany them. When a fox is seen, the hounds are unleashed and the riders follow them, shouting encouragement to each other and the hounds. When the fox is caught, the hounds are allowed to tear it to pieces as a reward. At the end of the day, much alcohol is drunk to celebrate the day's sport."

I shuddered. "That is barbaric."

"I always thought so, as did Judith. The thought that her husband—a big, brute of a man who must have been nearly twice her age—could prefer riding with hounds to spending his time with his lovely, fragile wife left me bewildered. Before I could help myself, I was pouring out my feelings for her. She said nothing, and I stumbled to a halt finally, certain that I had made the world's worse fool of myself.

"But I was wrong. She raised her head and managed a pitiful smile, and I was sure I could see a tear in her eye.

"'Oh, Ian, how perceptive you are. And how kind. I have never loved Patrick. I married him because my parents insisted. We were impoverished, and they said he would make an excellent match for me. I was very young and accustomed to doing as I was told. In those days, Patrick was very kind to me and there was nobody else interested in me, so I did as I was told and married him.'"

How very like a Japanese woman Judith was, I thought dryly. After all, hadn't I done just the same?

Ian had obviously not noticed my cynical thought. He went on, "I seized her hand and held it tightly in my fingers. When she did not snatch it away, greatly daring, I kissed the back of her hand.

"'He is a blind, stupid fool,' I said. The thought came to me suddenly that Judith had to share her bed with him every night, and I felt sick. 'I would never leave you alone, Judith. I would take care of you in every way.'

"I had no real idea what I meant by my last words, but to my relief, Judith seemed pleased. She took her hand away and stroked my cheek, smiling softly.

"'Dear Ian, I knew you would be different.' She paused, seeming to expect something. When I did no more than smile back at her, she added, 'Would you like to kiss me?'

"I had never kissed anybody except my mother, and that was long ago. But my heart sang at the thought of kissing Judith. I put my lips against hers very gently, and at once she put her hands on each side of my head and mashed her mouth against mine. To this day, I cannot remember exactly how it happened. We had been sitting on the grass, but suddenly we were lying side by side. I had no idea what I was supposed to do or say, and I almost howled with frustration.

"Judith came to my aid. She stroked my face and kissed me again and then took my hand and placed it on her breast. I could feel her heart beating like a bird, fluttering wildly, and I think for an instant I was truly mad. I ran my hands over her dress, kissing her frantically. I heard her protesting, trying to push my hands away, but I knew she didn't mean it at all. I persisted and finally Judith sighed and rolled on her back. Very shyly, without looking at me at all, she inched her dress and petticoats up her thighs.

"I could take no more, Mi. I grabbed the silken fabric in both hands and shoved it violently out of my way. Her underthings bewildered me, but Judith helped, tugging them briskly to one side. I was so inept and excited that I spent almost as soon as I entered her. I apologized time and time again, but Judith insisted she had enjoyed it.

"Perhaps she did, as after that, almost every day of the holiday, she came to find me in the library, and we would walk somewhere secluded and make love. She taught me so very much. Showed me what she liked. Made me slow down when I wanted to hurry. I had loved her from that first day, but by the end of the summer holiday, I was besotted by her."

Ian fell silent, his eyes dreamy, lost in his memories. Was it possible that after all these years he still loved his mistress? I could hardly believe it. He had been nothing but a boy—he had told me himself that he was only fourteen. How old had Judith been? Twice his age? More? And she had been in a position of responsibility. Her husband had had Ian entirely in his charge, yet she had betrayed that trust, apparently without a moment's thought. Or was I wrong? Had her own passion matched his?

I spoke warily. "That must have been wonderful for you. But what happened?"

"Nothing," Ian said simply. "When the start of term came close, Judith explained to me that our affair would have to be suspended until the next holiday. I was deeply upset, of course, but she pointed out that during term time, it would be impossible for us to be alone as the school would be full of pupils and teachers and somebody would notice. She sighed and wiped away a tear."

"'Don't you think it will be as difficult for me as you, my dear one?' she asked. 'Seeing you nearly every day but being unable to touch you will be torture, but it cannot be helped. If Patrick found out—' She shuddered. "—he would divorce me. I would have nowhere to go. Nothing. The scandal! And what your parents would say, I dread to think.'

"I thought of what Uncle Tom's reaction would be and I shuddered with her. She was right, I knew, but how I was to bear the time between holidays, I had no idea.

"I found solace in my books. I spent every waking moment with my textbooks, and before long, I was top of the class. I even won a prize for the most improved student. Uncle Tom was delighted and took me out for a long and very expensive lunch. It was the first time I had tasted wine, and I drank far too much. So much that I nearly confided in him about Judith. I caught my tongue in time, but from that moment, I vowed I would never touch alcohol again. And I never have."

FORTY

Winter will follow
Autumn. It is always so;
I cannot change it

At least I had solved one puzzle. I had often wondered why Ian never drank. But the answer did not please me at all. A stronger man would have learned to understand his limits and only drunk what he could handle. It appeared that Tom had been right when he called Ian weak.

I watched him quietly. He was still locked in his past. Almost, I told him not to go on. I had no need for him to finish his tale. I knew how it was going to end. Oh, not in any detail, but I could not believe that a married woman would seduce a child for anything but her own convenience. Surely, Ian must have had doubts himself?

It appeared not. He began speaking again abruptly. I shrugged mentally and moved my left leg to a more comfortable position. I would let him tell me. And then? I closed my mind to the idea for the moment. Ian was recalling deep pain. I would postpone the even deeper pain I was about to give him for as long as I could.

"For a whole year, I was in heaven. During the holidays, Judith and I were together almost every day. I managed to cope with term time with the occasional glimpses I caught of her, always telling myself that the days would fly until we could be together again.

"But then, at the start of the new school year—my last at the school, for I had secured a place at university to study medicine—things began to change. During the holidays, Judith started to make excuses for why she could not meet with me. From being together every day, it dwindled to every other day and then perhaps once each week. Patrick was unwell, she said. He was suffering badly from arthritis and could not ride often, so she had to be there for him.

"I believed her, of course. We were lovers. We were in love. How could I not? But the time without her gave me a chance to think about our future. I was going to university, far from the school. I was excited about the move. I had enjoyed my studies greatly, and I had decided that Uncle Tom was perfectly correct, I would be a very good doctor. But how could I meet with Judith in the future?

"I finally decided that I would be bold. Judith loved me as much as I loved her, I was sure of it. I would take my courage in both hands and tell Uncle Tom about the situation. Tell him that Judith wanted to leave her brute of a husband and that eventually they would get a divorce. If Tom would agree to support us—it would be no burden to him as he was, still is, a very rich man—then as soon as Judith's divorce came through, we would marry. I was vaguely aware that it was very difficult indeed for a woman to divorce her husband, and also very expensive, but I reasoned that once Patrick discovered Judith had taken me as her lover, then he would be only too happy to release her.”

“You didn't speak to Judith first?” I blurted.

Ian stared at me as if he was astonished by my question and shook his head. “I just took it for granted that she would be happy.” He sounded bewildered and hurt. “It didn't matter, anyway. Before I could find the courage to explain the matter to Uncle Tom, Judith found me in the library and told me that we needed to talk. I was overjoyed. It had been days since she had sought me out, and I thought she was looking particularly beautiful. We walked out to the school grounds, but instead of going to our favorite place by the lake, Judith stopped and sat on a bench just outside the garden. I tried to kiss her, but she pushed me away.

“I thought I had angered her in some way and tried again. She snapped at me. I knew then that she really was angry with me, and at once, I decided she thought I had neglected her and so I told her about my plans. She stared at me as if I was mad and then began to laugh. She laughed until tears ran down her face.

“‘Ian, how did you come to be such a fool? You expect me to leave a husband who dotes on me and would give me anything I asked for to live on the charity of your uncle? Really?’

“I was sure she was playing some sort of cruel joke on me, no doubt to pay me back for what she saw as my neglect of her. I took her hand in mine and held on to it when she tried to pull away.

“We wouldn't be dependent on Uncle Tom forever, I explained. As soon as I graduated, I would have my own practice. Money would be a little tight until I was established, but we would be together. That was all that mattered.

"She stared at me in silence for so long, I started to become nervous. Just as I was about to speak, she cut across my words abruptly.

"'You are very young, Ian. I suppose I must make allowances for that. But now you must listen to me. Our little affair has been very nice. I have enjoyed it greatly. But it is over.' She fidgeted with her parasol. The day was hot, and she always shaded herself carefully from the sun as it made her lovely tea-rose complexion darker. 'I had assumed it would end naturally when you left the school, but I have been overtaken by events. There is someone else, Ian. Do you understand?'

"I could not, would not, believe her. I was the only pupil in the school during the vacations. She never went out without her husband. Naturally not, no married woman would. How could she have met someone else—someone she preferred to me? I shook my head and spoke quite softly. I was sure I sounded quietly reasonable.

"'That is not possible, Judith. I love you. And I know you feel the same way about me. Why are you lying to me?'

"'Ian, stop shouting. One of the gardeners will hear you. I don't love you. I never said I did. And there is someone else. You know him. Richard Petty, the new languages teacher.'

"I didn't know him, although I had seen him about the school. He was very young. Somebody had told me that it was his first position. He was a tall, well-built young man with a fine head of hair. Handsome, I supposed, in a rugged sort of way. Many of the boys had commented admiringly on his prowess at rugby, a very physical and energetic sport. Those who took classes with him said he was a natural teacher, very sympathetic and patient with boys who were a little slow in learning. All in all, the very opposite of me. And as he was a bachelor, he lived in at the school, unlike the rest of the teachers, who were all married with families and had homes in the town.

"I realized I was still shaking my head. It took an effort, but I managed to keep still and speak without my voice breaking with the pain I was feeling.

"'You are just infatuated with him. You barely know him.'

"Even as I said it, I remembered how Judith had put me away from her for these many months. She sighed and patted my hand. The gesture was so patient, so unlike the wild passion we had enjoyed, that I knew I was deceiving myself.

"'Ian, this is very difficult for me. Please don't make it any worse. If you must know, I am pregnant.' My heart was in my mouth. I felt a wild joy. I knew that I had been right all along. Judith loved me. She had invented the romance with the new teacher to make me jealous. It was her way to be sure that I would accept my child joyfully. She must have seen the happiness in my face as she sighed and raised her eyes to the heavens. 'For goodness's sake, Ian. The baby is not yours. It's Richard's. And don't even bother arguing with me about it. When you and I were together, I took precautions, just the same as I do on the rare occasions that Patrick makes love to me. Patrick doesn't know that, of course.'

"My mouth was open and closing like a gaffed fish. Judith must have become impatient with me. She rose and snapped her parasol open.

"'I'm sorry you've taken it so badly, Ian. I wanted to be honest with you. Perhaps I should just have let things run on until the end of next term when things would have ended anyway.'

"I thought of my plans for our future and felt physically sick. Still hardly able to believe what I had heard, I said, 'Judith, what are you going to do? Your husband will dismiss your lover from his post instantly, and without a good reference he will find it impossible to get another job. And naturally, he will put you away from him. How will you both live?'

"'Do you really think I am going to tell Patrick who the father of my baby is?" She sounded astonished. "I fell pregnant once before, by another lover. I told Patrick the baby was his and he was overjoyed. Not that it mattered as I had a miscarriage. I will tell him this baby is his as well. If I don't lose it, my husband will be the happiest man on earth. Richard doesn't even know I'm pregnant yet and I have no intention of telling him the truth. When it is announced, I will tell him it's Patrick's child. I imagine he will be very relieved. Goodbye, Ian. You will soon forget me, I daresay.'

"She walked away then, Mi, without so much as glancing at me. I was anguished. Not only did Judith not return my love, but I had been one of many. How many? I had no idea, but the knowledge tortured me. Almost worse was the thought that she still allowed her brute of a husband to make love to her; that was truly unbearable. I even thought of killing myself until I began to understand that there was much more to what had happened than I had understood at the time.

"I finally realized that God had used poor Judith to tempt me. Just as our savior was tempted by the devil in the wilderness, she had lured me from the path of right-eousness. But it was not her fault. God knew she was a weak vessel, but He had chosen to offer her the chance of redemption for her sins at the same time as He offered me the chance of putting spirituality before earthly desires. Alas, both of us failed the test and fell from grace."

Ian smiled sadly, his eyes lowered. He was truly mad, I realized. I sat very still, each of my muscles tense in case I had to defend myself.

"What did you do, after that?" My voice was husky with tension and I cleared my throat softly. Ian stared past me, clearly not even seeing me. Was I as much of a shadow to him as Judith? At that moment, I thought so.

"I pretended to study. In fact, I spent each moment when I was not in a class in the library. For all that, my final examinations were a blur. I don't recall a word I put on the paper. I suppose I answered automatically, and all the studying I had done was worthwhile. I graduated near the top of my year. Uncle Tom was delighted with me. He asked me what I wanted to do when I was qualified. Did I want to set up in a surgery in London, where there would be plenty of opportunities for me to advance quickly? All I could think about was Judith. The thought that I might see her again if I stayed in England tormented me. Uncle Tom had told me that he was about to go on his travels again. He expected to spend some time in India, he said, so at once I suggested that I should join him there when I graduated. It seemed to me that it might help me atone for the dreadful sin I had committed with Judith if I could open a clinic offering free treatments to those who could not afford to pay for a doctor. I assumed Tom would pay for it—he had never refused either me or my parents when it came to money.

"'That is very worthy of you, Ian,' he commented dryly. 'But I doubt I will still be in India when you graduate as a doctor. I expect to spend perhaps three or four years at most there, and then I anticipate I will be sent to Japan. I intend to spend some of my time in India learning to speak Japanese. I have always been fascinated by Japan, and I intend to stay there for as long as I can.'

"'Then I will set up my first practice in Japan. I will join you there as soon as I graduate,' I told him firmly. It seemed to me that Uncle Tom wasn't very happy with the idea at first, but after a while, he had a change of heart and became quite warm about it and discussed my, or rather *our*, future in Japan enthusiastically.

"I was delighted. Surely, Japan would be far enough away for me to forget about Judith.

"It was, until I saw you and knew that I was the most fortunate of men and that God had given me a second chance in life. I realized He must have forgiven me for the sins I had committed, and I rejoiced."

FORTY-ONE

Snow is too lovely
To last on earth for more than
A fleeting moment

I knew from Ian's description of Judith what he was about to say. He had thought that he had found her again when he saw me. The knowledge made me feel ill. What woman wants to hear that she is no more than a substitute for her husband's lost lover?

Unbelievably, it seemed Ian noticed nothing. He stared at me and then spoke earnestly, cutting me with his every word.

"You were so like her. I was so full of joy, I could hardly breathe. Tom had already mentioned your case to me; quite rightly, he thought I would find it of interest. When I saw how badly deformed your leg was, my happiness over-flowed. I could help you walk again, I knew I could. And if I did that, then surely you would be eternally grateful to me, just as Judith had not been.

"I don't suppose you remember, but I watched you

intently. You were not only lovely and so like Judith that you set my heart pounding, but I saw other qualities in you as well. You were such a sweet, innocent girl. I observed how you acted toward your father. You drank in his every word, anticipated his every need. Clearly, you were devoted to him, just as Judith pretended to be devoted to me," he added bitterly.

I tried to speak and had to clear my throat as the words stuck. "It was Judith you loved, not me," I said flatly. "Is that why you insisted we were not really married, so that we couldn't make love?"

"No. Not at all." Ian looked at me pleadingly, his expression begging me to understand. I waited for his excuses in stony silence. "I loved you from the very first day I saw you. You, not Judith. You had all the qualities she lacked, and I was enchanted. But I could see no way forward for us. I am gaijin. I do not even speak your language. I could never hope that your father would allow us to marry. The only thing I could do for you was treat your deformed leg, and I threw all my skill into doing that.

"But it was not enough. That day I dared to pour out my feelings for you, I knew at once I had done a dreadful thing and that I could never allow myself to be alone with you again. If I were, I would surely not be able to control myself.

"I decided that the only honorable way forward was for me to leave Japan. I told Uncle Tom of my decision, and of course, he demanded to know why. I had to tell him what had happened, and to my astonishment, he told me that the best thing I could do would be to marry you and stay here in Japan. He would speak to your father, he told me, and all would be well."

Tom had told me as much. But now that it was laid out

plainly before me, my head began to ache as I tried to take it all in.

"I suppose you're going to tell me next that it was Tom who put the idea into your head that we weren't really married as well?"

"No, Tom didn't have anything to do with that. But he was very keen for us to marry. He said that if I married a Japanese girl, it would show that I intended to stay here, that I truly cared for the community. Fortunately for me, you appeared to be the perfect bride. He explained to me honestly that it would give him great kudos if he let it be known that I could treat my patients without payment because he was sponsoring me." Ian paused to gather his thoughts and I forced myself to take deep, even breaths in an attempt to control my racing emotions. "You understand that?"

His voice rose in question, and I nodded. It is the Buddhist way to perform favors with no hope of return. Naturally, it would give Tom great face if it was known that it was his charity that supported his nephew. Tom had been honest with me about that, as he had with everything else.

Unlike my husband.

I was puzzled by Ian's comment that I was the natural choice for his bride, but I let that pass for the moment. He was staring at his interlaced hands in sulky silence. Exasperated, I turned back to my original question.

"Tell me why you would not make love to me, Ian." I spoke bluntly, hoping to shock him. An ugly flush rose up the back of his neck, and I knew I had succeeded.

"I wanted to." He spoke so softly I had to lean forward to hear what he was saying. "I wanted you more than you could ever understand. But I could not bring myself to defile you, like Judith had defiled me. I knew we were not married. If I had taken you as my wife, I might as well have gone out and hired some yujo for my pleasure. I could not do that to you, Mi. I loved you too much."

My headache deepened as I heard Judith's name on his lips yet again. Still, I persisted. "But you knew of a priest who would have married us. Why didn't you ask him?"

"I tried. I went to see him very shortly after the ceremony, but I was told he had gone out of Edo, and nobody could tell me when he was coming back. I told myself I could wait, that I *had* to wait. To do anything else would have been to dishonor you. But as the days and weeks passed, something happened that made me understand that you were deceiving me. Oh, not in the same way that Judith had, but the effect was just the same."

I found that I was thinking very lucidly. I had been right all along. My husband was mad. I spoke soothingly, trying to calm him. "Me? What wrong did I ever do, Ian? I was always there for you. I supported you in every way I could."

"Supported me? Is that what you call it? You undermined me. I had no idea what you were saying to my patients, of course, but I saw the sly looks they gave me when they thought I wasn't looking. And I also saw that it was you they were grateful to, not me.

"The final straw came when I undertook an inventory of my medical supplies. I realized at once that my stock of some drugs was far lower than it should have been. I am a meticulous man, Mi. I have a certain way of rolling bandages and I always stack dressings so there are equal amounts in each pile. That was no longer so. Other things were disarranged as well.

"You were the only person who would use my medical supplies. I could hardly believe it at first, but finally cold reason told me that you had betrayed me. That it was you who had chosen to treat patients when I was absent. That you had flagrantly disobeyed all I had told you.

"I knew then that you were laughing at me behind my back. That you despised me for the weak fool that I was. As soon as I understood how you felt about me, all desire to ask the priest to marry us passed away. I did not want you for my wife. I did not even want to touch you. I would have put you aside then—I believe it is very easy for a man to do that here in Japan, and as I had not registered our marriage, I assumed it would be easier still—and I would have if it had not been for Uncle Tom."

Tom. Once again, it appeared that Ian was going to blame his uncle for all his misfortunes. At that moment, I longed to tell Ian that I had taken Tom for my lover. That he was far more of a man than Ian ever would be. I wanted to see his face when I told him that "Uncle" Tom had asked me to marry him, and that I was seriously considering it. For once, it seemed that Ian had intuited my thoughts.

He smiled, apparently with genuine amusement, and I watched him cautiously, wondering what was to come.

"Dear Uncle Tom. You like him, don't you?"

"Yes. I do like him."

"Naturally you do. Everybody likes Tom. Why shouldn't they? He's rich, but he never flaunts it. He's amusing company. He has the knack of making anybody he talks to feel as if they are the only person in the whole world who interests him."

I blushed. Ian was perfectly right. Tom had had that effect on me from the day he gave me the gold Victoria when I was no more than a child.

"He is a very nice man," I said stiffly.

"No. He isn't nice at all."

Understanding began to steal over me. Of course, Ian was deeply jealous of his handsome, popular uncle. Without Tom, he would be nothing at all, and he resented it deeply. How had I not noticed it before? Oddly, I felt great pity for Ian. It seemed that everybody in his life who he cared for had betrayed him, just as I was about to betray him. The thought made me feel very guilty. I told myself briskly that I had nothing at all to feel guilty about.

"Ian, I understand how you must feel about Tom."

"No, you don't," he cut across me savagely. "You don't understand at all. I'll tell you all about dear, kind Uncle Tom and then see how you feel about him. Tell me. When you went to visit your father this morning, how did he seem to you? Was he happy to see you—you and Tom?"

"I don't know what you mean." Ian's words had touched a nerve, and I guessed that was exactly what he had intended. I stared at him defiantly.

"Really? Did you never wonder why your father wanted you to marry me? Me, a gaijin with neither money nor influence?"

"Mother explained it to me. Tom is one of his best clients. It would have damaged Father's business if he had lost him to a competitor. And Tom is an important man with friends in very high places, so the marriage would give father great face." I added grudgingly, "Besides that, it was thanks to you that my leg was straight again. It would have been discourteous to have refused you."

I was beginning to babble. I heard the nervousness in my voice as I slowed to a miserable silence. I had always known there was something that Mother was not telling me, or perhaps that she did not know herself. In her world, Father was a god. She did as she was told, as she expected me to do.

Ian's eagerness showed in his face. "You've wondered, haven't you? I can hear the doubt in your voice. I'll tell you the truth now, Mi. And I promise you that it is the truth. Tom told your father that you were to marry me. And your father had no choice but to agree."

FORTY-TWO

If tears were jewels
Then every woman would
Be rich as a prince

Tom. Always Tom. I took comfort from the knowledge that Ian was lying to me because of his deep jealousy of his handsome, popular uncle.

"I don't believe you," I said firmly. "I know Tom's an important client of Father's, but for him to have that amount of influence over my father is nonsense."

"Listen to me, Mi. Please. I have told you the truth about my past. About our marriage. Why would I lie to you about Tom?"

I squirmed uncomfortably. I was beginning to feel guilty about what had taken place between Tom and me, and I acknowledged that I owed it to Ian to at least listen to him now.

"Tell me, then. Tell me how it comes about that a gaijin could have such influence over a well-respected businessman like my father." I sounded cynical. I *was* cynical.

"Tom has your father in his pocket." I had heard the phrase before, and it had amused me. There is no real equivalent in Japanese. We have no pockets in our clothes! But I understood perfectly what it meant. I was already shaking my head as Ian went on urgently. "It is true. Tom is not what you think he is, Mi. He is not just an important gaijin trader. He does trade, but in something more important than goods or money."

It was on the tip of my tongue to say that there is nothing more important in trade than money, but then I remembered Father's favorite proverb: *Prosperity grows on the tree of perseverance.* How many times had Tanaka spoken of Tom? Even the experienced head clerk had revered him. I had first seen Tom years ago, when I was a child, but he was still here. Still being greeted with great respect by Father. Respect, and—suddenly, I was sure—fear.

I was uneasy. All at once, I did not want to hear anymore. "Tom told me he is going to leave Japan soon. That being so, whatever you have to say about him doesn't matter."

"But it does. He has crushed your father. He will never be the man he was again."

I raised my hand in, protest but Ian's voice went on relentlessly.

"Tom is not just a businessman, Mi. He is a spy. A mercenary who works for anybody who is willing to pay him the price he demands. He cares for nothing and nobody except himself."

I almost laughed with relief at Ian's nonsense. There is a tradition in Japan of shinobi—what the ignorant peasants call a ninja. These men—and they always are men—are said to be able to make themselves invisible. They are true mercenaries who will spy and even murder for their masters. Oddly, the tradition is seen as an honorable one. But Tom was no shinobi. My skin recalled the feel of his hands and I shivered with involuntary pleasure.

"Without Tom's charity, you would have nothing." I was ashamed of Ian, and it showed in my voice. "How can you say such wicked things about him?"

"Because it is true. He has never kept his occupation a secret from my father. That is why Father refuses to speak to him except when it is absolutely necessary. He accepts Tom's charity only because it supports his work. If Father did not need the money to take the word of God to the world, he would never so much as take a penny from him. He says that it is God's way of making good from evil.

"When I was a boy, I knew nothing of all that. Uncle Tom was my hero. He would tell me tales of his travels in foreign lands. How he had duped the foolish natives and obtained information from them that was worth more than a king's ransom. When he said it, it seemed... right, somehow."

My mouth was suddenly dry. There was a ring of truth in what Ian was telling me, but I did not want to believe it. Father, a traitor to his country? It could not be so. I would not believe it.

"My father is not a fool," I said hotly. "He would never tell Tom anything that mattered. He would never betray *me*."

"But he did. He has betrayed his country, and he sold you to me. He had no choice. Oh, it all started innocently enough. Tom is patient and cunning. When he first came to Japan, he made inquiries and found out that your father was the most important money lender in Edo.

"As soon as he could, he obtained an introduction to

your father and began to borrow small sums from him. Naturally, these were always paid back promptly.

"Uncle Tom is very clever. He had learned Japanese and studied your culture. You know yourself how very charming he can be. He quickly made contacts in Edo society. He was a novelty, a gaijin who spoke excellent Japanese and understood how things worked here. And naturally, it helped that he was clearly rich.

"His acceptance into the higher circles awed your Father. When Tom invited him to be his guest at events held by high-ranking civil servants and even minor nobles, your father was delighted to accept. Tom began to groom him, pretending to be his friend as well as a business acquaintance. And gradually, he increased the loans he sought from your father until Tom was his most important client by far."

"None of that means anything," I interrupted angrily. "I already knew all that."

In truth, I hadn't known about Tom introducing Father to higher-caste circles, but I was not about to tell Ian that. Anyway, I honestly didn't see that it mattered. Times were changing in Japan. Traditional barriers between the classes were coming down. Why shouldn't Father rise in society, with or without Tom's help?

"Of course you knew. You are very clever, Mi. You see everything and say little. Very wise. But you are not as clever as dear Uncle Tom. Once he had established himself with your father, he began to move on to the next step.

"He told your father that as a result of your government's actions in reducing the traditional sources of the nobles' incomes, some of his new acquaintances—men of the highest status, important samurai amongst them— were in urgent need of loans. Naturally, these men could not approach your father directly; the loss of face would be too great. But Tom agreed to act as a go-between to broker the loans. Your father was delighted and agreed to a number of very high-value loans.

"Of course, there were no needy nobles. Tom kept the money for himself, and then sadly told your father that the nobles had spent the money and could not pay it back. Your father was distraught. He had advanced huge sums, enough to break him if it was not repaid. At that point, his good friend Tom suggested that perhaps he could help.

"Your father knows many people in Edo. Important businessmen. Thanks to Tom, he was introduced to men from the shogun's circle. Now, you must remember that accepted as Tom is, such men would never truly trust him. He is gaijin. One does not confide in foreigners. But your father is a highly respected Edo businessman. He is seen as being very much on the rise. The men Tom introduced him to would trust him in a way that they never would a gaijin.

"So, Tom hinted that he might be able to repay some of the loans himself, providing that your father paid him back by supplying him with certain information that Tom wanted but could not obtain for himself. As Tom still had all of the cash your father had advanced to non-existent nobles, it was an easy exchange for him.

"At first, Tom asked only for inconsequential things. Your father could see nothing wrong with passing information on that did not matter, but he didn't know that Tom was using it as a test. He already knew the answers; what was important was that your father told him the truth.

"Gradually, Tom began to turn the screw. He demanded more important information, the sort of thing that your father had to make an effort to find out. By then, your father had no option but to agree. He was tied to dear

Uncle Tom, who made it clear that it was in his power to ruin your father if he decided to be difficult.

"So that was how it went. By the time I told Tom how I felt about you, your father was entirely in his power. When Tom told him I wanted to marry you, he had no option but to instruct you to obey. If it's any comfort, I imagine your father hated the thought that his beautiful, intelligent, and, above all, loyal daughter was to be sold to a gaijin because of his own disloyalty.

"Uncle Tom thought it was wonderful. If you married me, then your father would belong to him forever. Your father might be prepared to accept the consequences of his actions if it meant only he was punished, but he could never bear to see you dragged down with him, which would surely happen if your father betrayed Tom, your uncle by marriage. I was so besotted with you that I didn't care what it took, as long as I could possess you."

Ian sat back. He was smiling. I longed to slap him, or far better, launch one of the powerful blows that Tengen had taught me. Straight fingers to his ribs would leave him gasping. A short, fierce blow to his temple could kill him.

But I did not move. For a moment, I felt deep sadness for my poor, foolish father. He had wanted nothing more than to be successful. It was not just the money, but also a matter of respect. He had risen from nothing through his own persistence and hard work. If Tom carried out his threat to expose Father as a traitor, then it would finish him. Father would have no option but to kill himself. If he did not, then the authorities would execute him for his betrayal of his country, and he would not only die, but die without honor.

All he had ever worked for would vanish like morning mist on water. Mother would be destitute. I would probably be arrested as an accomplice and tortured before being executed in my turn.

Oh, Father! What have you done? The moment passed quickly. I'd had a long time to think before Ian came home. Even before he had told me the truth about Tom, I had known that something was not right with what Tom had told me. That something was missing. Now I knew, everything fit together like enlaced fingers.

And I was angry. No, more than angry. Fury filled me, stiffening my back and making it difficult to breathe. Every man who had mattered in my life—except Tengen! Never my dear Tengen—had betrayed me. Used me for their own ends. Father had sold me. Ian had married not me, but his lost love. And Tom? Tom, who insisted he loved me? Perhaps he was the worst of them all. How was it possible to arrange for the woman he loved to be married to his own flesh and blood?

True, none of the three men had ever raised a hand to strike me. But the mental torture they had put me through was surely far, far worse.

I realized suddenly that there was one thing that I still did not know. I would find out everything this day. Nothing more would be kept from me. I spoke quietly. "And my brothers' marriages? Did Tom have a hand in that?"

"Most certainly." Ian was gloating. "Tom was well aware of the struggle for power that was going on between your father and Mikayo. To ensure he couldn't lose, he became an important client for both men. He whispered gently in Mikayo's ear, telling him how wonderful it would be if both businesses could join. When Mikayo protested that your father was a stubborn man who would never agree to such a merger, Uncle Tom pointed out how fortunate it was that both of them had children of marriageable ages. The seeds were sown, and you know the outcome. But the important thing is that Uncle Tom could not lose. If the merger had taken place, he would have had both men as his puppets. It mattered nothing to him that it did not. By then, he knew that your father was the man who mattered and he simply discarded Mikayo. It was Tom who hinted to many of Mikayo's high-caste clients that they would be better to move across to your father. He wanted to be sure that he had left nothing to chance."

I stared at my arms, folded across my ribs. Tom's self-serving cruelty had raised gooseflesh on my exposed skin. Was there no end to the evil of the man I had been pleased to take as my lover? I spoke softly, controlling my voice with an effort.

"That's why Tom took me to see Father yesterday. He was using me as well, wasn't he? To influence Father."

"You are very quick on the uptake, Mi," Ian said admiringly. "That's exactly right. Uncle Tom badly needs information about the Satsuma Rebellion, but your father refused to tell him anything. He told me he was going to use you to make your father understand that it wasn't just him who would suffer if he was exposed as a traitor."

I remembered the odd conversation that had passed between Tom and Ian when they had referred to a "mutual friend." Now I knew why they had been so careful not to name him.

Ian was still smiling at me, and I saw expectation in his eyes. I knew he anticipated that I would crumple. That I would cry out of pity for not just myself but my poor father. Did he also assume that now that I knew the worst of it, I would decide I had no choice but to remain as his wife? That I would follow his every desire? Worship him as I had Father?

I put that thought to one side quite deliberately. At this moment, Ian and his plans mattered not at all. Nor did Tom. Or my father. My time had come. Mine and mine alone.

Ian's voice broke into my thoughts. "Well, Mi? Now that you know the truth about dear Uncle Tom, what are you going to do? Even though he is leaving Japan, I am happy to stay here. Tom has promised that he will continue to fund my clinic. After all that has passed, I am sure you will be relieved to know that I am prepared to forgive you. I will speak to the priest and arrange for us to married."

Ian's gloating tone left me in no doubt that he was certain that I would take the only choice left to me. He was sure that I would beg him to find his priest quickly and ask him to marry us. That I would apologize for my unwifely behavior and beg him to forgive me. He knew full well that I would act out of concern for my father, but as long as he had me as his dutiful wife, he would not care.

When I smiled at him, I saw the triumph flare in his eyes. It lasted for no longer than the short time he took to understand what I was saying.

"No. That is not going to happen. I am not your wife. I have never been your wife. I will not lie at your side tonight or any other night. You can do as you like. Return to your opium den if you want. Or sleep on the couch in the surgery. I daresay you will be reasonably comfortable there. I don't care either way. You are not my husband, Ian. You have no right to tell me to do anything."

Ian's face was peony red. I felt no pity for him. Why should I? He had none for me.

"The world thinks we are married. You are my wife and you should obey me," he sputtered. "I will not be ordered about in my own house. If anybody is to sleep on the couch, it will be you, Mi. The discomfort might bring you to your senses."

"It is not your house, Ian. It is Tom's. Everything in this house is his, as are you. You have no right to anything here—especially not me." I paused until I was sure I could speak calmly. "Tom has asked me to marry him."

Ian's face froze with shock. His high color died to ashes as he whispered, "You are going to marry him? After all I have told you?"

"Oh, no. I am not going to marry him." I stood as I spoke and slid the shoji open, waiting for him to stand and walk out of the bedroom. He shook his head, but when I pointed silently to the shoji, he moved like a man in a dream, his eyes staring but not really seeing. "I am done with you and your family. Tom is coming for my answer tomorrow. He will not get the answer he expects. I think it would be sensible if you were not here when he arrives. You might not be able to control your temper and, remember, you are still dependent on him for everything you have. Your entire future rests in his hands."

I saw Ian's lips form words, but only a whisper of sound came from his mouth. I thought he called me Judith, but the single word ended in a sibilant hiss, so perhaps I was wrong.

He backed away from me then as if I were a patient with a contagious disease. Just as when he had arrived this evening, I followed his passage by the sounds he made. In the pitch darkness, he bumped into many of the hated tables and chairs. The contact must have been painful, as I heard him hiss and at one point, I was sure he had kicked something heavy—no doubt in a fruitless attempt to take revenge on the inanimate object.

He put on his shoes by feel and a moment later, I heard

the front entrance shoji slide back. It is very difficult to bang a shoji, but Ian gave it his best attempt.

Once I had closed the shoji, I threw the bed linen on the floor and made myself comfortable on the tatami. Almost idly, I wondered where my husband would spend the rest of the night. Would he return to the opium den to find solace in more of the drug? Or perhaps he would feel it appropriate to seek out a yujo and try to recall his true love Judith in her embrace. It didn't matter to me.

One thing I knew beyond doubt: in spite of all he had said, I was certain that with the first morning light, Ian would take a jinrikisha and go to pour out his troubles to Uncle Tom. I doubted that he would find the sympathy he was looking for. What interested me far more was how Tom would react to learning that I knew the truth about him.

On balance, I guessed that Tom would keep his appointment with me. Whatever else he was, he was no coward. Possibly, he would try and convince me that Ian was...not lying, exactly, but certainly exaggerating events. I wasn't in the least daunted by the coming interview, as Tom himself had told Ian that knowledge is power. And now the power lay in my hands.

Sleep came surprisingly quickly, but not before I had time to remember the old proverb, "The journey of a thousand days begins with a single step." It was, I thought, singularly appropriate for me. Tomorrow, I would take my first step on my journey.

But first, I would tell Shig to throw my brace away.

CLIMBING THE DRAGON GATE

https://books2read.com/u/brBxLk

As Japan stands on the precipice of transformation under the new emperor's decree to bury the past, Mi finds herself torn between the relentless march of progress and her loyalty to an old friend. When a trusted confidant arrives severely wounded after participating in a rebellion against the emerging order, Mi's world is thrown into turmoil.

Determined to heal her friend, Mi deploys all her formidable skills, but her impulsive decision to join him in his quest to overturn the new order unravels the life she had so carefully built. As the weight of her actions bears down upon her, she finds herself falsely imprisoned, facing the ominous specter of death.

In the midst of her darkest hours, Mi comes to realize the

profound wisdom of an ancient proverb—that the past is the future of the present. The echoes of history reverberate through her captivity, revealing the intricate tapestry of consequences woven by her choices and those of the society she once called home.

In this gripping culmination of the series, Mi's resilience is put to the ultimate test. Join her as she navigates a landscape fraught with danger, betrayal, and political upheaval. As she confronts the consequences of her impetuous choices, the line between the past and present blurs, leaving her to grapple with the true price of redemption in a rapidly evolving Japan.

ABOUT THE AUTHOR

 With a literary journey spanning more than a dozen captivating novels set in historical Japan and a collection of evocative haikus, India Millar has embarked on a diverse career. Her professional odyssey commenced amidst the machinery of British Gas's heavy industry, eventually culminating within the hallowed halls of the British Library, where the tapestry of knowledge and storytelling merged seamlessly.

Now, India finds herself in the idyllic embrace of early retirement on the enchanting Costa Blanca. As she continues to explore the realms of history and poetry, India remains deeply grateful for the winding path that has led her to this peaceful and creative haven. Each word written, each page turned, is a testament to the enduring passion for storytelling that continues to shape her life's narrative.

Website: www.indiamillar.co.uk

ABOUT THE PUBLISHER

VISIT OUR WEBSITE
TO SEE ALL OF OUR HIGH QUALITY BOOKS:

http://www.redempresspublishing.com

Quality trade paperbacks, downloads, audio books, and books in foreign languages in genres such as historical, romance, mystery, and fantasy.